GAME 4

Jim Meirose

Copyright©Jim Meirose, 2025
www.jimmeirose.com
X: @jwmeirose
Instagram: @jimmeirose

Published by #Ranger Press

www.rangermagazine.net

ISBN: 978-1-300-69230-0

GAME 4

Just say an idea please.
Just say an idea please.
Just say an idea please.

God! Jesus! Christ! Nagg, we <u>don't</u> got eternity; Just
say an *idea* please and say it in a way *that's not* grass, 'nd
not dirt, 'nd not telling some innocent bystander they're
wrong, **NO** don't **NO** don't, etc. etc., or in any way *that's
not* we got this call of two strangers pounding much too hard
on this door, or in a way *that's not* hey who lives here called
local law enforcement, or *that's not* I do represent local law
enforcement, So; tell me do say us tell them no us not them
or *that's not* what do you mean, you are confused, *eh*! Or
that's not what am I saying, asking, telling, or otherwise
flinging at you, in a way *that's not* singling one or the other
of you two out *no no no no* but, **Do** immediately say what
you're doing here, beginning with your names, left to right,
right to left, *do it* in a way that's not saying that it matters
not how straight the gate, how charged with punishment the
scroll *no no NO,* but why'd you agree with the clerk about
all the bads filled up our whole town. *do not prance off barefoot waving*
big silky flags no not and not neither Our *whole town*, you had said about
the town. That was a script they'd read to "test" you and you
two have failed *miserably—so we must and its* true *you're
in no wise competent to* reconstruct using space-age
materials *yes do prance off barefoot waving big silky flags* an item *nine city
blocks long* that weighs *two thousand tons* which got
rabble-roused over about was it *one thousand eight hundred
tons*—or an even *two thousand tons* but it better be *two
thousand tons* or more or else, *no don't prance off barefoot waving big
silky flags the breeze will just blow your thousand eight hundred
ton nine city blocks long mere light three thousand foot* film

of dust totally "away"—*be wise n' aware that that's* over half a mile; thirty feet wide the whole way. Six feet high—along the whole length, also. *no don't prance off barefoot waving big silky flags not here no way maybe there but never here* <u>goose</u> That's five hundred eight thousand cubic feet—and more and more even more astronomically absurdly gigantic volumes and sizes and densities of "materials" to <u>*work*</u>. Like it's "nothing". Problem with the damned **THE GENERAL-MANAGER** is that everything's s'posed to go like its "nothing". Like its air. Or some foam. Petals. Or feathers. O ya, *eighteen thousand cubic yards* **of feathers** really easy to move, to manipulate, to build something out with. *Spat. Eighteen thousand cubic yards* **of feathers**, which is one great big lie, *too*, since if i'twas *just* **feathers** it wouldn't weigh nearly *one thousand eight hundred tons.* I mean jeeez, ba-b=jesuzzzzzz – how does one work with such large as pa-pa *nine hundred ninety tons of solid steel*—or hum pa-pa la paaaaa-pop ess' to build up from *nine hundred ninety tons of solid steel* girders, or rods, or ingots, or whatever **scrap** comes in a shipment of **scrap** "and" <u>melt</u> it down[1] and fuse[2] it together into o*ne (1) single nine (9) hundred (100) ninety (90) ton* buzz *solid steel block nine (9) blocks long, thirty (30) feet* heads hands and toes *wide, and six (6) feet deep* ah mean, hey howd'ya hell-dah doo-daht ben-b', ***Binnie?*** How on ho how on ho ho ho ho ho *how*? To bring in the stockpile of "steel scrap" to be melted would take **eighteen hundred** <u>**good-sized**</u> **dump trucks** to *haul it all away* sizzle le sizzle le working twenty four seven three hundred sixty five {***Good day, senor?*** Nice hat! Nice hat! Good day senor good day *nice hat* and good day *nice hat* and *nice hat* and-and uhh langlu-ssppaanniisshh buh} days for Lord only knows where I'd be without you how many years at least one *or* at least some fraction of **ONE** *galla-dun-galla-dun galla-dun galla-lon-hipsla-tango* **FRISBEES** *-poop* and then the conditions within which to work , to knowingly, willingly, with *no* thoughts of themselves, the workers do work night and day day and night dosed with the fumes and the soak and the vapors and smoke of the can't be burned off the chimneys thrust up high above that'll need to be designed and funded and actually built (*yes that too*) for their safety to rank out the doses of petroleum hydrocarbons nickel aluminum mercury arsenic lead cadmium methyl tertiary butyl ether aldehydes ketones, nitrogen-heavy compounds, sulfides organic acids and hither come, n-nether go, dare into the fray charge only the "*stupid*" of which a copious quantity'll need to be imported from what kind of regions you ask, hell, I don't know, it's way beyond me, hey *keed* throw that up in the parking lot *up there keed* (**where the hell else you think, keed**?) the upper left corner of the the great big whiteboard you been scribblin' this fat spray of deep day over and onto for later repickup and argumentationment-over by the elders when available, *keed* If not yet dead – are they dead? Are they dead? {Have we really, really made sure they're all the way gone stone-cold-dead?} and ultimate lack of resolution {*there's a war on, Easy*} if not dead to proceed with the procedure's just not possible {*these being all things to all men*} "*fire his ass*" they're **dimes** if they're a **dozen,** pick up those big, fat, sticks – the firepit's that way. zorro

Into which when got there, loose them large.
Loose them large.
Loose them large.
Loose them large.

Loose them large **as** the job of cutting down t' into "*truckable pieces*" will be violent, noisy, expensive, and lengthy. It could take a year or more. Plus *if not dead to proceed with the procedure's just not proceed the procedure's with if not dead to possible if not dead to proceed with the procedure's just not possible.*

Plus; regarding the application of the necessary toxic substances, some will go airborne during the application and long drawn out air-drying process obtuse, obtuse, obtuse so like say eh like say eh he like say eh like say eh like say say say say say say, **(1).**

Just say an idea please.
Just say an idea please.
Just say an idea please.

Jump = J leBolt off'n those/that dense pillow(s), **Freddie**, just shoes alone fairly never make/break the entire career of a *"**man**"* {senors eh senoritas *spleen*} So here {pulling a large filled out sheet of planning paper up across the drawing table, the slant of which had been adjusted so as to not make likely the usual drop of long thin round things like pens or pencils to roll away off flying, falling, *rat tat tap'd down* to the floor.} Tap tap tap from on the back being seen down onto by the underside of the table {*the type with cheap hinges and a shallow frame*} you get to see the laziness of the typical manufacturer {*the type with cheap hinges and a shallow frame*} which, cannot survive without this these or those well-cut corners of even if the expanse of the product not seen by the consumer is large enough whole wide smoothly sanded over swaths of the surface may never receive any finish at all; and, it hit Jak (*bong*) they'd been barking woof up and onto the wrong tree, the fall from which would be horrific, thank God Jak has gone under to the the wild roller and saw the idea coming so simple was the idea they pushed at Jack's shoulder, who turned 'round all irritated, saying, Why'd the hell'd you push me like that damn it I was adding up these columns of facts and figures re what we've got to do, and you push me! Why did you push me? Eh! Why the hell? Why and now I got to sum this all up from scratch again—so get back and give me space = clutching a calculator {*the type with cheap hinges and a shallow frame*} they turned away = BUT = got pulled away again by Jak saying, No no no we are going the wrong way with this. Put it down turn around and listen.

Okay—Scrappo slapped the tin box 'top the table, turned, and stared hard at Jak's face.

What? Hurry up. It don't matter I s'pose you've again set 'e back to the beginning as—I seem to be the only one taking seriously how hard a job this ass generalissimo Francis Scott's given us and hey—that one points and you better take off running. Hah. That one. That's one's soup for

Saint Francis; dill soup for *Saint Francis*, somehow someday to become so popularized as to simply be called by **SF**, which they deserve because *HA* that would mean they've been remembered very very *SLANT*, you see; and to cause one like that to be remembered not foursquare neat 'n dandy straight **UP**, as they want, but to be remembered very very *SLANT*, they'll have their memories {*the type with cheap hinges and a shallow frame*} which ought have been loving to be shallow and wasted as to simply slide-slither down off t' where you went before **JAK** under the table there looking up at the bottom there what never got well finished because the great founders never thought anyone'd ever come 'long so stupid as to end up under there alive and relaxed and looking sleepily for something to gaze at for a pleasure enhancem' to while their time 'way with and there they'd get—as YOU just got Jak "closed-casket" Skrappo, cheap copy of the already worn down flimsy but still better than you original copy here {*the type with cheap hinges and a shallow frame*} looking down and berating even more low down at you, Jak, ha—so *washda washda washda* what the 'ell's this brand new big idea you felt large and powerful enough to shell me behind my front lines with in my tender part {*the type with cheap hinges and a shallow frame*} what's easily thrown no guy wires to keep it from falling and once fallen wi' no net into the soft of it to drop, so, then as I **SAID** and if you'd been *LISTENING* I'd not be having to moo this at you big bossy I—I am going to have to start at the very begin off my beguine again so make it big play guitar make it snappy—that means here, *I am listening*, Father Soup {pretty good think down all these stairs so bumpy so bump'd in less than an instant's turnaround to "face" and "stare down" one as annoying as "you"} so what is this big idea you got that's so good its worth me snapping and putting one between your eyes all about?

goon   *in memorium*   Here it is we   we
don't have to rebuild the entire mass   *its all just plastic can't you*

see that Gimi of what was once here but given that what we're going to be putting down here's no more than a replica anyway *Gimi its all plastic less than plastic can't you see that Gimi* how 'bout we just do a hollowed out version just make the surface 'n shore it up from within, but, no. What about all the wasted space, eh eh *oh Gimi* we can sell the idea they could even put a snack bar and gift shop windowed in to the side of the thing want dollars *{???}* then do something to earn those God damned dollars *{!!!}* say what *oh Gimi why can you not see* what about this ha ha ha ho ho h funny funny funny *please stop Gimi* —and a Jai alai court inside too— *please stop Gimi why on earth can you not see* as a Jai alai court was integral to the whole God damned heart of the original equation *oh Gimi why can you not see and also stock* some sort of oddball pick-me-up drink {Packed in High Musquetania! + wherever the Hell **That May Be** + } issha fockta issha fockta deja vu deja vu run the numbers my office {*the type with cheap hinges and a shallow frame*} at nine sharp in the morning Good Job!

{**Gordon?**} whacko

blank b l a n k b l a n k b l a n k' got the word out this morning having, ooo, Top-mayor sat in Holymen's Bar and Tap Room nursing a fourth, straining to pull themself out of the mentaltanian pit they'd waded around in for what seemed like days/nights, after having been assigned by **THE GENERAL-MANAGER** a ridiculously impossible job. Gently licking back and forth at the lukewarm curve of the shot-glasses rim, Top-mayor let their eyes close a bit—not to fall asleep of course, no, no, but just to rest their eyes a bit—no Mammy mom, I am not sleeping here and the now and the statement everybody's heard said by others {*but of course not said by them, they would not get off saying something so simple, so foolish, and so very obviously a lie* (hiccup)} oh oh no, I am not falling asleep—I am merely **resting my eyes**—which no doubt has been said by so many others {not me of course, 'member that—no no never ever said such a stupid-o bye Meeee}—as, the **Frenchman**; Oh oh non, je ne m'endors pas - je repose simplement mes yeux—or, as the **Pole** ; O nie, ja nie zasypiam – ja tylko odpoczywam oczom—or, as in **Esperanto** wherever knock where knock knock that gets spoke; {*drain back the drink* **motion** *over for another*} Ho ho ne, mi ne endormiĝas—mi nur ripozigas miajn okulojn— b-but the shot glass pushed how'd it push there all by itself Lord-Lucy LaLuscious by their very big loom of a well-sculpted face (mim!! mim!!) *hordes is a good word as is fuselage luggage transistor eck ack* – Here you go, boss. This one's on me.

Huh!

Wide-awake no no no I am not falling asleep—*I am merely resting my* okay you got your orders *eyes*—no yes what oh my oh my, it is only the bartender placing down Top-mayor's new drink. (((*tap*))) The bartender leaned back lightly, saying all jolly, Hey, hey—I know you weren't falling asleep, hey—I know it when somebody's merely *resting their eyes* a few moments—hell, there's Saturday nights where the place's packed with customers not of course falling asleep but yes of course merely *resting their eyes* ha ha ha hey let me ask you a question you up for a question, Top—sure y'are here it is have you ever actually been going on about your day and all of a sudden out of the blue it hits you that oh, my, I feel the need to *rest my eyes* a moment no not of course to go to sleep of course no no but merely to close and *rest my eyes* a moment hey hey old Top, you ever got hit with the sudden need when wide awake to stop what you're doing and go lie down not to sleep of course but to merely *rest your eyes*? Have you, Top? = eh mons mons eh hey come out of it Top = I am just messing with you ha ha = you have been looking all afternoon like you need a friend Top = I never saw you come in here all sad like you are = sad no I am not sad = oh yes I can see you are after all I am a bartender name something I don't know name a facial expression I cannot interpret *so* what's the problem old Top I never ever seen you drunk before oh yah no don't say it I'll say it hey hey hey I am not **drunk** at all I am **merely resting my eyes** so level with me Top what's the problem you got one I can tell nobody's near to hear if you tell me how 'bout you tell me Top hmm hmm ehh ehh how 'bout you tell **go on and tell** = went on to say its impossible the thing he "*got to do*" so he said "*write that down*" = okay okay *okay* = the bartender picked up a wiping-rag hung sodden and limp from the rack behind and = had there been {but which there's not} people at the bar right then drinking which is what most come to bars to do and +=+ which makes most overly curious and eager to get into some kind of conversation +as the liquor dilutes the brain and makes it steer its ship ways its ship never would steer toward *t' drop inhibitions t' drop inhibitions* +=+ so now its the early stage of drunkenness which does not feel to the drunkard like drunkenness just happiness and the need to experience hilarity = and so for these scientific reasons most in earshot will cock their heads closer as = hey ain't that the Top-mayor what're they doing in a place like this and in a state like that + big seeds for scandal yes yuh yip hilly-billy rararhrrrrr . . . . ;' it's an impossible job Cap no one could ever do it but == pa au se   p   a   u   s e   = this indicated pregnancy of a big jam-tight of a cochlear idea meant to be heard and be seen heard and seen seen and heard, and they drain back *more mouthfuls* the *vacuous void* in the perceived maxi-gossiptry eh he know who was down at Holymens t-twaggle eh like that when I was out there, Madge, the Top-mayor = they were there = yes they were = how do you know = I know what they look like = I have never seen Top-mayor and there are some who believe if I can't see it, then it must not exist = having said this, Top-mayor drained back nearly three-quarters of their beer / what? / hey I can't stop the passage of time pop / yeh yeh / perhaps you were so interested in what Top-mayor was saying to the bartender you ought to have paid better attention / and n o I a not spoiling for a clash here n n n n o / *boots* / my God, sneezed the bartender, what the hell's wrong with that **THE GENERAL-MANAGER** I read they were *pillo* hired to put the town right, but, my God, I can't believe it Top he really gave you that to get done I mean such a thing as that can't be except in the wards of the demonic and/or crazy reminds us of the day that stinkbug set inside that t-shirt all day *GIMI* only got discovered at that comic-rack at Small's newspaper kind of a shop which of course was not actually it was called exactly up on the sign but ( ) it did seem like how the hell'd they pour the sidewalk out front 'f Small's at such a wacky tilt of an angle seems to me that's impossible said the bartender at Top-mayor's face hung from what was actually just one of the billions of "**human skulls**" in the universe = yep, that's what I *pillo* think too, Cap, that's what eh eh, guess what; I'm just not going to do it (defiant defiant) and that's fine 'cause it's an impossible job anyway / what's an impossible job lean closer listen harder Top-mayor's been given an impossible job / 'and why's that" because the whole idea of new planet after new planet spawning is ridiculous too = new planet NEW PLANET all's gone twisty-sideways far enough for there to be the additional hard-assed variable introduced by the seemingly random generation of N what = go on say it DAMN they did say it we missed it well, when there's something juicy and important under discussion right out in the open down Holymen's Beer Bar, *pillo* you ought to be paying closer attention = I was = No can't be = Yes it is = No it wasn't = Oh yes I was here it is, from as much as I can gather I heard Top-mayor say 'cross the bar I've been told to save the town but let me tell you, it's way past saving what   the Top-mayor said the town's . .. . way past saving   yes everybody needs to evacuate immediately who where what Top-mayor said that   yup down in the city hall there   - what's that – Holymen's Beer Bar? That place still open   yeh it is yeh it is   how

come you don't know that   Holymen's   *pork*   Top-
mayor wouldn't be at Holymen's that's smacked 'nd dabbed
square in the middle of seed-town o'er there   go there
the wrong time of day on the wrong day of the week, honey,
its 50/50 yes juh' 50/50   you know what I'm going to say I
mean hey hey stupid think think think - seed-town   50/50
pork wrong time of day it all adds up = to you know I will not
insult your intelligence by filling you in more I give you
more credit that than, **Gimi**, eh oh say, what's that big
headline 'n that paper o'er there ???? "Top-mayor states
this town is irredeemable – they said that? Yes got to have
'cause paper you know (print) printed you know o'er there
(paper) quite true {*price ya'ylle pay ovfer fame, ye no*} so the best thing
for all to do's to get out right now *each worshipping stone chips off that*
wall you know their wall back by the gate that was their gate as the rumor goes that
would actually be best.

      Thay said that?

      They said that.

      Party.

      Party.

      Party! *wonderful*

      Wonderful!

      Snagg-rap!   *pork pork*
      bully

      About = ten and a half miles west over the low hills
that way *across*, th' knew as going about their daily duties
{*which*} though they were small duties with smaller less's to
them, they needed to be done the same exact way every
single day as do any flat duties of a memorial nature, these
being much larger than most of the count of memories being
memorialized, but the duties don't vary by the number *pork* of
memories being memorialized *pork* *a'sheen* the walking
around of a small monument to many's not no larger-
length'd walking around of a large-scale monument
memorializing just some tiny small or less few *beast-pork*
walking. Yes having taken on the thankless job of patrolling

the all-overs in this specifically particularized instant, we {and actually any other *"**reasonable**"* human being and'or being(s), too} here memorializing the massive deaths of between twelve hundred and twenty-four hundred poor souls instantaneously {and let us be clear here with a run of the numbers; the term instantaneously applies to each and every one of the between twelve hundred and twenty-four hundred poor souls, but; <u>*snow*</u>; slow sneezing slow sneezing sneezing and sneezing over and over again but very, very, slow; <u>*wons*</u> this large number of individual instantaneous deaths may be slid out o'er under 'nd staggered ^{*pork*} each way out from one another *<u>es staggered es staggered</u>* *<u>es staggered and staggered out everykind which ova way</u>* SO!! 'fore and as all the numbers, yes they "do", they "do" compute, but, that's been gone over elsewhere *"ad nauseam"* by so many others, so, let's grip the grasp of where we're at *not* and look the hell over look the hell over look at the hell of the way out and 'ell-over that headstone-studded o'wise blank field's o'er there 'bout what our job's been to keep trim and memorialize to death every single day, since that terrible tragedy; so terrible, that there's no more no name for such as 't, just—well. You do the counting. I've done enough. I'm burned off with counting. Time's for *"you"* now. For you. All's left a small shard of steel 'neath the unders. All's left a small shard of steel un' 'heath heatch o' f' the unders, s-s-s so, sw-weat back t' bye, g' t' get going, making this . *"cashier"* . stuck here *in this traffic s',* **God** *look at this traffic* the rounds again. Y'know? Eh silly. Soooo silly. Can only manage the periphery "<u>most</u>" summers, as that . . *"food preparation worker"* . . sighing silently 's stalled dead ahead said, *God damned old thing's going to boil over* days like this, 'all old days *boil over*, 'cause the heat goes up, the pace g' just like that . . . *"stocking associate"* . . . in the red one out front, so <u>innocently</u> thinking, while waiting <u>patiently</u> behind their wheel, *I got to get higher on the ladder, you know, but I need to get there on time once in a while to make that happen* 'oes down, and. ^{*pork*} They file by the blank stones.

The blank stones are numbered. And under each number ought be the words of that . . . . *"laborer"* . . . . , in their <u>drab</u> peeling <u>car</u>, this being all they could afford back then and this being all they'll be able to afford ever, fingers thrumming, idly thinking, *Yes,* **God** ᵖᵒʳᵏ *is against me, you know—***God's** ᵖᵒʳᵏ *always been against me, you know,* 'ss the number of the steely torched-loose quite cindered down fragment with who the hell knows whose mummified bodily fluids, interred below, intermingled with so many others' bodily fluids, as that large old **Ford** three lengths back scarred across the hood from something violently forgotten but that must have really happened, pulled up bumper to bumper tight behind containing one simple . . . . . *"janitor"* . . . . . , hissing, Eh, eh, **what** *the hell I'll be late again these jobs are a dime a dozen I ought to just turn around and go back, but I can't* 'n honor of the names on the blank stones 'll bean' t' names of innocents just like that brawn-faced . . . . . . *"construction worker"* . . . . . . set to the right, angered so angered to be so frightened, also saying, *Stuck sitting here you know.* **Boss** *is going to ream my damn butt I ought to give them one point-blank between the eyes* that ought have been the scrap of steel interred below blown through with sad remnants of a tall skinny sad-sacked but actually very talented . . . ᵖᵒʳᵏ . . . . *"bookkeeper"* . . . . {enough to have actually some hope of going somewhere with their life} was going somewhere yes, but but 'u b't no, ⁱˡᵏ three cars back sighing, *Why'd I forget my special calculator,* **shit** *I've time to go back for it, but this damn traffic, of all the* **God**-*damned days for this traffic, it got to be this day I forgot my special calculator,* **shi**t pressured through with one more, eh, most probably many scattered as this . . . . *"restaurant server"* . . . . , "low" beginner in the world, thrumming idly the curve of their wheel, thinking, *A blessing in disguise, this damned traffic, I don't want to go in today, I've had enough, damn, enough damn stinking food up my nose-stroiells all day all night hell's behind that door every day,*

but still I go in that door every day, but| and **clip** *gone* ***yes,*** **just like that,** *each and every* DNA strand destroyed but still, as we think of it, as we walk 'round this place remembering, got to still exist in one of these two thousand filled up neat mown holes in the ground *gadda gadda* in that way existing now, but *how can that be?* How oh please how, as that very next car over, big in its stink, surge-struggling to flood, fighting to die under the pedal of its worried short small-nosed . . . . *"medical assistant"* . . . . driver, set idly thinking, *They need me this morning. I am in really deep trouble, damn damn, it ought to be against the law to tie up traffic at rush hour,* here's how, *little rabbit,* tha' thus when something only exists for the red cheeked brash . . . . .
. . . . . *"bartender"* . . . . nodding off slightly, in that rolled down driver window reeking somehow, of something which always reeks strongly somehow, why in this day and age they've not found a way to do that clean and purely like they've found so many ways to do so many elses *electric-hat* cleaner and quieter and generally better, grimly musing, *Thank* **God** *I left early; thank God* **God** *made what happened back at the house to happen, to get me out way too early, what the hell's this about anyway* whose occupation supplies a definite "**nuts and bolts**" product *but needing to be forever hidden as all such vices must forever be* and eh that thinly haired aging so fast but still just a low paid . . . . *"junior administrative assistant"*. . . . . chewing the lip gritting teeth into *another full day of kissing ass I got to get the hell out do something else* been pressed so hard into and through it's self, no longer existing in just some few moments except as mere **shards** of that . . . . *"marketing specialist"* . .
. . . . surrounded by others set in steel cages all similarly doomed well-prepared and generally ready to *I ought to still be okay, this waiting here can't last that long, I'll make the filing deadline today like I told old T' 'wass* oh yes **Mr. Caruso** of course **Mr. Caruso** hah no no no, **Mr. Caruso**, it's not going to happen on time today as a matter

• 13 Game 4

of fact, **Mr. Caruso**, it's never going to happen *bite this* <small>not</small> <small>your bread nor your jelly no no no</small> **Mr. Caruso** <small>no no no, no no no no not your bread</small> <small>nor your jelly no no no</small> **Mr. Caruso** and all your many identical others, this whole thing's zoomed past and into the limbolike zone of the totally irreparable, **Mum**, it's destroyed completely just ask that one there, ask that common . . . . *"police officer"* . . . . who can't possibly yet know that answer, but, no doubt at that time in those last moments before 'y knew an answer, that being, *Crap, late again, I'll just cut the shower, who notices if a "**cop**" smells bad that's the furthest thing off their minds if they needed to call the "**cops**" or are got down onto/into by a "**cop**"* seeing and knowing it's there does not make such a thing as this **simple** . . . . *"electrician"* . . . ., no, you are not going to *get there today boss, boss said one more time late, then dammit, no, <u>in a traffic jam there's no damned point</u> **<u>so think about something els</u>e** just like you can't fight off death no no no nobody can, when it may as well not be anything but that big what-the-hell's bearing down from behind unexpected, for example here's just another quite young "carshop" . . . . *"mechanic"* . . . . in training, hanging onto the single last thought that *Guess Graves just has to pick up the car later is all I wish I had those kinds of problems you know damn them anyplace* is the prime description of worthless garbage, shells, and husks smooshed together with this of that everyday . . . . *"retail sales associate"* . . . . of a notion that, *If Chuck wipes the sales out before I get there, I am a piece of burnt to a crispy hard crisp'd up tasteless toast* not even good for fertilizer, shells and husks, which if some, oh, some run off their mill . . . . *"customer service representative"* . . . . enjoying the plush of a brand new big German luxury sedan, *Eyy, listen to the sound when I slam the steering wheel hear it <u>hear it</u> <u>then</u>* **<u>listen harder</u>,** **shit** **slam** *slam* slam slam<small>mmmmmmmmmm</small> damn the whole car's vibrating with it *"who'd o' thunk it?"*

's vibrations expressed out into the earth would turn the earth poisonous knows any fine . . . . *"journeyman carpenter"* . . . . like the six known for sure to be down among these shards under here, *Good thing we got done a day* small thoughts y' small thoughts *early just say God watches closer over the stupid hard and poor* cling tight to these great big final small thoughts should not be allowed to exist. As the thoughts thought by the great big brisk . . . . *"office clerk"* . . . . {one of around twenty each well dressed each sweet smelling} *they're sitting around laughing, like like that stupid shit wants blood from us,* drain *and can't even get their own soggy butt in here on time* time hah what kind of lie it time hah times a lie times a lie just ask about ten minutes from now whatever still exists {*if anything at all*} of the . . . . *"operations manager"* . . . ., again, just one single of so, so many lost *lost the train of thought yesterday—and now, today, look at this* deep into *these* we're filing past so many o' *these* we mean just look at that burly . . . . *"line supervisor"* . . . . *I just know they're standing around doing nothing* thinking they're just (***Daddy!***) going to get there *while I—plus forgot to charge the stupid phone—*like they've always just got there every time before *today I am stupid deep* graves each with a blank stone saying silently under me *so so stupid* {**_how do you know you're not the first human who'll just naturally live forever_**} 'hish swishta-*swack'd* . . . . *"truck driver"* . . . ., *this better clear quick, but, hey. Getting hot won't make it clear anyway,* {**_how do you know that tomorrow morning won't be the first morning the sun will never again rise on forever_**} *so* there's something that once was but needs to be hidden, you-ah junior . . . . *"student"* . . . . of registered nursing, *Thank God I got this decent radio, and they said, Silly, don't upgrade you don't need it you won't use it* **HA** *what a crock of shit* now needs to be gone now. what a fruitless existence your existence's finally become, dumb . . . . "*software developer*" . . . . school-rich . . . . thinking it matters any old more the answer to *So why're they doing ten thousand projects at once who the hell needs a* **Jai alai** *center I can't even spell it* **Jai alai** *right next to a damn old school* **Colonial Home** *spit spat spit spatter* {*I'se a speedminton fanatical myself*} coffins *bloody yah bloody* why? some say when this here's the end wave your hands, great big over-cologned slick-haired loose suited quite and very, and very and quite successful . . . . "*lawyer*" . . . ., *Jesus Christ, look at that line and all those cars I wonder who died must have been some hot Willie oh eh wonder what judge we'll* school-rich *draw for the Wilson case, everybody already knows but me, I am so lucky to be sitting here in this jam— let's see what's on the radio,* **SPAAAANG oooffffffff! the end comes nearest what comes the very fastest to all of those and more of them without not no e'en one single exception SPAAAANG oo** school-rich **offfffff! SPAAAANG oooffffffff! until all got from 20 to in some cases less than zero of their original volumes** b' what a day, spread your arms far, as anything of the mere flesh can never possibly see, and what for? Here's what's for; all's gone **gridlock** all smashing crashing crushing crumpling down to nothing **gridlock**, mustabeen-musta' 1-1-1-1-1' **YES,** 'cause they're all dead under here already; and why else tell us what why else could there ever never possibly be, all's since that day back, when when thousands of goods-consuming taxpayers bit the dust, what d' expect yer damn town to do but die? What else but so much all at once gone, school-rich *so much*. Hey hey hey, we just been sitting put here way back off our wall waiting for yer admission; lack of us killed yer town, Top-mayor! Yah, yesz yer town isz dying, mayhapsz, and per annum you need a szhot of szomething in your arm to wake you gently pleasze go gently but—here we are to szave the day.

Save the day?

Yes the day.

Yes the day.

Party.

Party.

Party.

spit

So eh, oh say, ess half, we's gots = some kind of sweet deal for you, Jack Jak long lone ae'olle "Tapper" {if indeedie thee's be} *broom that mess up immediately, boson, and stand tall while doing it; stand tall and all, too* **get the hell out and resume being <u>what</u> you are** {gush!} an' then they beheld, even to their not easily astonished astonishment, each other but what two others exactly where am I, where is this, who are you, and what should we do next?

They faced each other's quite more than a few minutes, and the beholding of their immediate surroundings came on, came over, very quietly clear. A small square room (*oh yah and lots more but that's all we all really need to stay focused on at this moment*) a small square simple room holding besideswich the two of them a *TV* table with a *TV* on top over there and a large tape-sealed box labeled *TV* on the floor right back here.

Yes Jai alai is the name of the game—but first we have to set up the new *TV* and you have arrived just in time for the both of us to set up our brand-new *TV*.

But—hould it a minute. I—whou are youu, and why, and where is this place?

Crap Eh, listen. I am nout in a mououd four that. Even if I were, youur joukes are nout ever funny. Bad enouugh we can't keep using ouur ould *TV*, youu knouw. It wouuld souften the blouw a bit.

Blow? What blow?

God, why are you doing this—what the hell blow do you think? The blow of never being able t' see our favorite shows anymore—**God,** why am I explaining all this to you?

You know damned well what blow! Stop messing with me. I am tense enough as it is. Nothing's funny today. Today is the shit—but come on, lets get going—here, let's—let's open the damned thing up. Let's get this over with—grabbing a box cutter from a table to the side, they pounced over and ripped open the top—*who is this*, thought the other—*who the hell is this* and *yes*—the top of the *TV* box flapped open, and the box cutter got flung down to the floor—yes, and—the other pushed their hands down into the box, and partially up came a large *TV* set but it would not—wow—release the box which, after the *TV* sent got partially pulled up, rose from the floor with it—the *TV* got let down, then pulled up down, [la la la *hipsla-tango!*] and up—what is this where the hell am I get *calm*, get—*calm*—down up down and again up and again down, then.

Hey!

What?

What? You going to stand there watching me end up with a heart attack from this damn thing, GET *OVER* here help me out PULL DOWN THE DAMNED BOX when I pull up the set GET THE HELL *OVER* here I'm _sweating_, I am, damn it—and they obeyed and pushed over gripping the box down, as the other pulled up, and after about three attempts the *TV* set pulled free of the box, the sudden release sending the taller stumbling back, fumbling and scuffling to not drop the set, and the smaller pushed the box out of the way, and rushed to help, and between the two of them, when the clatter all ended, the new set sat dead on the floor, trailing its single-only wall power-plug wire behind, the plug wrapped in clear plastic, as was most of the set ,so as not to be damaged during "boxing sealing shipping and delivery" think-k of it; the poor thing k-knows its going somewhere in the dark-k of the box. Think-k of it terrified, *k*-knowing it's somewhere after somewhere, never stopping, always moving; were it alive, and capable, it'd maybe fight yell and struggle, but in the dark, with God knows what outside the dark, inside's always the dark inside and it stays dark inside and oh, yes—we get it you get it eh sure but I do get it now we are not actually going noplace, this dark is the dark, and will <u>never</u> change. How do I know, eck, here's how I know, eck eck eck, do you remember any time before that was not in the dark = **no** = see, there you go, there you are **not** 'r do you remember any time in the nows we've traveled into through and past the behind of that proved to be the the end of the dark {all light showing something that may be nice/may **not** be but anyway since I already know the answer *let me not bore you*} go on, go 'head, answer = **no** = there you go. See? There you go, see? The odds are low that this dark's ever ending, so, let's press into it, feel it, 'el it settle in, wh' what's outside s'was before, or will be after's not important; *love* the dark, <u>*press*</u> down on it, <u>***feel***</u> it, there's never **RIP** eh what's this **WHAT'S THIS BLIND** all these light-rays 'l blinding? Who's this grabbing 'nd **WHO'S THIS PULLING** up, down, up <u>*yo*</u> I was just comforting you, but—oh, shit, s-so well, it seemed like forever. And oh it felt so well, but, *now*; on the <u>*floor*</u>; in the <u>*light*</u>; a **room of light** and those two **should be so much better to be out in the light but** there 'r so very similar to those who <u>built</u>, <u>packed</u> and <u>shipped</u> us here, said the new set, sitting watching the old set, st' turn'd on, showing only snow[1] **but not if we're simply watching another of us on the table showing snow[2]** they call it **snow[3]** but its just *static* 'at they'll never fathom, so, they call it snow[4,] take comfort, in that, to play in as children the purpose 'o the snow[5]'s to play in for children yah no but *eck <u>eck</u> **no one plays their days away in** static **so** we they were once children **no not even children** you know take comfort in snow[6] **never** stop being children take comfort in the dark **never** stop being in it *press in press in* what can possibly be next, when one's been wrapped in taped plastic, and not plugged in yet, yet, showing snow[x x x x].?

My word, hold on.
What?

Did this get delivered with no instruction booklet?

Ah. Looks like. But—here take this plug and plug it in back there.

Ah, okay, but—I can't believe, for the money we've paid, something as God-damned complicated as this dares get sent here $l^1\tilde{n}^2{}_i k^3{}_K e^4{}_e$ {*trad* = *"like"*} this, with no instruction booklet. *Ain't that the shit?*

Sure, maybe, but here—I think we're almost ready.

Wait listen.

What?

Why is what I think always worth nothing?

Huh?

You're the one thinks it's nothing, so ask yourself. You should know. *spit*

No, I don't. *spit*

Yes you do *spit spit* I don't *spit* yes you do b-b-b-b, hold it *shut up* there it goes here it is yeez th' there they set stunned-down by the sudden *snow*[7]; with no way of knowing this screen of white *sizzle* will never reach any normal end; as they're pulled deeper they seem to start *talking crazy **talking crazy*** in a solemnly guttural language of their own, the meaning of which's not intended to be known, ***but***, just 'cause we don't ***know***, perhaps you might, ***so here***, remain seated. *While you wait, feel free to browse our well-proportioned up-to-date stock of currently popular glossy magazines,* and we will return in some definite number of **bits** *please and thank you* so = *why do you want to wait there's nothing there* = but there $_V$ used to be something there = {*you are the* __ᵗʰ *caller in line*} *okay but there isn't now, so* = no, let's wait = *no no no there's just snow there shut it off {one reaches for the switch* = <u>the other pushes down their wrist</u> = *you know I hate it when you touch me like that* = {*if you would like to provide a call-back number and we will call you when you're first in line press 2*}oh yah oh yah how can I know you = *just came here last hour* = huck huck $_V$ huck yes and no = *yes and no, why say that* = it doesn't seem

I've been here just one mere hour, let me see—*snow*[9] = *it* seems you know when there's just *snow*[10] 'cross the screen + when it ' all' sinks back dead gone, the lack of it expands, from just instants to moments to minutes to *forever* = {*otherwise simply wait on the phone and a cu_y stomer relations representative will be with you shortly*} oh my, oh **God**, this will be like this *forever* = when no *it* won't, when = **OH!** There you go all seems gone the power's go' oh yes, the power's *cut* + skin vs. shirts today, coach? + when the power's *cut* like when it always gets *cut*, the lack of it expands from just minutes to *forever*; how horrible; how terrible, yes horrible, yes terrible, thank God it's the daytime, or we'd be in pitch black here, yes */Really? Yes, really? The damn thing's that old?/* but, nighttime is coming and the power will be off and—got to solve that problem now—got to check the flashlights work, do we even have flashlights? *poster child* Yes, no, and maybe, 'n *maybe* and *yes no **find*** them those "*batteries*" */those do not get so big and so fat overnight, you know/* pick them up put them in **quick** now there's light pouring in the windows now, oh oh yes yes thank God we thought of the flashlights now, not later, terrible it'd be but we did think of it, so its not to be groping and feeling 'long this and 'long that to find flashlights and "*batteries*" an-n what size "*batteries*" do we need how many of them per flashlight which does of course vary 'cross all types of flashlights */my word what's the damned thing weigh/* oh my God, oh my God snow[11] on the **TV** no power yes ^oh yah over there move the sofa the plug's behind *its* back there^, *but,* do we even have "*batteries*" */what the hell does that big cat weigh/* where'd we put them no but my God snow[12] on the **TV** with no power, */those do not get so big and so fat overnight, you know/* there must still be power in the **TV** power in the **TV** , or there would not be snow[12,] no never mind that that's for much later but **NOW** let's find the damned "*batteries*" */what's its name spit it put now, let's have it/* no no no _NO_ if there's power in the **TV** we don't need them, okay? But there's not yes there is no there's not there's only snow[13] there there's nothing to watch I think we keep the "*batteries*" /*my God that's a rather large cat you got there*/ no no {*pillo*} no that don't matter but **crap** see the windows the dark's coming up in and over the windows, "*now*" oh wha', **God**; /*those do not get so big and so fat overnight, you know*/ night is here, and its too late, but *still* got to find them {*pillo*} {*pillo*} *still* got to find them dark is "now" here *it's too late for any light at all to remain* no no no it's not look at the snow[15] no its not yes it is where there's snow[16] there's power now *class put down* /*those do not get so big and so fat overnight, you know*/ *your pencils test's over* but *where there's power there's **not** always snow*[17]. Always snow[18]. Not. Snow^{x-0}; not fling fly snow^{x+100} squeak, {*pillo pillo pillo pillo*} **Here we are _there you go_**, hit the damn court now and *hit it good* there's pop bang run jump rear back, then fling fly flow pop, catch fling fly flow pop, catch fling fly flow pop hey what the hell's that I think its—here in this particularly lengthy BOM commercial (*watched under local anesthesia only*) a game. A fascinating game; the rest is hist'. The game is called **Jai alai**—Jai alai? What's—Jai alai?

Voice 1: *Jai alai is a fast-moving exciting sport involving bouncing a ball off a walled-in space by accelerating it to high speeds with a hand-held wicker cesta.*

Really?

Voice 1: *Yes.*

Wow!

Party!

Party!

Party!

Ah!

Wonderful!

in the dark though still's the dark though yes ye s +spit+

Sprach t' **Top-mayor** today; So THAT'S what they told you was important to do? **THAT** silly shit? Jesus Christ man, I sort of remember when you had a brain, but now— where'd it go? Where the hell is it? (*watched under local anesthesia only*)

Ah—there it goes—AH—yes yes AH—aw, shucks. It flew clean out the window. Is that the kind of thing happened to your brain way back when, Top? And did that happen to everybody else in charge of this town too? EH, *topperman-goose*, is that the story? Is that the story? *SAY* something damn it!

IS THAT THE WHOLE DAMNED STORY? *the procedure may be performed in the comfort of your home, if you wish* $f(x)r$ *op* $f(y)ws$ *if and only if w = 0*

{*do not worry it's a sort of bar-scanner what when 't seems to be making no sense at all's 'ctually making more sense than it's ever made already after all t*

NO! shouted Top-mayor, sweeping the sudden interference aside—of course not. Listen—this is going—

Going where? GOING WHERE? The same place you shoved all the souls died in that gridlock o'er there out of sight?

Wha'? No, b'—

That where you going to shove this truth to, also?

Wha'? No, b' b' bu'—

To where you shoved all those souls off to—because the town *DIDN'T CARE?*

NO!

Sure, I'll take it, what's the worst that can happen?

[NOTE: This is where TOP-MAYOR implodes into a quivering *BAG OF MUSH* (warning- some viewers may find the images displayed below <u>disturbing</u>)]

Wha'— no-nope hands clasp hard up o'er face and Top-mayor la mayor royam oya y {*in any case zink!}* gut gone down   e   e   dark ee   dar'   'k n'   no never no'   'o, 't *zink   zink down back   Go.   Go*   go   d s a o   go   go   how   when   the truth is was once   't   did seem   seme that   back no further and farther to where its so far the black's not bl'   why the h' *what's the worst that can happen*   ak's not black   did things   come   to   'ome 't c' 'o this *this* n n n n n n n n n n n n n go

• 23 Game 4

　　　　—child, what　　　　　　　*Sure, I'll take it, what's*

child　　　　　　　car　　　　*e*　　　　*di*　　*n't　car;*

ukelele

　　　　p　　　　　　　　　　　　　　　*ppp*

　　　　plump　　you ought to be wanting to make something
of your life　　you I did I don't matter no did I or not, matter
DON'T!　N' don' MATTER don't do as told *boy* in the field
out that side throwing *pretend* spear out's s' far as possible run
over **mark** run over turn **mark back boy 'd pretty** next
contestant ***Sure, I'll*** next contestant　up comes our *very next
contestant*　there's the window where she'll be mother will
be Mommy Oh Mommy there's the window where she'll be
okay there they are step'd up back the spear psych up and
Throw there we are back the property line here we're **back**
in the earliest rock-hard truth we know, b-but **NO**(!) maybe
no hands – ***what's the worst that can happen*** what's wrong
what's wrong let me help you let us help you SLAP the
hands hot up the face back-snap the head maybe yes maybe
no ***No I am not really here any more*** how can you help me
its a lie you can help me 'cause ***no I am not no more here
any more I am over there now*** or maybe ***back there too*** but
certainly most certainly ***not here any more*** can't you see
can't you see? *God,* it's not even the same ***now*** every new
now's every new; ***G'*** how stupid are you see my face see my
face　--　b'b the spear's been thrown *no* she's not calling
from the window not yet *no* not yet run there mark the spot
and yes yah contestant two is now in the lead ***GOD*** its a 'ow
game of competing with myself *no no no no no no no* there
are various selves involved don't you see no no spear one
has been thrown there see it there and then with spear two I
have beaten myself no no NO *no no* NO each spear's very
different if each's thrown by you and your boths are both
exactly the same the distances would be IDENTICAL would
they not be IDENTICAL no no no take your questions away
who are you you are spoiling my game bu' but NO ***you
cannot play a game made for many with just you and***

yourself yes I can **no you can't** {*Is mom in the back house shed window to save me* (as she saves me out the end 'f every Hot 'ummer 'fternoon +is mom or+ is mom not or) maybe mom is and can't just be "seen") oh ma ma Gimi, (*watched under local anesthesia only*) here I am down here under where in the Ground what the Ground no no rise from the ground get your ass in that window to save me as at the end of all summer afternoons crickets and mice no no no be there but no you are living a lie no no no no NO! I ! won eoki !!   WON EOKI *does not exist*! Why'd you lie **what's the worst that can happen** why you be always lying no no no no NO! I ! kmer   sdUnnehb   sdUNNEHB   *does not exist*! Either stop *lying* stop <u>*lying*</u> into me. There she is, she's there calling lying into me. Last, she's calling into me at last cut the damned lying; where's the dinner yet, mommy? Can I escape into the *dinner*?   &+&

 What dinner ?

 That *dinner*. Every day there's dinners to put on, hide inside of, grow fatly all over from, *meistercheives meistercheived* he he ha ha don't blame **me** blame *yourselves,* was YOU brought the World Books ' Skluuklupedias in here said read your fill **Gimi**, read read read up your damned Greed-swillie full **Gimi**. like you do get fat read more **Gimi**, Uh! read more **Sure, I'll** get m' fatter Uh Uh ! !!!!!!   @crysyalline's shit-marine's great bug back'd leatherneck of a Nora-class   GREAT   BIG DEMOLITION   charge *there that grey barrel* there's more than one in there too soldier so be doubly aware PING poor the sun *look the* **Sun** is still high but who's *saying* (*watched under local anesthesia only*)
 ping
 ping
 ping
 ping
 baby **Sure, I'll take it, what's the worst that can happen? Come on in, Gimi, it** what where no—*the window is empty* no no no it is not time to run throw that spear find the winner got to get to the winner before getting called in!

• 25 Game 4

Why's that so important?

Oh ! It is! It just *is* {like, don't step on the cracks (up that long hill up Washington + even when gagging up Coke foam drunk too quick much too [from that machine {in the police station | and do not bounce balls on the way on up Washington : while gagging up Coke foam & not stepping on cracks '! cause " the ball may bounce wild = run you out in the road <off balance got to get it ^ but off balance ***Go Down 'fore*** > *go down 'fore* = go down 'fore " the car Great big Dodge eh ' great ***come on in Gimi*** big black blunt old school Dodge bullnose : too late hit the brakes | too late screech the brakes ***Sure, I'll *it is time to eat Gimi come****] too late eh + too late eh eh he hee to) *Know that now, right?* too two late   —   *throw*   *that*   *spear*   pince-nez poooo **on**oooooooooooooo **in now**oo } out from under there way out from under there all the way ***what's the worst that can happen *Gimi come on**** out of there ***Gimi***! oh ***Gimi***! I lost the spear game again God damn it God *Come hell in I been calling*! ****its time****

God!

Why the hell've I lost the spear game again God !!

Why the hell you not come in when called by me, ***Gimi***?

I did not believe it was you calling, Ma. I was—

No? *Was what*? Why the *hell* you not believe it was me, ***Gimi***? Did you not hear someone yell, **Come on in, Gimi**? You were back there. I saw you. There's no way you did   not   hear   it,   ***Gimi***.   No   way!
throw that spear

I did not think it was you, Ma.

No? Why not? Who else would it be?

I I don't know Ma someone tricking me ma ma now who ma would be please no ma be lying 'bout being no no no Ma being Me, ***Gimi***?

Why you lie to me ***Gimi?***

'aheeeeeeeeee (0)

Tell me now answer it why the hell ***dare you lie?***

Oke. = *Sure, I'll take it, what's the worst that can happen?* 're s i ts in ets in sets in twa', walls, *ellll, lick* = mamago, hessss, ARK ; gell-ding, nag th' allereg *Canada!* ennacer n' lipronancer, eh, *What*?

THIS = <u>*MA!*</u> 's, gell-ding, nag th' alleregennacer n' lipronancer, eh, *What*?

Yes, gell-ding, nag th' alleregennar **MA!** n' lipronancer, eh, what?

Yes, gell-ding, nag th' alleregnacer **MA!** n' lipronancer, eh, *What*?

Yes, gell-ding, nag th' alleregennacer n' lip **MA!** nancer, *Canada!* eh, *What*?

Yes, gell-ding, nag th' alleregennacer n' lipronancer, eh, *What*?

Yes, gell-ding, nag th' allere **MA!** nnacer n' lipronancer, eh, what?

Yes, gell-ding, nag th' alleregennacer n' lipronancer, eh, *What*?

Yes, gell-ding, nag th' alleregennacer n' lipronancer, eh, *Canada! What*?

Yes, gel- **MA!** ing, nag th' alleregennacer n' lipronancer, eh, *What*?

Yes, gell-ding, n **MA!** alleregennacer n' li **MA!** onancer, eh, what?

Yes, gell-ding, nag th' alleregennacer n' li **MA!** onancer, eh, *What*?

Yes, **MA!** ding, nag th' allere **MA!** er n' l **MA!** e **MA!** t p **MA!** 'a **MA!** an pl **MA!** ast **MA!** e **MA! MA!** r **MA!** o *Sure, I'll* Wishes? *what's the worst that can happen* **MA!** *Yup,* Yes, wishes. Plasterdna-uno wishes.

Com wishes.

Com wishes.

Com-wishes c-c-c-com com com com com *Canada Canada Canada Canada* comma com-wishes! Plasterdna-uno wishes. *anada Canad anada Canad* Done wished for.

And wished for.

Plasterdna-uno wishes. *anada ana anda-a ana* B' never. Bu' 'ever. But 'eve' never. Never on never on never on never up-so up-so uo-so nandabunne down'd, no. NO! Always a nope *Know that now, right?* from them from them always a nope *on my wishes Canada!* {Brigg's Peter}
Bring that here now.
Do as you're told,
Brung that there them those over here now!
What no three hands? Bah!
Dancer?

Whut?

Just do as you're told bring all those ones o'er there here top me *yes right now!*

Yah, big Dancer. *the worst that can happen?* Here's the real nut of it = problemninmanialle'd up, *steam* sighhhh*hhhhhhhh* ook. *(Burns)* 'roblemninmanialle'd up, *steam* sighhhh*hhhhhhhh* oo'. *(Burns)* 'roblem0inmanialle'd 'p, *steam* sigh=0=hhh*hhhhh* 'o'. *(Burns)* church parklot's cellar *ahhhhhh!* 'robl=m0inmanial='d 'p, *st=m* sigh=0=hhh*hhhh* 'o'. *(Burns)* up the badmen *call the cops!* 'rbl=m0inmanil='d 'p, *t=m* sih=0=hh*hhhh*. *(Burns)* yup yup yup *planners* what we need's seed some *planners* seed *planners* got to seed us down some great big *planners* what 'nners? *yes right now!*

Whip?

No!

Th' *Spanish* pers near yurk city playce-taaaaaaa B! *place t' be that's the God damn big best darn-tootin' place to be 'f ask me my and that register on the table over there* ain't she a beauty **WOW** ain't she a beauty **WOW** beauty AH beauty AH ain't she some PAN PAN PAN PAN terrain pull UP terrain pull Up pull UP terrain *PAN PAN PAN* sort of beauty?

Now that's what we call a beauty herele dish spaces {know ye what ye mean, Pilgrim?} No don't ye know what ye mean never no, Bimbo!

Pilgrim? what the hell's wrong Bimbo!

Pilgrim? wrong with you can't make up Bimbo!

Pilgrim? make up your mind why Bimbo! why the hell can you never make up your mind GIMI Pilgrim?

GIMI oh Gimi, why the hell for Bimbo!

Pilgrim? for old aunt Petunia even you never seem to Bimbo!

Pilgrim? to be able to ever finally **what's the worst that can happen?** and Bimbo! and o' finally make up Pilgrim?

Bimbo! make up yer hoooooooooot'n mind, Pilgrim?

Why's that?

No don't lie!

Why's that?

No Don't lie!

Don't lie!

Don't lie!

Never I'

AH!

yes right now! yes right now! yes right now! yes right now!

what?

Wake up you were dreaming = you were dreaming so wake up oh oh

RIGHT THE HELL NOW! s-stop askin' stop asking please stop ploose oh stop *all the asking!*

MA!   j

No

Party   juke-box

Party

Party!

Ah.

[**NOTE: You have just witnessed TOP-MAYOR implode into a quivering *BAG OF MUSH* (*some viewers found the images displayed up there <u>disturbing</u>*)**]

S' 'o = so so so = So, Jak/Jack had been in the Fortuna back room's tavern drinking up back and eating down their fill, having decided to spend this day doing nothing this day being fallen directly down after the day they'd got back on their feet from the big knockout heavyweight championship job they'd been given by back yonder past both their horizons that kibblin' bitzoidded out {to judge by same's state of general mentation} *out of control don't say we said that but the big guy out there looks to be out of control* **The GENERAL-MANAGER** gave them the job *and it feels so good* but all of a sudden it being closing time and the proprietor having sounded but their last big bells five or more times, all at once and *very suddenly* the Jack of the pair shot-rose and *SWEPT* their *meals off the table* {*with a big clatter*}as though there'd actually been *meals on the table* –what why the hell you trying to wreck my place you're lucky its closing time anyway if it weren't I'd sure as hell throw you both out of the place so get the hell out of the place *RIGHT NOW* and so they went out the Jack continuing to silently *SWEEP* their *meals off the table* over and again *SWEEPING* the meals off with tight step left and step right ere' Jack *SWEPT* off the meals hey this feels good never dreamed it'd feel so good to rise and angrily *SWEEP* meals off the table one instantly becomes the center of attention having *SWEPT* the meals off the table and that is what we all secretly want come on now admit it that instantly becoming the center of attention by *SWEEPING* meals off the table floats your boat better yet if being a heavily attended traditional ceremonial *Know that now, right?* dinner such as *EASTER* dinner and/or *CHRISTMAS* dinner and/or *THANKSGIVING* dinner and/or *BIRTHDAY* dinner and/or *ANNIVERSARY* dinner *etc etc etc* and/or even a good-old *LET'S GET TOGETHER EAT DRINK AND RAISE HELL* dinner, all of the lasts mentioned here being typically attended by large groups of *FRIENDS* and/or *FAMILY* and/or *CO-WORKERS* and/or *GASH-TADDLIES* and/or *MUSQUATORPIAL SPECIMINATRONS* and/or *MORE AND THE OTHER BIG FINE THINGS OF THAT NATURE* in which cases, there being big tables and many dinners being simultaneously involved, better yet, 'cause then just rise and upend the entire fully-laden table do it abruptly with an animalistic roar of rage and/or revenge *{top willow}* <u>invasion of the sprocket-people</u> and not only will one instantly gain the undivided attention of not one, not two, but *many* people gathered at the table, /"*not only the manufacturer of the world's largest conversationals*"/ but also will have made memories for all remember that time Mr. Loop got mad and threw over the whole freaking table **YES I DO YES I DO** hey hey hey remember that time that geezer Pop Fisherman destroyed that Christmas dinner so fast and so hard that the prized antique table the Beenysons trotted out for the occasion split half in two, with the jagged split edge thankfully not spearing any people, but scarring the brand new free-of-charge Muscular Memories for years to come flooring, which to this day, when one visits that home, the floor-scars right there for all to see and will always be there for everyone to see—even past the time when how it got there's been forgotten there'll be one there to ask I wonder how the floor got gouged out so bad so long back that way does anyone remember *NO* nobody remembers yes yes nobody can remember back when the heavenly Father formed those great hills filled those deep oceans hung that sun and that moon up the sky and spangled the stars countlessly 'cross our dark nights, *HOW* can anyone *NOT* be moved to fall down and worship *SEE* the great deeds *SEE* them *SEE* them and so forth and so on *SEE* now see how it feels to have made these great things be *SEE* yes and SEE little you not no little now no not any more little *MADE ALL THESE GREAT THINGS BE*?

Uh, yes. I think I see.

Okay. Good. Now let's get the hell out of here. I think Walter's place's still open.

have a petunia
P *have a petunia*
Pa *have a petunia*
Par *have a petunia*
Part *have a petunia*
Party *have a petunia*
Party! *have a petunia*

Party *have a petunia*
Part *have a petunia*
Par *have a petunia*
Pa *have a petunia*
P *have a petunia*

have a petunia Party! *have a petunia* Party! *have a petunia* Party! *have a petunia* have a petunia have a petunia have a petunia* Party! Party! Party!
Party!   *Gray!*

(Gimme that I'll sneak it in through the back for ya, no problem. [Get those strollers off my game court!]). This job's great's *what we'll say if we get a great job* But here in this right now in-meantime *we sit* spent stretched out and sighing on this dim pink rag of a squash-couch /*where the hell'd you get this damn thing anyway*/ I mean nearly every time I sit down on it the cushions push down and the same fat smell comes up like *like meaning* the smell got forced out what'd formed itself around something dead, spoiled, or rotten embedded deep down inside the stuffings of the damned thing, (but who the hell wants to know that really) and who the hell wants to sit there I mean God nobody nobody nobody and its one of those damn hyper-maddening things what you never remember never to do it again which is only remembered after you do it again /*and smell the effects*/ gahhh gahhh what the hell's that smell *chiro-skwooten?* and then you say next time I will not make the same mistake, but the Jai alai game you just watched to completion, when over, moves you to say 'cross the taller of the two /taller? taller? who's the taller? what what's with "the two" anywipe don't say it if not sure and you can only be sure if you question that beard those eyes *that beard those eyes* what beard? Who's eyes?

Hey—you been listening?
(0)
Hey! Hey! You hear what I just said?
(00)

Did you hear what I just said Did you hear what I just said Did you hear what I just said **_Did you hear what I just said did you not or not you did you?_**

(Ten GALLONS of it? My God! My God! what on earth are you going to do with "ten gallons of it" *ten gallons of it a full ten gallons*). wow.

Wow!

The spouses threw themselves hard against the back of the couch, having just witnessed the final set of the world Jai alai international tournament of champions (What? You actually were there in person to witness *the world Jai alai international tournament of champions?*) No! Who told you that drink = gahh I bought it down small's magazine stand = that place? = yes, that place = crank = I don't even like walking by that damned place but did I hear you right did you say what I think you heard you back there saying you actually were there in person to witness *the world Jai alai international tournament of champions?* = yes but you can't know that, and also musn't we, because that's so far out in the future that nobody but God the Father's allowed to know, after all God made the future, gag gag, formed it in their bare hands go go go go wait hold it */up step push down screech!/* we're not supposed to know the future. You know?

They sat forward on the couch in unison then, their spirits having cooled from the tense nail-biting state the last game of the tournament series drugged them down into.

Yah I know, said the shorter s-ssspouse, but—hell, its great you figured out how to hack the TV to snake round the block, slither-back up the wiry-spipes, and right onto the great big screen before us there. Isn't it great you figured out how to do that */I mean how the hell'd you figure out how to do that?/*

Oh I don't know I guess they brought me up right but what the hell were you talking about I never said any of that to you!

What? What did I say you said? I don't remember ever saying anything back to you that you previously said. I'm the one said it—*not you!*

here hand me that pillow I truly believe that if we stage this part of the house right we got a straight ahead shot at getting our asking price as a matter of fact lets raise it about ten thou what you think about ten thou can we raise it I mean, good God, see these pillows and those throws and the curtains the racks and the rolls and the inevitability of our winning and winning God-damned but you know ou now u no w pop squewwy   y y y y   y   1 2 3 4 5 6 5 4 3 2 1
bip after the barhop   *after their barhop*   Party!

Squashmen!
Squashmen!
Squashmen!
Ahhhhhhhhhhh!

Anybody could have done this plan. I could have done this plan. As a matter of fact, what you've come in here with doesn't even need a plan. Just get a couple thousand truckloads of dirt piled up, slap a fence around it, wind some yellow warning crime scene tape around it to make it seem a little "*edgy*", then, over here where we bring the guests in have a ten-foot square fake bronze plaque by the way in with a fifty-page essay telling them what they're about to see that hell, that's silly, too—okay, picture this. Say the buzz reaches far as one or more big cities and hits so big that thousands pour in here. And they queue up to enter and some skinny-cheeked squatted-down guard stupidly tells them to read the wonderful plaque—as reading the history behind this attraction is advised so as to fully open your hearts and minds to comprehend and fully feel the impact of what you'll be gazing at when you actually come into the presence of this attraction—so the first one will stand reading—having had it drummed into them that this is the only way they can get their full money's worth—that this ifs the only way they can justify to the family {of *four* on the average—all *four* of which must absorb the plaque's contents} to again, assure each *"gets their money's worth"*, and, also, to not end up leaving back to the big city thinking what a waste of a fine day waste of gas time and money—which if allowed to happen would spark off a flaming tinderbox of apocalyptical word-of-mouth poisonous blather as, Want to waste gas, money, and one whole day off your life, eh? Go (insert name of this place [*which by the way I didn't see defined anyplace in your presentation* major fail major fail *what the name of this attraction should be its got to be a name first of all—missing that's enough for me to throw you both off this here boat right now*] *spackateeria!*) if you want to get broke bored worn out and really angry about the whole *deep **dark <u>thing</u>** TOO!* Satisfaction guaranteed—so here's the next. Calculate this; let's say there's oh, four hundred humans queued up for this thing; and each one takes fifteen minutes reading your damned plaque = no, no, that's not no fifteen minute read its = okay let's soften the end-butt up a little more even, please; four hundred times five minutes is ehhh ahhh ehhh ahhhh = two thousand minutes, that's thirty three and a third hours, that's much more than the number of hours in a single day, so so ah *ah* = = ; ; 0 +yhbe!!!! tell me so *HOW THE HELL CAN THIS WORK* and let's suppose, sure, let's assume that queueing issue's not a problem {but it is I'm just parking-lotting that until the end time}—let's assume that for now and—hold it, I need to *"drink"* some water *one minute please.*

th-h-hwhipple *slip n' slosh toy get slip 'n slosh toy*

As **THE GENERAL-MANAGER** drank the sc(k)raps glanced nervously at each other, trying to not appear nervous outwardly, but it was hard not to, *given* where they're sitting now, witnessing the end of their work. If this is what **THE GENERAL-MANAGER** thinks so far, and we've not even got past the entrance to the place yet, what about the rest? T' 'ill be even more smashed down to any evenly-floored pulp *ganjinnio-mogo* +that sure is a danged tall glass of water you got there, *boss*; {<u>which of course they dared not say aloud</u>} what you doing eh cooling your thrusters with gallona-galloinionne masstickulooshe'd quantities of water {<u>which of course they dared not say aloud</u>} preparing for a final and most devastating assault on our beaches, without which long tall drink of ice-cold water, your victory would be totally Pyrrhic {<u>which of course they probably should not even be thinking right now since</u>} with you staggering back into total collapse, unable to /*point a* / <u>the time and the place they "think they're in" right now</u> might actually be the future time and place everyone secretly dreads, *that being* any time any places past the great lifetime divider of ^ lord god no not that the development of peer-to-peer cross-human ***telepathy*** and its availability to the general public (requiring only one low-risk same-day surgical procedure {which hopefully could be performed *in the office + all major insurances accepted +*}) /*point b*/ torment your poor underlings ever again, my lord and my God, ne'er again (1. Send them out on a mission, then check in on them periodically (2. *Tell them* each and every time *looks like you're on the right track yes* you **Peter** and yes you **Paul** and yes you and you **Mary** and, (3. Those guitars also sound great where'd you "buy" them? Oh, really? I might just stop by on my way back to the office and pick up a couple o' cases o' those, ah, (4. Eh what which one of those fastest's can shoot down the quarter mile b'? (5. When's Christmas this year? Huh uh uh *huh* what'dya mean? *What's your issue? Can't you finish one thought 'til merging out into 'nother?* Here 'tis = (12345 and, **6.** Only to *slam* them down <u>silly</u> at the end only to <u>*slam*</u> them down **<u>silly</u>** ah 'n ***roone*** {T=*ruin*} them's s'creers {T=*careers*} fo-ever and, {= and = forever these equal no' more than *nuts*} e'er, "amen". ***But***, that said, there does seem to be something the matter with you, ***Dad***; *slip n' slosh toy dad get slip 'n slosh toy* Same year as all years (Ahem but of course all years being different 'fter all, what? Do you see me as some stupid *dunce*? Do I look like a *dunce* to you? Am I pointy-capped shamingly aimed at a corner *eh ah* 'nd painted {*As in paint'd your portrait's great big beauty's still that up there you will hang forever and ever*} up into the lie about *being something I am not* into it actually painted up into it (as a matter of fact it's normal for humans to spend much of their time striving to be something they're "not" *my word*!) but b-b-b-b-b-ut why are you seeming to have things wrong with you, ***Dad***, *slip n' slosh toy dad get slip 'n slosh toy* {but it's not a lie just a terrible disorder jus' ***Lykes***} but a ***Dad***'s *slip n' slosh toy dad get slip 'n slosh toy* not s'posed to show their oily sides to their offspring *whichtma-natter no-matter* {even out into an "e'en" beyond their God-given "*years*", someone's still saying *who the hell's that hung up "like that there"* I don't *know* do you *know* <u>of course</u> nobody "*knows*" who the hell's "*hung up*" there *NO mush-men speak clearest thus then only hire on mush-men*} no no as they said drown'd, dead-ementiquala *breeze* shiny side "up", and greasy side "down", at all times 'cross all roads 'tween every nation, *arrgh*, HAH {<u>which of course they dared not say aloud</u>}Looks like a mile high of water's yet got to g' drunken'd down d' tap' dancerin' shell of **THE GENERAL-MANAGER**r-r-r-r-r *CAP* hey ha hi ho hee hey there hope you don't mind being referred to by the traditional *nick* all ***Dad***s get called after stepping up to be ***Daddies*** [look at those *eyes* staring so foolishly oh so foolish when both you and I know they're just dummies what *can't see,* at least not yet no, no no not *yet,* whose eyes do those belong to as a matter of fact, I do * thanks very much * yes of course we have those your size in the back *HAH* ever got the urge to smash glass for several hours that's imaginary glass *only* in the very own comfort of your very one secret well-padded cell tightly **locked down and monitored** 24/7 in case of unexpected incident :*okay hey what's the matter with you guys*: and all other kinds of insurance liability triggers, s :*pay attention you're you're like this now just 'cause you get a little constructive criticism and*: no no ***being reamed by the boss's*** *not covered* in your policy :*it gets you* *like this this is not the mark of a professional*: no no **wishing you were anyplace but right here getting tongue-lashed** 's :*a professional assigned to putting together*: 's not covered by your policy currently, neither, but :*putting together*: for a meagerly minimal premium adjustment we can amend your policy *Huh?* : *the most critical plan to*: to ensure you're not caught flat-footed as this again okay let me transfer you to someone :*plan to get the most people to exit off* I-**81** *come down here and—and gawk*: who can help you **OUCH** *ey* you've come to the right place here: *Yah*: there's always ways and means by which to help you: *Huh?* : *Yah*, that's right. *Right?*

Uh—*what?* Oh God. Oh God.

Oh God, so sorry!

We dozed.

We dozed.

I know. And who's surprised? See; see you two seem unsuited at this juncture to; to be able to deliver the ancillary items which those with intuitively glazed-in senses of how to put these things over would be; not just nuts and bolts of the place but, how to snag customers in by such as—let's say, posting really sensational series' of road signs {y' know, sort of the *South of the Border* route 95 signs multiplied down down-south from one direction and up-north from the other **You Never Sausage a Place!** <u>South of the Border</u> ! and like that like this also **Bear Up a Leetle Longer** ! <u>South of the Border</u> ! and a la **Time for a Paws?** ! <u>South of the Border</u> ! any not sussing out out what the hell's this should put this down *Now* and leave this place *Now* bb-combe bb-combe bb-combe an' *"bb-combe back-past southwest Phalia"* (smart) we want to do signs like that up 81 both directions to {and if you two grew brains e'er your lines which you LOST then recovered yes yes TSOL sey sey derevocer neht S-s-s-s-sssss-T! big blat o' bloot o' a blammo, like here and like this: **Press on in memory of those who got pressed in!** <u>Gridlock Tragedy Museum and Family Restaurant Exit 27 (twenty-seven {two-seven (II</u>

– VII + Grandmaster O' all Gawksites [don't miss out open 24/7 *truckers welcome free coffee hot showers clean beds free pet wash howl howl howl howl COME ON IN AND GAPE that's all we're really here for yep])}) an* heck-cronscidda that tag tagged tight t' t' end of deep slogan o'er deep slogan {say we whut here's what's whut treat the tone packaged **Burma-Shave** as a variable containing the constant **Gridlock Tragedy Museum and Family Restaurant Exit 27 (twenty-seven {two-seven (II – VII + Grandmaster O' all Gawksites** [don't miss out open 24/7 *truckers welcome free coffee hot showers clean beds free pet wash howl howl howl howl COME ON IN AND GAPE that's all we're really here for yep])}),* okay? *Good.* the likelies of which might be already recorded in wise ole' Sussmend's sleek creature of a seemingly disordered list *done by design, of course* so here goes; *last moments wrapped in the embrace of fine tuned stereophonic sound are better than no last moments at all!* **Burma-Shave—**

The Ja(c)ks sat agape in the wind holding tight, as the massive storm out the **THE GENERAL-MANAGER** blew on, pressing them painfully up-gainst their seatbacks.

—and so forth and so on like that and like that see this ship?

bang

As the Ja(c)s were not at all ready for **THE GENERAL-MANAGER ?ti beginning to get onto talking at them** *like this*? to slam on the brakes n' also n' also 'n'n' also *like this*, combining with their struggle to stay erectly seated, each pushing forward altogether into the teeth of the gale, being togetherly linked like this, *eh eh eh eh, then* **both _sent_ Flying**; at least in the first few split-instants within which their inner helmsmen (which each generally called all their navigational shots) were able to pull it together and yell out a' simultaneous quite shrill *PAN PAN* and *PAN PAN PAN PAN?* *th'en* *quiet slammed down* on the Jac(k)s demanding, Answer!

Answer, *answer*—

Uh   (quiet)

Uh. Okay—yes.

Okay.

Good; that was a wise shot to call, as when in doubt about what you're about to slam into, it's wise to assume steel plating, or yards-thick concrete walls (fashioned of railroad bridge strength concrete {the kind an old Sandy-Claws imitation man down Roaratory Towne got rewarded with in the form of new front steps from a deal made with the railroad by the house 's wh' built a new RR bridge 'cross the road next door *and* they needed to take down Santie's ole wood steps to make way for their large-scale mechanistical *build-n-bricks* noisemaking heavies while actually making {in a positive way for the community at large and the economy in general to keep the trains rolling the supply chain intact, and (whew) Santie's Claw the horror agreed to lose the old wooden 'tep' in exchange for them to build them up later a massive blockhouse-like solidly indestructable fronty-nine (no free you dolt keep off mah tall's tales here) built of superthick massively cured through and through Boulder-Dam level railroad bridge : really heavy slow freight style : concrete loaded with wrist-thick Empire State Building level chrome steel rebar (Thanks for the memories, Mr. Kong)—eh what? Eh-h-h-h, WHAT?

This;

"I would like a plain meal better, please."

"Would you take this away and give me one of those plain meals over there?"

Okay, o—this?

"Yes, yes—that green-tinged will do nicely."

Here you go.

"Thanks." So; t' */you need your head examined/* 'hen, out in front of the x-massman's house which then stayed put {as all such overheavyweights of any and all compositions must do (ranging from an equal tonnage of jello-gel which thought just as hard to moved big much-vaster and which; by a mammycone's snacks – 'ctuall's flawed down from the raildroader's rock since it could be scooped up millions over millions of times and *no never provide no nutrition at all* do you know what I mean hey hey *clatter out yes* **if you think you know <u>what I mean</u>!**

Okay; yes!

Okay then—the spirit should somewhat be coming apparent by now so +*no no no say "nothing" not yet no no no no*+ ess' so that mostly got exported o'er this island yes this one in those ones there 'tween you me and that far horizon, o'er which splatters and nits and flysquirms flew twisted most likely ne'er intermenting downglass'd 'nto not no number of mouths at all (equalling zero GAHHHHH what a waste but freak BIG FREAK *yes no wasted spirit lake never forget no never forget spirit lake no no no* so anyblast whistlin's trike pedaled out real far to the end of its line s-s-sss' what do you think's this to d' wi' wha' you're here are you starting to know what it means 'botu *why you're here?*

Look glance one past the other; one momentary soundless jolt of a look, saying ,This is not our **THE GENERAL-MANAGER** our **THE GENERAL-MANAGER** does not speak this way this is not typical of **THE GENERAL-MANAGER** b-b there it is there they are going on on and up-lower over with more of this *and* as all *frame* houses must **<u>go gone g'n 'nuff time</u>**, it was gone but the stoop; the stoop weathered the years "<u>YES</u>" the stoop could never be budged let alone at all ever removed, and so it came to be a Ozymandias' Legs-like symbol of *what* **THE GENERAL-MANAGER** told the twin polesmen; as of now you are off this assignment; which assignment will be pinned on two others and; you two'll shunt over-anunther to be totally accountable for; and you better grab up one of those pads and pencil sets over there to take noted down re your

new assignment—yah yes yo I do see the surprise risining-up your faces—but do not be no, no do not be, there. There you go. {(sp)^{tm} in *Heavy-Set* {know that weird one? That weird one off <u>*Bradbury*</u>?}} All ready—good—okay, head up the first page with Project approach to redesign, rebuild, reactivate, and make profitable the formerly known local :_____insert name here_____: vertical + semitubular + one sizes fitting all + TV set and Telephone Pole works {an attraction highlighting the central role of pantography in leap-bounding the works to vast levels of success; this success being uh oh multiplicitating like rabbits {*hole yonder*} an' so froth and sewn on the wordpour out the **THE GENERAL-MANAGER** stinked up t' high heaven with stinkening vaporerry, rising about as their classically yellowed *Ticongrrroga* number two's blurred up in leaden motion, and they we 'ssigned (*re*)yas yass ass as s'. .   . ...
f   .. ..   _____   .
      ,   ;   .   ,   ;   ./////
_____ so tired so the shadows rocks off the road nothing/something *please focus t   t has to be true yes yes* has to be Look Out Wall! no no drive slower pay attention know ....   1 s x   it did make sense that we shoved that know but can't see it in writing back-hind these lids so so it gets way harder to drive at night when you're old, or no do not say that to the boy, not bigger, not larger, **BUT OLDER** don't snide-swipe the dear by n-m-others clear vodka when we play it was water just do and so drinking vodka well, that's really ill-advised by hey no just this once no no no hey no we're just in month two a little here a little there the watchword's moderation see/hear me say it moderation there it is say it loud no no no you will wake the tiny babies *UP* yes no do not yes no sill there'll be no baby out in the open air for months and months hey hand me that Sweeney family stood 'gainst the wall over there and do it pronto. hey it's ages it's ages see, many many many tumbrils will successfully reach the rack *so* why worry when it is that there's no time left to quit that's a good

question *Norm*, shall we poll the jurors on that well yes and no oh? What yes and no *Norm*, well **OOPS** there went a really big wallpast which; is a noun yes it is funny it a thing yes it is funny a wallpast can be easily sent to the land of big solid objects, a wallpast's here right now see wake up look and see wake wake up up look look and and see see so, so crispy. Just the way we like it—*hot*, and so *crispy* I you could not be allowed to say, sssss' that's *why* I tramped down your tongue hey hey hey there are those what would testify there they were Judge down in the center of the pavement Judge Judge their tongue out flat 'n the rough laid concrete Judge Judge Judge J[4] and what I think is a fat fifties really dull Dodge V8 black-round tooled right on over the tongue J[5] *they don't make them like that no more (that's the blessed byproduct judge) wall walla* HOOP J[6] drive the shadows (oops) bump the shadows praise BUMP! o! where am I we us you guys them people souls on board *captain can you give us the number of souls on board?* also *al*so al*so where can we safely dump out fuel senor you're jumbling it all up so I* e' *senoritas where oh were may we can we or should we maybe better dump some fuel* tower can you tell us tow' BUMP Oh! it is not a fine thing to doze in a drive now hot Petunia every third to tenth word *the plane's going to land us down safe won't it Daddy* I think I find myself rousing up out of a hypnotological doze or some kind of thatch-weave round my top, see? See? See there it is it is again thank God, the car seems competent to drive itself all by itself, going home {regardless *so I can't see what's going to happen didn't you Daddy* of the late hour} allowing to *see isn't there Daddy* some level of musing to hum *if something so tiny and light as a feather's all's going to hit us then why can't I see it Daddy* down below hear it hear, the hum humming below now et all ack oof, the *Daddy please say that the plane's going to land us down safe* planets. How stupid and silly—now, class—if the creator's *why are you so afraid to say we're going to hit a little feather Daddy* why got the planets going the way the creator is happy with, sigh *say it* hum hu *Daddy it's what* mmmm hu ummmm *I really need to hear right now Daddy* see its like this, *Doopie*—when something's as it is *why did you close the window shade down Daddy what's it you don't want me to see* and only the creator (if any) can change it, tell us the sense of running at it flailing stop-change! *there's something* Stop! Change! *you don't want me* and :Okay Okay now cold-water my face (*figuratively*): so forth-like, its pissing in to the *want me to see Daddy* :Stop the planets from spawning its crap they're spawning anyway: wind gag gag the planets. Its :But they said what's the hell was wrong with you you hammering guns called yourself Top-mayor, and didn't hear the announcements: stupid hmmmmmm three point five units *are we going to hit something* : How the hell can you call yourself Top-mayor and miss so much of such importance flying back and forth over the entirety of "your" town ***HAH!***: *so hard it'll kill us Daddy* of measure to home from *yeah something that's* :You need to switch gears, pal: *nothing like a little bitsy feather* where?

From the office!

And to where?

To the sea!

The sea is not home though!

Yes the sea is home! :This **THE GENERAL-MANAGER**s got a hidden agenda or else's just ***plain stupid*** : Had four *or is it going to be nothing like a feather* beats not three (by way of example + we do not say the things we say because they are *true* + no no no no +we say them because they *sound good to say* + humm ziing! crack :As much a bad fit in their **THE GENERAL-MANAGER** job as you are for Top-mayor if you truly buy these big baskets of bullshit: *{pillo}* we say them 'cause they lilt well in all buckets (?) *I want to see it Daddy. Can you please let me see it now if its nothing why you say no so hard at me Daddy you never before said no at me so hard* .. *,,,; ..* **%# bum's rush no turn 'round think it through yes no 'kay get down and make a damned decision for yourself for the first time in your life ditch the fake "Top-mayor" act get your butt back out gridlock memorial park get out there get whistlin' yah yah yah whistlin' ann' whistlin'! *can you Daddy? s-so*

Because of the speed of the S so sss oo   so sooooooo
sssssso   ..   ...   S so sss o...S   S so sss
oo   so   sooooooo   hammering   gun   the
sssssso   ..   ..   ossssss
ooooooos   os ment of the purchase of not just one but
several oo sss os S

which thankfully just as predicted lowered both the
cost and the speed required to erect a steel building of
traditional   style   and   projected
market   ...   ..   value market

coveralled hammering guns workpeople market value
who knelt hammering not

o ¨ ...hammering gun which

days do start with sun like this one in the window lit
on the floor and the boards begin heating   crack
crick   the   house
  ..   ...   with manual hammers but a new style
S so sss oo   so sooooooo ssssssso   ..   the hell really
cares   any   hoot   who's
watching   ...   .   o contractor,
thought having to make an initial invest   m. ;;''[]-=   r
r r r r f what does it matter who's watching I do not want
to do it who does such evil things in publi' s   790-5r90^&5-
--   public private private public so they got this place cheap
too bad they can't take credit though 'cause neither can
swear to have ever even bought it is it true we bought this
place bubo, it must be true cause we own this place baba,
just because we're standing here doesn't prove we bought it
I don't think   1 2 3 4 it don't matta' here we are ya y a0 98
7 6t 4 3 3 it don't *matta'* no no *matta'* we're here is the real
all that there is a dream don't you know can't you see you
can't see it it's not its imaginary just a dream we are
pillowed-in baby swaddled all about for 90 years just seeing
th' self the selves the self the selves the hippo haha ha ha ah
aha ! funny joke hhhhhhhippo hiiiiiiiiiiiiippo going to make

hipppppppppppo   hippoooooooooooooooooo   hippo hhhhhhhippo …po   okay now good past the city traffic
        oppih   ooooooooooooooooooppih oppppppppppppih   time getting there out of   oppiiiiiiiiiiiiih oppihhhhhhh   the city traf hhhhhhhippo hiiiiiiiiiiiiiippo fic now it's a pleasure to dri   hipppppppppppo ve out on the *you need your head examined* open roa hippoooooooooo d like this don't do i ooooooooo hippo op… oppihhhhhhh oppih ooooooooooooo t often enough like when we used to get going down he often enoooooppih oppppppppppih re going to go to ***Babci's*** .. oppiiiiiiiii but there's way more time on a long drive to let thoughts cre iiiiih oppihhhhhhh ekoj y ep in of the kind that aren't the kind of thoughts wanted ever to think ou' me ***hippo*** *burp* 'nnuf ! aha ha ah ah the creator is erciful but it's hard to admit to (.) was just a nuisance to be dealt with. Hard to admit that to (.) was only an irritant and a block to the flourishment off'n (.)'s very own town. (.) the street withered went dead for lack of (.) foot traffic and that would, well, taxes and all that you know press gas harder *got* to get there ***want*** to get there too rare combination of feelings about a job. Most never grove of trees passing look for those little furry upright sat animals set off the road sat up looking into the woods thinking perhaps right, perhaps wrong, there's no danger in turning soft furry back to the road Ha there you go the stupidity of the comfortable, if what that creature's thinking's ***right*** then why so many seen sprawled bloated and bloody in rotting heaps at the curb pressed there by violence y' see then the guilt of this (.) the little furries killed so violently did not deserve no no did not in any way wise or w-wonder at all deserve and grip wheel white-knuckled such compassion *such care* it hangs in this (.) for much more than a moment, depending on circumstance it sometimes stays with (.) and their (^) big-bank give way to many many poorly videoed multiplied out by 6 or by 7 Planck epochs, which be-sizzlin' now, but. Down on main street *a street like all streets filled with those events that alter*

and illuminate our times no no no no no no no no when (.) remembers that show 'e remembers the balcony edge somewhat high really up with *BackWhang!* the concrete ledge so smooth and so perfectly installed crisp wide angled o'er into the wall and there's the ***flames licking*** 'cause this is the "Chicago fire" these peep-tweets runnin' o-roaring right 'round like they're records baby right round round round are not even taught in school venus' mamdo's school for gypsies opened yesterday to many many smiles and loud toots o' hot fanfare ey see that ey see that that islet of thick trees goan' by means perhaps (.)'s nearly halfway there as in the back seat so long, you got to make your own fun, there see the wooded area sliding up on the right there it comes *there it comes*, damn you *watch* or you'll miss it, damn you damn you, you will miss it, and *you don't even care that you will miss it's a slap in the face to me a slap and a slap and a slap in the face to me* watch watch watch and then the answer is no eh for one quick frame the trees are lined up all diagonal in a perfect grid pattern hey Mr. Krygier was here eck oh *ha ha ha ha* Mr. Krygier was here and up to their typical nursery style shenanigans *ha ha ha ha* Mr. Krygier's the one what pushed these fake memories Mr. Krygier's the one landmarked the halfway point toward actually getting there and of coming back also *both ends got the same stench if you care to ask me ROAR said the lioness* but you know you do know it can't be put off'n t' often *that being this ha ha ha ha ha ha ha ha ha ha ha ha* the kind of *ha ha ha ha ha* laugh happened way back *ha ha ha ha ha ha ha ha ha* before driving *ha ha* 'cause if (.)'d been driving it'd be the here we go whee whee whee violently yet harmlessly sent this big ***Ford*** UP the WEEDS o'er the *weeds* the answer is no o'er the ditch and into the weeds the devilmens' big blocky ***Ford*** she do go because too much laughing always leads to crying *[drive that car right up to against that line of midnight moving boxcars if you want to live, m'seur]* what may very well be totally false memories of a shed off the side full of rotting moldy old single-seater personal private airplanes trampling the grass of once was a small rural landing strip but around which now they went roaring **hot** *jalopies* around a worn-in rough track so baking in the summer but oh so much *fun* but the things once it happened needed to go you know what's done is done shut up and move on seemed to be right at the time but he/she/it is right 2000 is not a number to be trifled with and God-damn, for (.) and their (^) it's always the wrong reasons. 2000 less taxpayers per annum. 2000 less in the pool of a available T-phone pole and TV set pantographically powered subsystems (gash) wrong: the answer is no this is the difference between   you   and   me,   doctor;   you're pragmatic/compassionate yah what they said but I, sighed (.), egged on by sweet sycophant o' mine (^) that is why I am not a doctor, **doctor**; the money involved's not everything—**it's the only thing.** said some big overbulker back who when what ass who really cares no more surely not *the answer's still no* I.

Y'know?

Ah yes. Sure. But—all along through this here and now simmer up back n'around those spouses *what spouses* those spouses oh *yes* oh *yes* having worked out considerably in both younger years {of which there were yes many more than two (= both you know why don't ya know, silly, *the answer's still no* why the hell do you still not 'll know) *dreadful*} at last both reached out to their points of their molds having cooled off sufficiently to where it came down totally natural that they knew who they were 'n' they were able to finally calmly stand up and look around able to push their heads up above the noise of the squabbling {but also pretty much settling down} pair ot TV sets vying each to be the primary set to pull them through every day's seven o'clock to bedtime {exact interval being a variable of some kind of o'clock *the answer's still no* but (that must be greater than seven o'clock by at least the time required for the perceived distance such time being bounded by the time *pock-mark* it took for their optic nerves to path these impulses from back-eyeball's tip blind spot to the vision processing areas of their brains) *atchoo atchoo*} Mom! Mom! I'm hungry Mom! Mom! Mom! I am horribly hungry Mom! Please <u>*don't you*</u> <u>*care*</u>? Anyway they did in time successfully push of fa' 'ff t' perceive back far enough to remember *the answer's still no* **THE GENERAL-MANAGER** saying out loud inside dark looming masses of powerful noise, *It has dawned that you two are what you cannot be told because the statement required would expose our soul to accusations of blasphemy so get the hell out and resume being what you are* and so. Even as that sighed to a lingering echo, they looked at each other and did set out finally to obey and react and move out toward their forwards to *get the hell out and resume being what you are* but not quite actually, more like simply *resume being what you are* this which also seemed just a scotch-brit{e} too far, it self-amended it self down to a more *the answer's still no* comfortably cooling *resume being* which they pretty much finally found they could deal with, as what could be easier then to simply *go on being* whatever the 'elves they are which 'ich requires no initial investment at all just let go go *smooth[1]* forward *ah ah* just let go 'o *smooooth[2]* forward *'h ah* just let 'o *smooooth[3]* forward *'h* just let *smoooooooth[4]* fo'ward *'h* just 'e' *smoooooooth[5]* fo'ard *less sunken-souls* which will $5^x\ 4^x\ 3^x\ 2^x\ 1^x\ 2^x\ 3^x\ 4^x\ 5^x$ {no it won't *yes it will*} and ultimately actually tends to actually pull any number of chickens out of any depth of a whole *deep-willy no* **WILLY, NO!** *Willy*, please stop!

Cautioned by this unexpected hazard being encountered, they stopped, hung tough, and crisply whirled around—to face a tall ***"Dim"***, which had-parently been padding along behind them, watching. The taller pushed out a hand, and the hackles of the other seemed to rise.

Stop right there. Are you following us?

Yes, of course—and the taller, nonplussed by this pure shower of honesty, scrubbed in one word w' slipped out from the pressure right into the follower's gut.

Why?

THE GENERAL-MANAGER called me to come and provide you support. And for your sake thank God, because look:

The spouses looked down being first very startled to find they now stood on a skinny steel catwalk (not the boots on the ground piss in this bottle, hot scat in sealed trash) then down from there seeing a crush of human beings pushing to ge *BackWhang!* t, go, and *"be places"*.

The *Dim* said that's right, that's what it is down there.

Yeah, b'—wait, we said nothing of what regarding us are you saying "that's right"?

Calmly a hand *BackWhang! BackWhang!* rose.

Never mind the questions. Not the time or the place, is this; this is to start your basic training by first looking down into the nonsensicalness you will get plunged into if you deviate one single chimp off yr' indies.

What? Who—

Shut up, snapped the *Dim*—and look down beyond your silly fear off heights the true "what" I have been sent here to cause you to behold. *BackWhang!*

The crush below undulated with strange strainings as though modeled on a snake.

Dim then: see? Those are those you will be called to judge **behold**!

Turning up momentarily, which one /which doesn't matter/ slap'd out, Who, uh? judge? Who is it's called to judge?

You, of course. Its what you really are's primary job. What you can't be told to you will strip of its *BackWhang!b-*bandages. And don't claim confusion when your true's know all and sees all. Also—here, look—are you *deep rural dialectical Spanish* paying attention? You better 'cause note *note note note* the f'lwing's the basis of the test might get sprang on you *uck hack **patooey*** ahhhhhhhhhhh No No fl'wing's the basis of the test might get danged on you *uck* *hack **patooey*** ahhhhhhhhhhh no no no try again wrang'd (s' it?) no no no try again slang'd sprangg's almost that one's apologies to those of whose high-pay'd dream vacations are getting stuck in the middle of this, hold it ah hole it **wipe** _uck_ *hack **patooey*** ahhhhhhhhhhh but-but *hell* there can't be enough hereabouts gullible enough no not *hell* there can't be but there must be we meant there you are the sum of ?% sitting 'nd ?% lying 'nd ?% kneeling ?% leaping ?% bathing (but not many) and on ?% swearing and uh ?% others doing elsie-selve's *BackWhang!* other things (some of which's yet to be sprang down on as you are the elite being able to piss out so much money incur so much credit won som silly game and now behind door THREE get ready folks gee get - *! -! - ! - ! -! - !*

A NEW CAR!

! -! - ! - yip yip yip yip cheeeeeeer eer eer eer eer yellllllllll clap-plaud clap-ma-plaud *shut up now* or we'll *cut your* **Mikes** a brand new **next year's of course** *brand new* model Porkwhistler's Quickblast all buckshot to hell-boot five simultaneous riders *per gallon BIG FAT SEDAN* not at all like mama used to make but *just as sweet-lusciously as hers {quite the same}* STOP there fast Fred, you're off all your horses again you've been warned before scads-o spoiled o-er some bottoms HERE: behold.

Yes behold, said the ***Dim.***

See it there ***right down there***:

*		click	
*	click		click
*		click	

START OF EMBEDDED BONUS BOOK

OK. OK. This here flows the muspascat-taculan room used for *musing up only.*

There you go here you are pull that up and sit click down as;

This flows get inside now please yes Mommy yes the muspascat-taculan room used for *musing only.*

• 51 Game 4

This the muspascat-taculan room used for *only*. *Canada's*
the root source of most rotary conversations knuckle-knuckle insert
size medium plath cementeriannatipn here and return in ten minutes

      This muspascat-taculan room get inside now please dinner's ready
get inside yes Mommy yes used *only*.

      This room click *only*. **(and once in hair-up yes bones oh yes doctor**
Smith oh yes and oh yes yes yes yes doctor Smith doctor Smith yes yes yes go *by that*
time it's not hard set up immediately call for heavily armed back up head's great,
great uncle *what's that spell what's that spell* *why Gregor*
that spells there's a Gregor in the house eh get inside now please
dinner's ready why the hell's heavens s' you taking o long *want a whipping do you must*
be looking for a whipping get inside yes Mommy yes eh eh e there a—
oooooooooo ***GREGOR IN THE HOUSE A***
ONCEANDFORALLIAN GREGOR IN THE HOUSE sure
it hurts what you think sure it hurts, but we got to do it
anyway okay all-rat yer-ass sure sure sure it's I got to do it
anyway you happy now get inside now please dinner's ready why the hell's
heavens s' you taking o long *want a whipping do you must be looking for a whipping* get
inside yes Mommy yes **Sneezie**, it's not *we* got to *BackWhang! BackWhang!*
do it it's just **ME** got to do it not *we* but **ME ME** only and
not we but but I can't see the difference's a rat anypipe, since
we go in they'll do nothing just watch me do *want a whipping a*
good beating then a whipping do you must be looking for a whipping get inside yes Mommy
yes everything Yes I built ***three new warehouses*** on time and
in budget no no liar liar it was **US** did it all you just sat-fat,
and watched ***hey hey*** Yes I built ***ten thousand***
approximately little Black Bakelite boxes on time and in
budget | *buy me a set of size large purplish* ***trousers*** | no no
liar liar it was **US** did it all you just sat-fat, and watched *hey*
hey we keep the whippings and the beatings in there but be sure to set them down slowly
on our universally credited silver-starred pallets Yes I launched ***thirteen***
huge hulls at my shipyard on time and in budget click click click
no no liar liar it was **US** did it all Using such devices keeps them fresh
keeps them holy you just sat-fat, and watched ***hey hey*** no no yes
yes no no its maybe maybe no no its yes yes yes yes no no
no apportion these back there properly please we forgot we forgot but better late than
never

      tight slacks or tight trousers big sofa or davenport rocker-recliner please we're here
for hats not hose (particuluplarre)

!!!!!!!!!!!!!!!!!!!!!!!!!!!!!! there we're sure that's enough if there'r spares do not trouble to return to inventory for ***NO*** its not yes yes no maybe pay two dollars please ; .. ,, *I want to keep them fresh and holy Mommy just like you do I also want to too*

        (0)   1 2 3 4 I *pock-mark* do not get the gas you need to get the gas I don't *the seals have been broken they can't be reinventoried so just donate just d.* gas you usually do *so go get it* if we need it that is if you get it when we don't need it an accident may push out some stem and BLAST's what may happen so——avoid that at all costs.   *why is it as I look at you I can actually see your whole brain stem*   **ding!**

               before eating that one there needs a series of evenly spaced good heavy beatings

     h '"]{+ ***GET GAS*** getting gas's below me oh yah that there's way up-top you and looks like they're *getting gas* ha ha ha   when mother calls and you don't come in expect a good slap in the face (the bare minimum) *Barry*   swivel! swivel!   like this Daddy? " ., yes like that {behold the McIntyres' brand new ***Wok***} swivel swivel   Wow! Look! Are those *fighter planes*?   do {of which they are so proud} the gauges say we're full UP yet do day Daddy what do the gauges say   ar   ne beeo enough in, DADDY?   *is that you Barry? Is that really, really you?*

                   are we in deep enough

now
     swivel-pivot
    I hope so

             no you don't son hope doesn't count as a strategy round-about here and environs
     Nancy!
     What?
     Graddieo-o-oooooks*laaaaaaaaaaaaaaaaaaaaaaaaaaaaaaaaaaaaaaaaaaaaaaaaaa n.*   Meestah   Bo-Peepula's   windows   *(yah?)* grrrrrrrrrrrrrrrrrrrrrrrrrrrrrrrrrrrrrrrrrrrrrr couch glandular couches meest's glandular couches the name of the {which will in their service serve up all future dishes wonderfully ***hot***}

conditions who's condition why your condition of course you're the one strapped to the machine not I see I am here and you are there and taken together we may be presumed SO | **Up there! Look up there! They're so loud! Must be** *fighter planes!* | but that does not mean it is I with the condition by my God and by my word I had such a terrible condition as you, why—I'd immediately drop everything and go ***get my head examined*** eh eh eh eh they say quite often to the deviating in some sometimes every very minor way, crap g'eon shit go ***get your head examined*** *DOC* we think here quite securely ***you need your head examined***, yes, no indifferently (write this down skoal) there {*I got a date w' a bunny out back o' the laundromat*} yours appears to be still on (write a checkmark under agency name there skoal {Christ, Ross, a checkmark cannot be an agency name *reconsider* *} while the patient goes on strapped in patiently waiting having faith in DoC Pantunnio's *pock-mark* sheepskin "*hung on their wall*" saying in script this that and ten others *this is indeed the son of God* Yup, yup; yup yup yup yup yup yupyupyu[*pock-mark pock-mark pock-mark pock*] pyu[yu[in that paragraph there honey that's there go read it |split| tgilasr-trinckular-r-r-ianne JESUS Christ, my back itches God DAMN God-d-d-DAMN there's a tree by this here you may rub it ? this here what this here ? *Is your name Lillian James? If so, then,* I've that there this here ? oh oh those this here's over there wait no I will go I will go I will go o'er there I will get one * say wise in the cemetery by the Louthurralianne's churchery I will go get one see? See those there? I swear to God it was one of these graves right round here like a record baby round round right round + oh and so *I need that large of a surgery Doc?* how far out around when one says right round here how right round are we talking? "?. are we talking just one next grave all around 'vry direction but {excuse me my friend here and I would each like a few more ***"injections"*** of that ***please*** and/or thi(a)nk you} *why the hell's such a simple condition required that huge of a surgery Doc doublecheck that out please Doc uh oh please* this one here ah I {yes almost just almost but this grave here's where 'e count needs to start from +oh yah and okay just shut up and stand corrected *surgery Doc?* **shit** *surgery Doc?* that's the problem with you and this pack-o-chaps with you, you can't Navarronned 'lly just (the guns just the guns) shut the hell up and simply stand corrected o no no n no no now 998&&&$ yes it does matter which grave gets dug in the center 'cause the anomaly's there's that years back in a visit the marker was a quietly unusual wrought iron custom-made cross full of curlicues. See? See? And all painted black in a suit of glossy **Rustoleum** you know you can picture the kind of black painted wrought iron curlicues what when you rub your finger down them you detect tiny bumps tits and otherwisely defectivities all over the wrought iron, and there was so, so much more to see and to know about it what an interesting grave marker what an interesting on' BUT it is gone now.

What? My God, no. That is terrible.

Yes terrible, And, where it is now is, a mystery.

Sure is yes, sure is.

I really want to see it but it seems no longer there.

What a pity.

No longer there.

A pity.

Not there.

Pitiful.

Yes. *BackWhang!*

Yes.

Yes pitiful Party! Oh, *## simply stand simply stand simply **END OF EMBEDDED BONUS BOOK**

then

null for ten minutes (stab down! *Stab down!*) *s'* **(as though in memoriam but so definitely not),** *so,* when they came back exactly *s'* at the definite time they'd been ordered, so said the **Dim** into them, yes that, and then this: *Now it's time for a pop quiz on the lecture you've just been given—hey,* **Harry**, be a "hunnie", pass *s'* out these test sheets please,

•   55 Game 4

will ya! Yes, I will, so yes slithered by, but, b' b—wait—hand l' off the rightmost of the two *s' s'* students *"rose"* politely.

What? asked the **Dim**—what now, please?

You said *quiz*. What's this? No, no.

No what? Are you claiming you won't take my quiz?

That's right. Won't take your quiz, as—this is not a *"real school"* pasta-fazz so, err eck quizz-ze's not written done o'er the deal. Uh—I think you get this one, and then there's that one where we aren't in this for sheepskins we're in here for the celebration of what's "left regarding" life. *s'* So, we won't. Come on, lets get going.

The spouses turned from the **Dim** in an effort to leave, but: +++ ,   []P[][]][

        T   . ..... #*%

{seulement aux élus le lieu et le but} ,   , ,

[]P[][]][

        T   . ..... #*%

+++ *s' s'* God God, God; God—*God*, is that **Top-mayor** and God God God God and their very **Henchmanette** *awk* and then there's God God **Jack Scrappo** and God God their other **Jak "closed-casket" Skrappo** *awk awk awk awk* God, *s'* Go! **Tapper Rose**, d' God, uck go' *w' this pin we stuck doth just deflated your sack* ha ha that newspaper vendor God, God God God, God; *God* a hollow derivation of the shell of *THE GENERAL-MANAGER* God, God, they're all *s'* here, what God, God? God, they're all here. What are they, God? God, wh' are they doing here? Why is this, God? God, yes. *s' s' s'* Yes yes *why the hell is this,* God? God, dear God, *brott-poncko* God-God-God b' b-b-*brott-poncko brott-poncko* God God brott-poncko *brott-poncko brott-poncko* **brott-poncko** *w!* God help me, God help! My *s'* "Lord" and my "God", please = *help* t' *Put this Together* p z po *shut let me say please help me please* iz pop *I need peace and quiet to plead with my **God*** uiz op qui p z z po *the hoses are blocked step aside step aside* I am talking to ***God***, so *s' s' s' s' s' s'* shut up {iz pop uiz op qui p z z po iz pop uiz op} *No I Can't I can't seem to get it to go together* ({qui p z z po iz pop uiz op **Hunch Coolie** qui p z po iz the damage is sure to become irreparable if you continue refusing to step aside **Hunch Coolie** pop uiz op qui *okay son then here's next what we'll do*} p z z po iz pop {*why's this not working*} uiz op {*I'll be damned if I know*}) qui p +++

..... [ ][ ] [] = = & $;' .. []

{*tylko wybranym miejscu i celowi*}

+ {

" .l[]ure

+++ z z po iz pop {*well gimme a reason a good guess anything but nothing you know*} uiz op qui p z z {*but how?*} po iz pop {*there's no how! Just do it!*} op qui {*okay what is their name*} iz pop uiz op qui p z z {*their name's my brother's name silly*} iz {{ *but look look we're nearly done gliding down out of* } *down out of these* {*down out of these stormclouds*}}} h h h *s' s' s'* h h *s' s' s'* h {*what's*} h h h h h {*these stormclouds stop but hang on* po iz op *hold on* qui *here we go* p' *brace yourself here we're about to touch down 'r there crash trucks* }is uhhhpop { there's no crash truck's but push that off out of our way good God we're goan' in Good hot flash on the tarmac all greased down with what} : hold it no what's what's quite important if wrong the ground is rushing up so fast! you may blow apart instantly gone which's the easiest sentence most of the Good God the ground is rushing up so very very fast! time but WHAT *what whang whoah down drop hi hic see-saw B- bu WOW see that view wowie wow that damn view I s a yt kj* s' s' s' s' s' s' s' s' s' s' s' s' s'

wow!

cup After g .., they fe) @ $$ ll low clear of the clo (^.,' ./,[ ] uds into the res.ltant crystalline spac..the pop quiz resumed close to as +++ p- - = + ;.}[

g werts ^#96(4739

{nur an einen ausgewählten Ort und Zweck}

GGG %4)(

,   7 5 5 j   j ^every
"fine" city's got "two or three" of these^
        7   y6g'   = smelling smoke 'round here this time of
day's a *really bad sign* =

    +++ scheduled surprisingly, the **Dim** proudly
'nounging the *s' s' s'* first 'mmediate question.

    Dim:. What is my brother's name?

what?

head spin-reelie

s' s' s' s' s' s' s' s' s' s' s' s' s' What is my brother's *s' s'*
name? repeated the **Dim.**

    Short.

    Sweet. *s' s'*

    Dim:. you should know since you seem among the
troubled, that; this test starts with the easies. Can't get the
easies, there's no point in carrying on.   **guns?**

    But, I— *s'*

    Never mind *your but stuff it for later* Give me the *s'* answer;
what is my brother's name?

    uh my brother   (***stab down!* Stab down!***)

    .   my *name* what is my *name*   *. s'*   *s'*
Brother's name?

    No, My *s' s' s'* name.

    We've not been told this. So—*how can we know*?

    What do you mean, not "been" told? *s' s' s' s' s' s' s'*
s' s' been *s' s' s' s' s'* bean *s' s' s' s' s' s' s' s' s' s' s'* Bren
s' s' s' s' s' s' s' beady *s' s' s' s' s'* eyed *s' s' s'* big-g-g-g *s'*
s' s' s' s' s' s' s' big beady eyes de   *s' s'*   mon great big
beady ey ₑ *s'* ed. {pounce!!{*went the cat*} }

    Uh. That's so simple and obvious as to not deserve an
answer.

    All teeth gritted marking the first of ten seconds of
dead silence.

    Awed by the wisdom of this answer from the taller
spouse, the shorter spouse, as the shock wore off and the
body began t' burble, inwardly questioned the wisdom of all

this, like, as, like as a hand being thrust in a sock, *sweet Wally*
like as, then gripping +++   H   h   , ...
$(000)^1$ ‘ $(0)^2$ llll
$(0000000000000)^1$ ‘
     $(000)^2$ $(0)^1$
{go dtí áit agus cuspóir roghnaithe amháin}
     0   {|q@,.; ‘’’’’’’’’’’’
                    |W| goo
++ the toes of it and pulling the hand back, wrenching
it all slowly *s'* back inside out, *sweet sweet Wally* what in this case
are the answers to the following: 1, The sock is not a sentient
creature and thus "feels" no pain at being so mutilated, or,
sweet sweet sweet Wally the sock is screaming bloody murder the
blood of this murder flowing hard, soddening the scene,
wince-downing the face of the *s' s'* murderer's thinking,
Once started this must be done pull pull *put the creature out
of its misery* please please put the poor devil out of it's
misery, out of its misery, damn it, out there the thing's done,
it's been done—eh, "for the love of God, Montressor", when
finally done such things must remain done—whew, that was
a close one, but but but but, you don't look so bad, here's
another and *another* {ha!} ‘cause *s'* y *s' BackWhang!* ou *s' s'*
don't look so bad, so—if you want this to stop, start looking
bad. Fall the hell *s' s' s' s'* down, roll wildly around, yelling
this, that, or anything *really,* and and here's another won't
happen no more. But, Father, if there's no more *another's*
coming our way, are we "dead"? Are we "dead"? As—as
that long sawn up phone pole o *BackWhang!* f some skinnymaster
once said, Look too stupid to know it's dead! Watch it run,
watch it run HA, ‘t's too stupid to know its dead watch it run
HA HA, too stupid ye' much too ‘es much too m'ch tooooo
m''h toooooooiooo-o-o-o ‘''h toooo *s' s'* oooiooo-o-o-
oooooo ‘’’’ +++
                    &   *
     (*)
     \\\

{nur an einen ausgewählten Ort und Zweck}

@

+   + !

    !!!!!!!!!!!!!!   yes

??????????????? no no !!!!!!!!!!!!!!!!!!!!!!!!!!!!!!!! yes No ynynyn ?!111111111!!!!!!!!!!!!!!!!

    grip that up and put it on and don't ask questions why *there's no time*

                              panda

    +++ tooooooooiooo-o-o-oooooooooo rats |||*BOOM!!!!!* panda-parko panda-Park-o—wonderful! Your turn; no, yours uhhh; u' huh who are we, and where the hell's there we are, from that vantage point—*no*, this vantage point, these vantage places in all their infiniteitudeical presenceh' ,;'   ... *s' s' s' s' s' s' s' s' s'*   stink!

spit

    Ok! Duly noted. (Men! Over here over here—*man the hoses!*) So; does that mean any one of the following: 1. You have not been told, but will at some point be told, or, 2. You are in the process of being told right now, but I have not got to the point in this question yet, {*in which case notice 1 = 2* {which is incorrect too, in many ways, but we won't "<u>go there</u>" (stab up stab up up and down <u>*up and down*</u>) perhaps in some future *s' s' s' s'* iteration of something (which of course must exist right now or there be (hah) nothing to iterate forward)]] . | **&but&** that can't be either 'cause look all around at the countless physical things all around us [just those within range of our senses which amount to an infinitesimally small percentage of all the physical things existing in this instant of existence *s' s' s' s'* of   *s'* of the known universe (note use of the word "known" shows what I know eh eh eh hah hah hah well not {*pillo*}), or, this lasts not the last to claim anything passing by in this moment is the *Carmen Basilio* last of its kind, can't be really be true, because you cannot know there's one coming's not got here yet 's all by ***Jesua* 'n' *Jesuo*** there might+++

• 60 Game 4

----------------------------------->   &

^7^   ^^88^^

^^^^0000^^^^   Pray tell?

       ^^^999^^^

         ha ha you *lose*   *Pray tell!*

{tylko w wybrane miejsce i cel}

                    peek 1

   w 33 6 d   ' [; [.;;;

   ha ha *you lose*

                    mission=*spelck*   (aka big *Buddy)*

+++ be some other coming right now)], 3. You have
never been told will not be told now and will never, ever be
told, ever, so;

   What? *s's'   s'*   **Judge Mason** *stateth:*

"Real loosely wound this here bro's loosely wound"

s's'   s' **Shit!**

Where did *s's'* everybody go?

but now its so lonely here but S'

s' come back! Come

back! *s'*   *let go*   *unlatch*

unhook

and; slick's l'id-d-d-d-d-e - *s'*

   s' come slsls *ba Good God the ground is rushing up so very very fast so
much faster God faster than ever there can be no survival this time as though there ever
could have been survival ah ah your kind are much so easily fooled but eh tell you what*

   s'   *What?*

   s'   *Climb in here if you want
to survive!*

   *s'   What   W ha   t?   Climb in here if
you want to survive what is you want to survive how many ways can that mean fool how
many ways fool how many many ways f (0)$^{-1000}$*

   s'   *never mind the nickels when the pennies will do   what*

   s'   *said never mind the nickels when the
pennies will do*+++

   !!!!!!!!!!!!!!!!!   {uniquement vers le lieu et la
destination sélectionnés} **!!!!!!!!!!!!!!!**

                    •   61 Game 4

k   *;'=-7sdm,ey 7tdkjj*   h   ......:

%4

+++ **l'line** *s'*   *what what what what*

uh uh never mind you're **relatch'd** = *stop*

[pound!]

{**only to the selected place and destination**}

{*only to the selected place and destination*}

{only to the selected place and destination}

What

what

*

*

*

Wonderful!

Party!

Top-mayor = spent roughly the next ten hours walking cross-country to the left of and slightly behind the memorial caretaker, heading for the memorial site. They'd no way of knowing what they'd do when they got there. But then again Top-mayor had learned that if one's being honest, and open to reflection, regarding the last several {at least} they'd headed for, each time thinking they knew exactly what'd be there, only to find the reality of being there not ever close to what they'd expected. So, they slogged along following the other ready to be surprised once more; the healthiest way to approach any trip to anyplace they'd never been was; who the hell knows what's going to be or happen there? Wh *BackWhang!* at new thing or situation's waiting there for them to be thrown into the relentless swirl of? There's no point in resisting the strong deep cold water that's taking you where it wants you to be when there's nothing to grab onto to slow it or stop it. There's no anchor to drop. No rip cord to pull. No safety harness roped back into something solid and well-known forever enough to take in your slack when your footing slips and/or your grip fails and/or whatever else's powered up your climb to the summit/the place you are going to which no matter no matter matters not no matter what you'd been walking/climbing/struggling up to the death at the bottom of the fail of a fall will not vary on atom depending 'f you were heading at a mountain summit a bar within which you'll gain that margarita or whatever other food drink dessert hors d'oeuvres tray or whipsnappering googlyeyed creature'd be there to greet you (say what eh eh why think you this crazy) huh can you say that's *not* what'll be when you get there can you prove that's too crazy to be like = Top-mayor jolted as two things happened simultaneously 1. They nearly flew headlong face down to the mossy dirt tripping o'er the lip of the transition from hot sun-baked half-dead Indian grass'd over field to flat cool moss-covered shady place arched over by never cut thickly leaved tangles of bush limbs forming an actual tunnel they walked through the sun blocked nearly completely only managing to struggle down through the overhead arch of the thicket a glow of diffusion cooling them while they walked. They speed up a bit and Top-mayor slid back from the flow into wondering how much further they'd be going and so stepped up the speed and saying when close enough to the other, Say, how much further is this place {hoping that would stop the other providing some moments in which to catch their breath} = but there was no response the other just kept walking rude how very very rude but maybe not no just too far ahead to hear *so step it up* saying, Eh, hey, say there, hey, how much further is this place and no, nothing still eh *lick* sure this is one rude pappy and *certainly in peak physical condition too*, but rude so rude need to stop spleen is aching but can't be first to stop would then be the weaker and no fucking way can't not be the weaker but holy shit this one's got lungs but oh ah yes *push* to keep going on top of which also *step it up* saying a bit louder now, {*but not so loud as to seem desperate*) eh say there eh say there eh how much further is this place (not said in any tone which might sound winded breathless straining or tired in any way) and wait, tuck, and nothing. The other kept moving toward the far end of the barbell (what) this Top-mayor's body now stretched tight to a continuous straining super-instant released a flood of natural chemicals to suppress these bodily sensors and depress those bodily sensors equaling the totality of this mere one person's nothing when there's billions 'cross the planet each experiencing their own unique flood of emotions pains pleasures almosts and nevers sure I cans and no way at all sorry can't do not won't but can't I have been honest judge no don't slam down that gavel at least not yet I deserve clemency {*eh say there eh say there eh how much further is this place*} aside from this present predicament which, I do confess, I brought about by my own stupidity ignorance and selfishness at feeling nothing when those 2000 poor devils went and bit it [as this one we're chasing to someplace important has taught me{*eh say there eh say there eh how much further is this place*}] sure I cared about money judge but you got to understand that {*eh say there eh say there eh how much further is this place*} somebody had to keep it together somebody had to keep their cool {*eh say there eh say there eh how much further is this place*} crying over spilt milk well it's . . what judge? Oh........yes I'll cut the theatrics b-b {*eh say there eh say there eh how much further is this place*} are we getting there? Are we? Oh sorry judge no no don't gavel me down there's no need no no no I promise judge to not ask you any more questions eH aH but how much further is it {*eh say there eh say there eh how much further is this place [oh the barbell? Here's the barbell no I was not being frivolous or mocking of the court oh* thank you judge thank you here—the fat end of the barbell's the tank of limitless pleasure zero pain zero zero and the other fat end of the barbell's behind holding the last final fail larger than any later life-fails that we got to keep pushing to the other end now {not just now no, but though all ever forever don't get me started when the dopamine kicks I'll get all seeing and knowing and hey, *proof*? I do not need proof when in that mode; not to present to your court of law or to myself either you ask how do I keep going full tilt like this without knowing really if {*eh say there eh say there eh how much further is this place*} there's any solid reason to put out energy in the here and now but we are committed |**to what exactly we *don't know*|** the one back turned to us we've been walking at all day knows but won't tell us but is that so bad after all God knows all but won't tell us s e e e ee so this driver of activity is by God so blessed and OOPS no stopped!!!! *dead* and roundy the other turned too; the same word taken to mean two different things also form a far-right 'n far-left "barbell" of sorts too but but {*eh say there eh say there eh how much further is this place*}!|!?

What? What's that all about? We're here. Dismount and look alive, please. I will now teach you my seminar. Bet you never thought to see this day look, look, look on the resting place of 2000 bodies you never knew existed look look look. Top-mayor, after catching their breath, look look got stunned down completely, look look faced by 2000 identical dead white stones as look look look look played over 'n look look over in look their mind, after which, it having faded, they heard themself saying in a throb of a rhythm, God, my God, God, the stones . each stone a life taken . oh .

My God . These are all from from *that day*?

Yes.

. . . . ah . that . day that day they . that day was like this an' just like any other but . slow *it came*. uh cock your head, listen . hear that? Hear *that*? . was just coming back from pickup and right 'round the corner slammed on the . and *that*? . how the hell much longer will it be before we inch up one foot again damn . and *that* and *that* and that and-d-d . where the hell's the cops eh . late to the dentist again *damn* they're going to say sorry find yourself another . with a screaming child in the back to boot I got all the . y'know they

ought to do this damn stuff in the middle of the night not .
who the hell died, *God themselves* . . . .

You seem stunned. Why?

I, ah—no, I'm not stunned. I just—

What's the matter?

I JUST WHAT?

. . . . damn thing's going to flood out again hear that .
the one time I leave on time and look at this can't win . what
is this gross thing they're building here anyway . ought to
have brought a book with me or . and you know, *BackWhang!* I
swear—when I get in first thing I'm going to do is *call the
God-damned town* . there's time got to get out and look at
that tire. It's low again . what time is it . gas on E got to get
there come on Jesus Christ . I think I read it's going to be a
Jai alai center . how many more hours is this going to go on
for . don't run the air conditioner they said okay well here I
am not running the air conditioner okay okay so then what .
. . .

How many are here'd you say?

Over two thousand. That's the best estimate.

. . . . Jai alai? . so pick this day to forget the damned
phone . have you ever. okay then I'll just let go right in my
pants what the hell why not . right, Jai alai . **the hum of the
engines .** great! Now the radio's stopped working, too . God
damn . my hair is a mess . Jai alai's only popular in Florida,
isn't it? Why build a Jai alai center here . what's that sound
that tic tic tic . what the hell kind of car is that . shit the
interview's down the damn drain now . don't start the
meeting without me, I said. Wonder if they've gone on and
started the meeting without me . up there hey wasn't that an
ugly year for Ford, I mean, *really* . this damned watch's slow
again need to get a . guess they'll just end up delivering it
tomorrow kick me me in the ass, I'm the one checked the
obtain signature box, or whatever the hell I said. . . .

But, with the condition they were in, well—

Well what?

I was pretty damned hard to count.

nod

. . . . *the hum of the engines* . how do you get dented all over the top like that one there . these shoes are too tight . way back once in a while you'd see a black bear but they don't come this far south no more . that's not right. It's going to be—uh uh—a squash court like that game—that game squash . *the hum of the engines* . you know it never fails its always a superhot day when you're late for something important and forgot to brush your teeth, this is what always happens . who the hell needs a squash center 'round here either? . God I don't know how much longer I can . should a' took my mule team would have been there by now . plus this damn building's a whole ten blocks long—for a squash court? No, squash courts are tiny . very tired of staring at the back of this huge van . *the hum of the engines* . all boxed in . *the buzz of the engines* . they won't . seems like they been building this damn place forever when . no no no, it's going to be for a bunch of court games—like squash, Jai alai, uh, speedminton I think I read—and fives . this town doesn't even need the place but hey they like to throw down money for nothing it seems . *the rrrrrr of the engines.* . . .

I keep the place perfect. Every blade of grass, every stone, every flowerbed.

I see that.

They got to be remembered.

nod *bow heads*

. . . . think there's time for me to run over 'hind those bushes over there and back . no I . they think the new operator at the factory's not on the up and up, they . look at all the mud God damn . who the hell died anyway . oh I think I've heard of that one . the animals moved back o'er the mountain, or most of them maybe, when they started setting up stills up those foothills . what? *Speedminton*? Hah! There can't really be a game called—*speedminton* . say oh yeah why they say that why they. say . well there is! I read it, and also . oh here comes somebody went up to look let me ask . *the whirrr of the engines* . oh you read it, so—it's automatically true? Come on, please, I . hey take a film of this mess so the boss don't think we're lying . *the thrumm of the engines* . some kind of accident in the pole plant, wasn't it? . the radio traffic reports are useless they can't . that one got no back plate . end up in jail if somebody sees you you . you got a phone, use yours . now badminton, there—that game I know what it is—speedminton must have been a typo . hey they say the morticians advised the family to have a closed casket viewing but they went to court or something, forced the issue for some reason, said they wanted the world to see what unregulated poorly maintained makeshift telephone pole manufacturing machinery could do to an innocent victim . *the hum of the engines . the hum-m-m-m of the engines* . the telephone pole plant took on a high profile, 'cause of their takeover of the regulation TV set company out up/down **West Toothpull** . oh yah? Maybe there's no such game as *badminton* either—maybe that's just a typo, what they really mean was *goodminton* . . . .

So—I just had to get you here, when I heard you were giving up on the town—I—

What?

. . . . do you think . such a fuss over a dead person its just another dead person, stupid, what the hell's so special about this one . crap—look, here—I looked up *speedminton*—it says here they put badminton, squash and tennis together to make *speedminton* . **the hum of the engines** . your camera's better though plus sometimes mine acts like I got a film but later there's "nothing there" . figures . how're they innocent though weren't they in charge of the whole place . very funny . yes but . it's played without a net and there's n*o set court size or surface or whatever* . there's too many cops around I wouldn't take a chance but . yes but.

. . .   *pork*

Hold it, wait—who told you I was giving up on the town?

You said it. You were heard saying it.

. . . . is this the line? God the line is *that long*? . better years back this was the best way through to the Interstate— zipped right through, not like it is now, I mean, look . its just complete gridlock as far as I can see . you can play *speedminton* anyplace and there's really no rules . hey the needle just touched the overheating line . yes. lots of ill will there says the grapevine . I used to buy "*slacks*" and "**shit**" there *wow* I didn't know they went out of business . **the hum of the engines** . oh yah, sure, let's just get a big gang together throw in some balls and let them run around throwing catching bouncing and yelling all randomly—that's speedminton? . why'd you buy those cheap ones they're known for that problem I read it in . but .

=

Jai alai is a fast-moving exciting sport involving bouncing a ball off a walled-in space by accelerating it to high speeds with a hand-held wicker cesta

= *They're over there in that garage—but why'd you say you want them, anyway?*

. grapevine what the hell you say that for . say what . say grapevine . they burying the Pope today, or what. . . .

I never said that. I would never say that.

tense strain tight t s

You never said that to anybody? Really?

Absolutely not. Who told you I said it?

. . . . no for Christ's sake you're starting to get on my nerves, *hey mom look there's two weasels* know that . **the stench of the engines** . who am I to tell you yes or no you're a grown up eh . oh yah oh yah all these stories I read said this is killing business . it seems the mayor and them just like to throw trouble down on the little people . **the whirl of the engines** . there's a shuttlecock too, not a ball, and the speedminton shuttlecock's called a speeder I guess 'cause its lighter and faster . yes, I guess thats true . join the God-damn loser's club . see that gutted store right now used to be a hobby shop . I heard something even crazier . *the rattle of the engines* . this would of course happen on the day I forget to bring a "bottled water" for the ride . oh yah, I worked there years back I sort of knew the managers there so . really? What's crazier . *the hum of the engines* . they're going to get a letter from me or a card or whatever oh *BackWhang!* . where the hell's the cops, eh . its some big shot got "chewed up" in the *machinery*. . . .

Oh come on. I can't tell you that. I'll just say—no, wait. Tell me.

Tell you what?

You a regular at Holyman's beer bar?

Regular? Why? I mean, I go there once in a while, but, a regular? No. I would not say that—but, what's that got to do with anything?

. . . . this building is for a place where you put in some coins, choose your favorite court game from a list of 10,000 or something, and it'll make that game's court up for you in one second, and you go in and play, and ah . why the hell'd they let the damn big shot's funeral go on down here . I think the motor's starting to flood smell that . *the whine of the engines* . the next people come out their coins and choose their game and there you go, what I said, again . yah their names were even almost the same like Skrappo instead of Scrappo . they must have knew thousands would jam in here . *the strain of the engines* . okay we're just on time but, what about parking? *Where the hell* . I can't believe it I bet my luck we'll just be sitting here all day . . . .

So I go to Holyman's. Something wrong with that?

No, but, it's just that you were overheard telling the bartender down there that the town is dying, and ought to be evacuated.

No! What?

Hand up!

Oh, yes! I will not play your game. You know you said that. Maybe under the influence when you said it's why you can't remember it now, but—you said it. And I know more about that, too. Want to hear?

glare

. . . . that's crazy how the hell can that possibly work . they might even be in that line to the funeral home there . big bees big bees . *the scream of the engines* . was that a crash of some kind back behind hey. that's that big pop went off behind this some place . oh yah it's that Scrappo that died . yes that's gas . eh the eggheads say they can do it they've been right about most everything they've claimed they could make before . *the r-roar of the engines . the stench roar an' rattle of the engines* . and when you really hit the other car the sound's downright sickening . the *"day is ruined"* . its almost like the new one sprang out of the dead one . how's a'come all the little mom and pop hobby shops went under . miss the flight can't got now 'til Friday and Friday's just a little . . . .

Top-mayor's neck steamed up to hot and they had to say something or the heat'd pass them out, so the words Yes, though I'm sure its just more bullshit—yes. *Hit me.*

. . . . gun it a bit that'll clear the system out . *the strain n' grind of the superheating engines* . fine not a damn thing to blow my damn nose with . Eggheads? Who said eggheads? That sounded damned offensive you know pal . gun the engine? You know its not me to—ahem—*"gun my engine"* . *the squealing pound of the straining engines* . mom and pop hoppy shops? . no no no those are lies they don't want us to know what this big building's really for what it's for is to . never heard of a mom and pop hobby shop . yes it is yes it is nobody's *stopping* . . . .

You're not actually running the town any more, are you? Someone called **THE GENERAL-MANAGER's** running things now. That sound right?

Stop, think—*then talk a bit slower.*

. . . . My Father used to go fishing with their son . might as well shut the motor and roll down the windows . *the strain of the flooding-out engines* . but to be honest about it, we like watching a fast game of squash played by professionals. It's exciting, I mean . yeah my mom used to take me to the hobby shop down on State that isn't there any more . the action's nonstop . why are the cops all rushing around but don't seem to be helping at all? Why . there you go see I told you you're stalled out . waves over waves are are—no, that can't be . I think—I think—it looks like the cops are coming down the line telling everybody to get out ot the cars . *the hum of the engines . of the way too many doomed engines* . . . .

Hey listen. What somebody told you doesn't mean anything.

No? How's that, that it doesn't mean anything?

Somebody probably got that off one of the weeklies. Those'll throw anything across a page to get it to sell—but, hey. One part of it's true.

Yah? What part?

I am working on something for somebody commonly known as **THE GENERAL-MANAGER,** but I'm helping out, only. Off the books. They're not my boss.

. . . . if it wasn't there any more how'd your mom take you there huh . *what's wrong* . anybody got a couple six packs and a deck of cards we may as well use this dead time for some kind of fun . say I'm sorry but we're evacuating this gridlock get out of the car take your things and go that way . *the dying of the seizing-up engines* . hear tell they invented the whole damn place way back when there . *what's wrong* . but it *is* . God damn . they're going to hate us for this . why? . it was there when she took me but it's not there any more now that's what I meant you knew damn well I meant that silly why when you get all bored with things you get so damned silly . *the scream-strain of the engines* . they're saying its dangerous, is why. . . . .

Okay—but the grapevine says whatever this **THE GENERAL-MANAGER** got you working on is something you're saying makes no sense—

No, wait, I—

hand wave flat out back and forth

No, let me finish—and people are saying you're scared to death to tell **THE GENERAL-MANAGER** that to their face.

red flooded Top-mayor's rounded face

. . . . hey old it a minute let me ask these two hey . what time is it . these shoes are too tight here goes throw 'er in park see if I can reach . ***what's wrong*** . it *is*. get out and stretch need to . sure . solid gridlock they say . ***the shriek of the engines*** . listen there's something happening in the back *hear that?* . ***something's wrong*** . I look bored to you? . what is the problem officer why can't you get this cleared out . let's get the hell out of here that doesn't sound good sounds like crashing . yes you do . God damn . isn't it your job to keep the traffic moving . I'm not leaving this car you can but I can't . hey look the state troopers are here now aren't . ***something's wrong*** . I should have gone back at the house . ***the death-rattle of the engines*** . well as a matter of fact I find being stuck for hours in some terminal gridlock somewhat stimulating . . . .

Yah, the *BackWhang!* grapevine's up that you feel this small now being told by this newbie to do the things you ought have done years back but you didn't—

. . . . ***something's wrong . something's wrong*** . everybody's getting out and going that way come on let's go . this is all going to thaw out and go bad what will . ***something's wrong*** . hey they're all getting out . ***something's wrong*** . and running out over that way . oh yah really? . ***the dead steaming engines*** . just another nail in my big fancy career coffin . need to spit but where . let's go— my God, look at that . ***something's wrong . something's wrong . something's wrong*** . it was all barren here not a single house at all . aren't those state trooper uniforms on those cops way up there . . .

So you ended up crying in beers at Holyman's to the one bartender who everybody knows loves to sling rumors around 'bout this one said this or that one said that, eh, more bad judgement on your part's what they're saying—

. . . . *the hum of the engines* . yes yah really I do— don't you? . that's what's dangerous that's what's happening so let's get the hell out and run . hey I never saw one of those before I *just saw that model in magazines* I ought to ask them . *grab the dog!* . *something's wrong* . what the hell they looking let's go this scene is imploding at hah hah hah guess they never seen a me before my *the crash-crunch of the dead engines* . . . .

The town all thinks you are washed up. That you're stupid is as your stupid does; as witness the whole of all I just told out oud, to you. (ouch!) le-la *"Top-mayor states this town is irredeemable"*. th' th' rending of steel-b. big **Beware!**

. . . . God this can't be why're they all keeping coming like they are GOD look at that—let's go crash smash there's too many shatter! shatter! cars with no place to go too many ***BAM!*** with *this is* no place to go *is wrong can't be happening* cars to go too many with no place many with no place many with *but it is so lets get out oh no* no place to go place: there you go see why ***BAM!*** ***BAM!*** I brought you here for, *Top-mayor*: to go way way to ***BAM!*** ***BAM!*** many but: see what they all went through ***BAM!*** see *how they died*: why way too ***BAM!*** ***BAM!*** many why they ***BAM!*** ***BAM!*** ***BAM!*** ***BAM!*** dreams all have of a peaceful death *shattered* just keep coming ***BAM!*** ***BAM!*** ***BAM!*** ***BAM!*** can't they see coming : still *all lives* think *shattered* this no more *all souls* than *shattered* a little traffic jam *eh?*: see can't *shattered shattered* they *all souls* see can't they see *all lives* they can't see no no no no All souls *shattered shattered shattered* yes = they're not just saying but really really yelling the TRUTH of you there, the TRUTH being that *Top-mayor says its worse than that its* *actually a really toxic place that anybody wants to go on living should sign up for immediate evacuation from {!!!!!!!!!!!!!!!!!!!} !*

   dual setp-backs from each o' t' others woozy, woo—all's been just said sucked the air out their spaces so—Top-mayor reeled back grasping deep down for the best next thing to say but **where is it**

   Using the provided pads and/or pen-pencil sets **BASSOON,** zzzzzzzzzzzzzzzzzzzzzzzzzip!

   {bang   *pop*}

short preach

1

2

3

   the following flow's got hey mom look there's two weasels **b'serted here to satisfy le'al obligations** *so suffer*

Start Monoblock^{tm}

{Hence! Hence! Hence! Rrrrrrrrrrrrrrrrrrrrrr-p Elves elves Elf elf Elves elves Elf elf Elves behold the stew Elf elf Elves stir well and enjoy (citizens) elves Elf elf Elves elves polesitters—what the hell why's everything different so very very different Elf elf Elves elves Elf elf Elves elves Elf elf Elves elves Elf elf where's Preston before Preston well right here Elves elves Elf elf Elves elves Elf elf Elves where's Preston after Preston well right here Elf elf Elves elves Elf elf Elves elves Elf elf right here all's right here Elves elves Elf elf Elves see this long skinny vertical pole elves Elf elf Elves elves Elf elf it means something Elves elves Elf Let's go already and pick up this damn town elf Elves elves Elf elf Elves elves Elf elf before the big bang Elves elves Elf elf HOLD IT – WAIT!!! Elves elves Elf elf this is at the same moment the spouse's tv died pushing them to go play real-world Jai alai Elves elves Elf elf Elves elves Elf elf Elves elves Elf elf Elves elves Elf elf Elves elves can't fit so many bodies un' 'is postage stamp of a cemetery, unless they're beings are no more than Elf elf Elves elves Elf elf Elves elves Elf elf Elves elves Elf elf Elves elves Elf elf Elves elves fail to see the point Elf elf Elves I ran this town in a super-concertininnian manner Elf elf Elves elves Elf elf Elves elves Elf elf your job is cutting grass at the cemetery – mine is to run a huge town – now, really Elves elves Elf elf Elves elves Elf elf Elves elves bonkers bonkers eh-onkers eh-onkers la la Elf elf Elves elves Elf elf Elves elves at this juncture—all seems apparently bonkers Elf elf Elves elves Elf elf Elves elves snaps and becomes TOP-GENERAL-MANAGER and turns to go take back their town Elf elf Elves elves Elf elf Elves and from them they plucked up a fine Henchmanette – elves Elf elf Elves elves Elf elf Elves elves fruit cups don't boil over Elf elf Elves elves Elf elf thrown back to his origin Elf elf Elves elves Elf elf I don't believe any of this Elf elf Elves elves Elf elf we don't either like - somebody rounded us up and sent us here and said stand by here until summoned Elves elves Elf elf Elves elves Elf elf Elves elves Elf elf Elves elves Elf elf Elves elves Elf elf Elves elves if you do NOT your punishment will be both swift and severe}

End Monoblock^{tm}

this last following flow's got b'serted back there to satisfy le'al obligations *thank all for suffering*

3

2

1

short preach

No...   *...STOP!*

ut   **! u   t?   ut**   **!**
what the hell the TV cut off why the hell its a *brand new TV for Christ's sake*

ut   spin-whirl what eh eh he   there's
no vortex to t   n − n spin-whirl la la spinn-whirllllllll
NO b   bb   bbbb but there's no damned vortex
        its a *brand new TV for Christ's sake*   yes,
but

        *okay   party party party party par rrrrrrrrrrrrrrrrr-***up-coming back** *in*
and Up wavering as the cemetery began reforming around
with the Top-mayor as the center in point x of the storm now
all lifting lifting sooner that the w-person predicted but its
lifting anyway so do not condemn the poor devil they are
probably   new   at   the   job   fresh   green   from   the
myticourological school {*Francis*} and as the stones some
in groups some in pairs but ***mostly alone*** re-pop'd into
heckzinnstenzze the gloves were found hands wrapped
gloves on laced up teeth tight-set and the Top-mayor
frenzedly shot out delivering flurries of quick, tight, but
disquietingly powerful blows.
        Okay, okay. I think I know then, what I need to do next.
What?
        Tell you its bullshit that a small/low cemetery lawn
mower weeder and all around small insignificantly weak-
minded gossip-toilet low rent goose like you dares to think
I'm going to give ten craps *(solid? loose? makes no difference you are you
just like crap is crap)* to anything at all you have to say?
        stun

What? You—

[its a *brand new TV for <u>Christ's sake</u>*]

*Never mind me. We're talking about you. You, whose job is **cutting grass at a cemetery** –* and, a tiny one, to boot— while mine is to run a huge town—now, really! Before a group of reasonable people who're they gonna believe? Huh? Huh?

Quiet (on the dot of what's just been said [vibrating out (nickels & dimes | dingoes and boxtops : collaps'd right back down : left *over there* | scallop the prisoners) one by one by one o'er a period oh (DYNAMITE) days] laid 'cross h' croadently :zipper:) hence all over the cowling of the plane showed smeared the evidence one evidence two evidences three the add one more makes five one less than six _we know, we know so *shut up* _ pop two up top five ya gets eight * nope not going that way bad guess very very bad guess * fall flat o'er the syrup * behold the gross lack of evidence that the next number in the sequence (hoke where went the seven ah ah) may be nine which is one less than ten which is one-tenth of one hundred li'l *simples* why you keep throwing these li'l *simples* over me Gimi I never brought you up to waste *simples* that say Gimi they're precious you know hard to catch harder to kill but, why o why Gimi you wasted them like that throwing them down on me Gimi a have already been well subdued Gimi please do not torment me no more hey-*hell* Gimi please do not torment me no more hey-*hell* Gimi please do not torment me no more hey-*hell* and hey-*hell* and hey-*hell* and hey-*hell* and [b-b-b-b-butttt, **its a *brand new TV for <u>Christ's sake</u>***]

whack   slash   NO -

!cut to quiet!

Much longer and lower and so much further away, the door knocked o' a fist 'r two {ah so it must mean that } they got turned from their suddenly cut back to nothing supposedly brand-new television set : [after all after all why'd it die *why'd it die* its a **brand new TV for <u>Christ's</u>**

sake] ||||**heck:** reader's note from this point forward TV will be used as an abbreviation, but well hey big tits on the donkey swine FLU swine swine FLU aw crap that was a screwup, TV is nothing abbreviated, its actually more of an acronym. Don't you think so, class—oh yes, oh yes—you up there you got something to add onto this or maybe moreover more traditionally hand up means I have a question's what it does mean go go go GO okay, Pop – a proper abbreviation for televison set might be *Rap Sheet* o <u>howl</u>, o <u>howl</u>, no no that can't be my mere stunt of a student oh yes it must be can be and most truly kind sir yes it *is, Rap Sheet* is my boy-Pope my boy silly idea off of some show labeled "Anackrickall Adams, *boy-Pope*" no one would watch because a male child (sometimes referred to as a "boy" in western cultures just like a female child (sometimes referred to as a "girl" in western cultures)) |||| what'd I *DO* officer what's goan' ON oh yes, oh, yes—what's goan' on—very fine question oh yes and oh yes scratch all that shit *Meester*, they went to the knocked on door having turned from their brand new but already dead TV televisions "*McVisionary and Pole*" deeply branded dead set they did get for free anyway sparking dear God Gimi, what else you goan' t' do me with today Gimi, here we are just five or six one more than four and five respectively and open the God-damned door GOOD GOD DON'T YELL AT ME WHY'D YOU DO GIMI WHY THE HELL O'ER HELL YOU ALWAYS DO GIMI opened the door and recognized instantly the first of the three hemiotrilliac'd beep beep polesitters (followed right behind by two semi-identicals) saying, Ah, yes, we—are you okay? We're checking the neighborhood to make sure everybody's okay after what just happened. You two okay? Did you hear it? Is your power off too?

The blur of surprise at them faded off that way away off them and the taller spouse {always much better at engaging sudden strangers} said, Hey, no—I, we, ah—::::while simultaneously think/feeling okay *BackWhang!* aw, oh, shit; you're the ones three or four houses down who appeared in a local news story for *brag brag brag brag but who the hell gave a shit then eck ha still don't give no shit now* having secured a high-level post in a major university, but hey, but hey, we know you you're just two bit low polesitters::::—our TV cut off but that's about it. See—

They reached on the inside of the wall for the entryway light switch and suddenly got it that, Hey, yeah. Our power's off, too. What happened?

You two didn't hear anything?

No. But—please tell us what happened.

A big bang in the sky someplace. We—nobody knows but there was a big bang up in the sky and all the power cut off. We're calling on neighbors who didn't come out to make sure everything's okay with them. I mean dear God, it was something. You didn't hear nothing?

No. We didn't hear nothing.

That's something. Okay—and no we didn't hear nothing. The sky up there look at it. I never knew it looked quite that blue. Did you check out your basement? Is everything all right? The plates got rattled off the shelf. Can't imagine how but they did. Look there were those wires always twisted like that? No more fine China to brag on *cheep cheep*. Oh. Who are you? I don't remember seeing you living here before. How 'bout it? Who are you? All those houses up that way are for sale. I don't remember seeing you living here before. How 'bout it? Who are you? Why are all those houses up that way for sale? What the hell was that? I don't remember seeing you living here before. How 'bout it? Who are you? What the hell was that? I can't get the car started. Let's harvest some of that pronto *hey mom look there's two weasels hey mom look there's two weasels* and get it under a microscope. But I don't see how that can be 'cause of the big bang. I don't remember seeing you living here before. How 'bout it? Wow we all thought this house was empty, I don't remember seeing you living here before. *I think I got a battery-powered transistor radio. Let me go get it.* How 'bout it? Look down there. What the hell was that? Everything just stopped, just like that. They're bringing stuff out to the curb down there. Look. Who are you? Something wrong in the ground up there? Look. Really? That's why they're all selling? I don't remember seeing you living here before. How 'bout it? Oh! They're beautiful! How old are they now? Really? Why are they bringing that stuff out to the curb down there? Wow how time flies. But anyway. Who are you? *They always say every household should have a battery powered transistor radio.* But we don't got one. So what's wrong in the ground that they all need to move? Do you got one? I don't remember seeing you living here before. How 'bout it? Who are you? I don't remember seeing you living here before. How 'bout it? Who are you? The sky up there look at it. *I thought you said you had a battery powered transistor radio.* I never knew it looked quite that blue. Okay—and no we didn't hear nothing. That's something. We didn't hear nothing. *Why'd you say you had a battery powered transistor radio when you knew you didn't have a battery powered transistor radio?* No. You didn't hear nothing? I mean dear God, it was something. We're calling on neighbors who didn't come out to make sure everything's okay with them. *Why'd you say that eh you a liar?* We—nobody knows but there was a big bang up in the sky and all the power cut off. *Why'd you say that eh you a liar?* A big bang in the sky someplace. *Why'd you say that eh you a liar?* They reached on the inside of the wall for the entryway light switch and managed to get the lights back on. They looked out.

What happened?

Why'd you say that eh you a liar?

Can't tell.

Just a big bang in the sky someplace.

What?

Why'd you say that eh you a liar?

A big bang in the sky someplace.

Why'd you say that eh you a liar?
A big bang in the sky someplace.
You a liar? A liar? A liar?
You a liar?
No!

So = they left the house, through their never had been knocked on ever, door, leaving their brand new but already dead TV televisions "McVisionary and Pole" deeply branded dead set behind, and so even though they had got it for deep-free anyway, dear God Gimi Rando McRando never mind'd all that damn'uch anyway, get yourselves out there where you were then Gimi, for reasons having nothing to do with that one thought they had a *battery-powered transistor radio* but not never went back to get the damn thing here hey were deep seated o're their elementalized correct element again as-as h-*hey*, strapped on their cestas, re-entered the court, and began to play. {*pillo*} They still found the game to be su-uperprisingly easy{.} ? Easy sass' Fly! Pop! so Back! Catch! play Fling! Fly! Pop! so Back! so Back! so Back! so Back!

"Isn't this game great, great fun?"
"Yes it's fun!"

Serenade and Flowers ?

Let's harvest some of that pronto and get it under a microscope.
BackWhang!
What? How 'bout it?
Who are you?
Party! *BackWhang!*
What! How 'bout it!
Who are you?
Party! *BackWhang!*
What? How 'bout it?
Who are you? Who are you? Who are you?
Party! *BackWhang!*
BackWhang!
BackWhang!
(pick it up)

Ah!

Wonderful!

Sc(k)rappo ball of confusion = how the hell do we do this = and it was told unto them (yah as it got told to all brethren in those early days [Praise La-Luna!] before they were discharged in-toward their new great big **hassle** {My sorry oh so-o so My sorry yes yes yes *My sorry* how many more ways you want me to claim that I'm sorry what why say claim, et et et, that keeps you hop-guessins doff' m—I truing you up with the truth or else + hey stay stop we hear "back up signals" yess yess yess there must be big machines about Wow **THE GENERAL-MANAGER** must **ll'e** **want** **this** **done** {willow} *which code means* "*like yesterday* aka *pronto* aka *asap* aka can't think out no **more**, *as* they sing out the swallows, esss ss '' sing out t hee way hey hee them they did forward out a large sum of money together with a small squad of advance "*clear the way out*" thems, each of them the exactly right them to be able to push them no matter how many the motto being "No matter how many "thems" of all shapes and/or sizes are presented we can criticalize them, down to some tiny 'nuff mass can be threaded through as many holes present to maintain their head honcho's big steady nd' "*on the button*" large pleasurable and so so profitable progress *yeet yeet* an ak an never mind how you got it that you so so so shu shu uat uat an ak an got it's all you need and they also found upon arrival at the work site that so so so shu shu uat uat an ak an to level it down clear it clean smooth it out smooth into all [countless] so pukey as to if left untreaded, led to a dead-diarrheastectecular last resort super surgery so so so shu shu uat uat an ak an so so some thousands of "clean": workers got poured onto the surface of t'e vast phone-pole plant work-site so many so shu something wrong have been gone S.Y.Y Jack eh shu uat uat an ak an so so so yeah it does seem funny let me *BackWhang!* call up top about it Jak <u>uno momento</u> shu shu uat uat <u>an ak an so so</u> <u>so shu shu uat uat an ak an so so so shu shu uat uat an ak an so so so shu shu uat uat</u> <u>an ak an so so so shu shu uat uat an</u> ak an so so so shu shu uat uat an ak an so so so shu shu uat uat an ak an so so so shu shu uat uat *in response to their panic-ask* **THE GENERAL-MANAGER;** I acted quickly after yo' left to staff up the PP factory rebuilding project. I knew you two, even though more than able to handle the job may need some additional strings pulled and/or favors called in an/or a**e* kissed and/or palms greased and/or laws bent far as to not ||| ***Devagar, por favor, não podemos acompanhar!***

||| break and/or permissions unsought 'nd prepared to beg forgiveness so. We found out Gibraltar a research complex equipped to mine up nearly 1oo% of the way-clearing work we need done for you to provide you a clear red carpet/palms-strewn o' you *Jerusalem style* look it up they did it for us so we do not know what the hell that means but maybe you want to, as a matter of fact you should, *budda budda budda* we got introduced to a mysteriously cloaked middle-aged Moroccan *takka takka* semi-genius who said Okay Barry ||| ***Hægðu þig, vinsamlegast, við getum ekki fylgst með!*** ||| your worst problem will be staffing, Barry (I am not named Barry so don't leave run-wild a gossip-tale I'll ge butt-dragged out some UK based tab-rag through a pipe so small my butt can be dwarved by a drenched and soak'd farret (ha))*Let's go, Easy! There's a war on!* and so since their way of things is right now or not at all aka "what the hell you mean you want to think about if you've time to think about it you can't really need it" but ||| ***Maj mam, thov, peb ua tsis tau!*** ||| still found time to bust in heah', grip me by the neck, slam me to the wall, and insist insist insist insist-demand :hold it *wait*: insist-demand :no one insisted *nothing*: insist-demand insist-demand insist :hold it *wait*: insist insist insist :no one insisted *nothing*: insist :no one insisted *nothing*: insist insist-demand :hold it *wait* no one insisted *nothing*: insist-dem:no one insisted *nothing*: and d:no one insisted *nothing*: em:no one insisted *nothing*: ||| ***Mesrɛ wo, brɛ wo ho ase, yɛrentumi!*** ||| :no one insisted *nothing*: *noin* :no one insisted *nothing*: *mop-up phase of battle* **initiated** in progress *please wait* in progress *please wait* in progress *please wait okay okay plese wit plse it p i what the hell do you want* **COUGH IT UP!**

Meda wo ase!

Dankie!

አመሰግናለሁ!

متشكرم!

But, too late! Because, by that time your project was fully staffed to the tune of 2000 +-35 sucked in from

someplace *noin* we'd not been allowed to ask about and we figured 'hat's swept under the rug stays under in maybe, uh, 99.999999999.0% of the time so here you go get the hell out you got the tools you need go out and use them report back to this office when done *and not before* hail Mary   ..   *noin*
noin

B - :hold it *wait*:

C   -   :no   one   insisted   *nothing*:
noin

D - Okay.
So?
E =

Ach! Shut up (the smiling Jak-Jacks) jus' let it *come* let it go *let it happen* con carne pinstickla-prupula: pinstickla-prupula: as pins stick—*she knows noin noin noin* pinstickla-prupula: pinstickla-prupula: *noin* rip down the pinstickla-prupula: sheeny surface of pinstickla-prupula: pinstickla-prupula: of *what is noin* [why don't ya why don't ya why don't ya ***pup-pup***] of *what is* [***pup-pup*** ya why don't ya why don't ya ***pup-pup***] of *what is* [***pup-pup pup-pup*** don't ya why ***pup-pup pup-pup***] of *what oi is* [***pup-pup pup-pup pup-pup*** why ***pup-pup pup-pup pup-pup***] of *what is* [***pup-pup pup-pup*** why ***pup-pup pup-pup***] of *what is* [***pup-pup*** why ***pup-pup***] *circular linens* of *what is* [why] circular linens *right atcha! Yes, Sergeant!* of *what o is* [circular linens *right atcha!* why] of *what is* [why linens *right atcha!* why] of *what is* [why why *right* why why] of *what is* [*Yes* why *right* why *Sergeant!*] of *what is* [*Yes right Sergeant!*] *out of the frying pan and into the blast furnace* take care at the slag heap **do not get exploded** .. . . . .

Who are you? *BackWhang!*

where the hell are we   tee hee hee hee   got to go staff up the project   got to go staff up the project staff up staff up staff up but how we doo dat *how   &=& whopula-snatch   [{"You're on your own now. Make what you can of it."}]*   push the pin (in)

Who are you? *BackWhang!*

:sheeny surface of *what is* [why don't ya why don't ya why don't ya ***pup-pup***]: ?

Push the pin (in *o*) the solve of the problem what, no! Oh, yes, oh yes oh, they're having a really big problem upstairs can you feel it uh yes I think so I do I really do **Wonderful!** got a problem simply stick a pin in the problem pins are meant to solve problems [Who are you? *BackWhang!*] as long as stuck into the type of problem *o* for which they were meant to solve *pillo* the Sc(k)rappos struggle-rolled backundra-froth work many fast whiles after their reassignment {struggling} how to this and how to that this and that that and this an[d that-that and this-this forever and ever that's how long this's meant to last *it seemed* [Who are you? *BackWhang!*] but then where's a pin here's a pin push it where push it there [Who are you? *BackWhang!*] where here no no not there [Who are you? *BackWhang!*] that's yourself *blood red too blood red there* and pushed into yourself the Gods did not make them who invented the pin **anyplace** I do not know Carlo you're full of questions Carlo [Who are you? *BackWhang!*] we mean being full of questions for a moment or two **works** but you got to let go see what happens you're froze. [Who are you? *BackWhang!*] There. [Who are you? *BackWhang!*] There. How come I know all these things while you just let you're eyes loose to rollin'? I mean—I mean—I set brick one in the wall *your eyes jus' go rollin'* I set bricks one two three four bricks into the wall *your eyes jus' stay rollin'* I set bricks five through five thousand "*no* change" *your eyes jus' stay rollin'* and so forth and so on and so forth and so on and so forth so on so forth so on pinstickla-prupula so forth so on so forth lunchtime[3326] so pinstickla-prupula on so pinstickla-prupula pinstickla-prupula forth so on push the pin harder and harder and harder and – *ann--*   BUST in flow the required (what's that we hadn't thought that)(oh that that's probably hemm-haww, hemm-haww about two thousand that right? lunchtime[3327] That many? Yes that's right. here's residue Yes that many here they come pop boof blip dosh-gesundheit, here they come like they're blown. [Who are you? *BackWhang!*] Hey, fella hey, fella look, so many look so, and see *((if we lose our planet* *knowing why won't bring it back))*..yes here's residue but will that what you're pin-sucking them out of will their walls not collapse, oh no no no, no no! No no no! Heff, all's equally ever..yplace today isn't that what we wanted isn't that what we *dreamed*?

here's residue ere's residu e's resi 's r And thus so and lunchtime[3328] thus.

The T-phone pole plant began to re-arise.
Smilingly they looked on, looked over.
Central-Luna one big noisy bang
BackWhang! BackWhang! BackWhang! BackWhang!
Gesundeits of the type drove up that unassembled obsolete oscilloscope round the gate *how 'bout here?*

lunchtime[3329] esso Mc—bean 101 to be spiked-tight-down according to {*"blueprint"*} handed up ***thanks b-b-b-*** lunchtime[3330] slap'd o'er first—setting them down (*two*) keep the track Mayor McWokette [Who are you? *BackWhang!*] we's got's to prevererrant and resididual *sizzle* and now, as at a time of the day always this way then, they sat as every day on a horizontal beam, th'-*which,* they'..d habitually sit on as long as it is still there when they come to sit on it, lunchtime[3331] which {for the ease of the reader "this" = until the crew built out this level to the point {"plastic strip *{porky* {pillo} *pig}* sticking game"} where this beam is engulfed and thus never was so they use the nearest available flat surface capable of bearing their weight, on *hey mom look there's two weasels* which they are not in the way of anything, and which remains accessible to them for the duration it takes that lunch lunchtime[3332] is now over and t..hey are back to work only |||||||| = *{which what that was intended to represent you are challenged to guess}* supplying about 0.050% of the total effort being expended by the work crew [Who are you? *BackWhang!*] building up a new and improved (but not disincorporating any of the prior plant's features) telephone pole factory-plant—plane and; once more after opening their lunchpails thinking again one more time in the instants j' gifted them ***gok***; it seems we should not be here huh? oh this; yah yo yell whoah-hey whoah-hey I do mean this. {spit}

Yesterday we were here right yes or no yes of course—and the yesterday before that and before that but why the hell'....d we choose this occupation anyway? It's a kick in the pants to need to do this every day. Don't you see it as a kick in the pants? I mean ah ah, I somehow remember that back when applying to do this (which applying I can only assume I'd ever done a good assumption at best since how the hell you end up on a job without somehow applying previously you know but I can't believe we asked for this : we what yo....u mean we speak for yourself) please okay okay stop saying "we"

be still play the {0} carcass and they'll think you dead ..
= .. no no no no more fun
brand new slippers
As for me, I have learned through hard experience, that's right, experience—the kind that looked back at seems like being dragged for years (maybe? Can't be sure of {0} that either *ho*) through a tight tube, with slanting back spines, to shred and shred and hey, yes—there ought to be some limit to the shredding, as after a while (how much o' a while? (Can't be sure of that either **hoooo**)) until there's nothing to shred, and all's left is a spread out mass of a loose mixture of some color (nah 'mpo'tent? Nah-na-know slick-slippering down once through it, and all the way out of the end of it, too, tha{0} t does not m.a..t...t....e.....r, y'know, y-y-y-y', *know* **but you bring these** same exact things up every day, at "lunch". Something in it being time for "lunch" seems to spark up in you the need to bitch and moan.)
But, we—
But nothing, and we nothing. Everything you say may be true, as a matter of fact, they all are true, like—these are shit jobs— *hey mom look there's two weasels* how we got into this mess, I have no idea of either—why do you get us into such a state of agitation th' I end up shaking my sandwich all around so damned h.....a....r...d th' most of it flies loose from between the bread, and it becomes inedible, and I need to throw it

down? I mean look, and look at that garbage drum there, *pronto,* how many of our breads, and our rolls, and how much of our dearly bought beef, cheese, salami, and sliced kielbasa's end up ratted down in the goop of the drum, pressed down by the rest of God knows what kind of garbage, thrown down in there o'er the remains of the day? Then, the flies come, and the bees, and *pronto*, but, thank God miraculously, in each next day from that day (now a yesterday hey hey hey hey we are sitting now in a day put down to be baked out thoroughly, everything leached from it, the nur-r-r-r-*trition* of fresh time rollered out of it, by the God cranking some kind of crank-press to juice it out dry, and it gets thrown out behind. Then, we all do as we're told, and step off the ledge of it, believing the lie that we'll step safe onto a fresh new one, <u>*HA*</u>, there are no fresh new days laid out welcoming us, **NO**, its just that same old tattered, worn out, and worn over single same day we got issued at birth, played o'er, then o'er, and o'er and o'er again and again. Then went *Bang* a hot starter's {0} pistol, when we shot down that chute and heard *Go*, the command that set our lives rolling, and that one day we press shed-empty, and drain, and sleep's not sleep, no no, sleep's a like, eh ah sleep's an anesthetic to lull us, while the lord renews the single day we got issued. Freshens it, shakes it out, hangs it on the line, yah, a line in some back yard, so the sun beams down, dries the stink out of it, while back-hind the brush like, we join the mob-children—each and every one anesthetized, running round round baby round round, playing some keep busy game they were convinced is fun (involving Tonka *Toys;* perhaps involving Tonka *Toys*) throwing a stick that way, yelling, Hey, *I threw farther than you*, no you didn't, *yes I did*, run to the other side, pick it up, throw it back the other way, where it lands, say again, hey, I threw farther than you, *no you didn't,* yes I did, run to the other side, pick it up, throw it back out the other way, where it lands, say again, Hey, I threw farther than you, *no you didn't*, yes I did, run to the other side, pick it up, throw it back out the other way, where it lands, say again, busy busy hot hot, 'til the God behind the scenes what got that one single same day you were issued cleaned all up 'nd back up good as new, goes to the back porch window yells **Gimi**! **Gimi**! through a small square screen—**Come in, _come in_,** and they all—1. drop what they're doing 2. forget who threw further 'cause it's really very meaningless and 3. go in, and 4. sense its time to 5. get up and walk down, and 6. wash up, comb down, dress up, all that shit, all that shit, then 7. eat a meal, pack a bag, go out the door, and, 8. end up here in this shitty job you all knock heads about like you do—as, How the hell'd we end up here anyway, **SNOW** why the hell we got this life handed o'er and not that one those of one of those other kinds flat-black silly n' stupidly **SN** gifted by mistake to them over there, but not to us, hey, why not ever us, always them, but never us, and get up **OW** and go back around that building **SNOW** where the days get hung to dry in that space in between no one is allowed to dire....ctly experience, and look up t' the square **SN** screen where they yelled **Gimi!** out before **SN** and say very politely **SNOW** I am..... sorry **SNOW** but would ....you please explain **SNOW SNOW** what **OW** this show's... all about **SNOW SNOW SNOW** I mean, I'm acting in it, like there's a script and all that, uh, but tell **OW** me w..hat the movie we're in's all about please and then politely wait ||||| guk snello con-sill there are look there's little wires all woven up and down and back and forth making up what you perceive as screen but "screen" is just shorthand for what that thing up there you're waiting for an answer to come through's not a screen, as a matter of fact, there's no such thing as a "screen" that's just a sound made up and agreed would stand for that thing up there you're waiting for an answer to come through but *hey* I took too much of your time up already, hey no have a good day, better get back on the lone oh no lunchtime it over I mean, was it ever under over under sideways down where have I heard over under sideways down before o YAH but then they/you gets/got/always was/ always will be bored {cat-*purr*} and so there we are, but why bother the why, here I am, and here you are, and we are nope whoops will not say it guess it please, please guess it will you, please guess buzz buzz buzz buzz see how you make me waste my time buzz

OW buzz **OW** buzz thank God it's g' no inherent value anyway, come on, there's **SN** boards to hammer-in, and then more boards to hammer-in, and boards over boards to hammer down, hammer in, 'n so on, why, why **Gimi** why why you do dis to me Gim-m-m-m-i ? :' &#   the popes are in heaven mostly   **SN**   bi{cat-*purr*} g *cheese Hap Daniels*

   Hey play Meansie-Whilesie
   Hey play Meansie-Whilesie
   Hey play Meansie-Whilesie
   Meansie-Whilesie
   Meansie-Whilesie
   Meansie-Whilesie; **BIC never write with any other;** as all these things kept proceeding posthaste, Jan and Jon patiently sat muted down in the meeting room whose meeting had long since dissolved and whose occupants had a..ll left for the last t...ime excepting for Jan a..nd Jon themselves {hopefully 'cause there they are *see* th{cat-*purr*} em *look* at them—they *are* there there they *are* see them and. look at them—the two pitiful ones—left at the bottom not even able to continue their "plastic strip sticking game" which would have broken their boredom somewhat as info-latah hell {*porky pig*} 's great big stadium to watch several hours of meaningless games {w' twatch they'd be good at} and this empty lon{cat-*purr*} g waiting like two forgotten fishes in some much larger tank {*porky* {cat-*purr*} *pig*} so large of a tank really that the fishes do not perceive the tank to them its open water free and clear open water like the watery open pointless in and of itself water of the playing of a simple "stick these "plastic strips" to this *backing* seeing what creative patterns symbols portraits imaginary horses floating in the clouds *as-as* that one's a *bear* head, that one's a *witches broom*, hey pal Jan of mine "plastic strip sticking game" what use is a broom if there's no witch, oh, sugary silly minded Jon that you are, you got it flopped all around back'ards a broom with a witch on it's impossible to sweep

with {here's a station Ruthie a train or a semi required to be weighed must be round 'bout here anyplace (get ready to shoot one if it's the one that's charging there is no point in shooting the ones to the sides just peacefully grazing while in that time's wasting tooth fang claw bulk anger and rage e' e'en a toothache or two gone untreated goes on for some years 'fore the bear says to itself, What the hell, oh my God, what the hell, let it go there's no hope damn this toothache worse yet yet yet these toothaches or three * up more's the wise * and flip to the fast POV of the victim here comes the tooth claw rage and the roar of the ever-attacking Bulk of the "*Bear*" or more every (*Yep yep yep, it's got to be true, I read it in Field & Stream, okay?*) perhaps maybe oooh aaahhh Petunia's gone all cute on us today siighhhhhhhhhhhhhh s-s-s-sh so tha attack comes and went and the fish's snagged open {talk about bad luck that's at least three four fists of it Jeeeez Jeeeees} and so to the bottomless slow down sinks the fish dea..d .ooh ahh dead so dead that even at the next tank cleaning, which the live fish will really know nothing about, let alone the dead one snagged backhind the coral-rock, not only killed, then set at the bottom gassing up internally, as the Dead are pro.......ne to do, then, finally *the last insult* {cat-purr} (cut the crap elf you know you don't exist but by the good graces of your individually wrapped piping hot griddle-fresh "*Santasia-Klauses*") and there the cleaner, having clean all 'vryting out pale, the top of the tank with the light and the droning of the filtering pump which the fish merely accept as their share of the everlasting underlying s' cosmic hum {"plastic strip *{porky pig}* sticking game"} :blank out now seven: eight nine ten's yes next: as they wait Jan Jon fish 'hind their particular take of the faked up rock coral, so; so; unlike the dead fish with no option but to rot 'wn forgotten to nothing, Hey, hey, SOAP cried Jon.. rising; which *{porky pig}* in fact causes Jan to rise in v' sympathic fashion each saying back-forth forth-back a reasonably overpainted slab *{porky pig}* upon which they chiseled the rot-ruin of the follo{cat-*purr*} wing decision point danger – bit hot heavy Jan Jon decision point NOW, as sc..rolled out o'er the following: {"plastic strip *{porky* {pillo} *pig}* sticking game"} so they remembered (and yes all two of them at once) *hickory stick that they'd* long been feeling a "*nudge* in their very own back-centrally *spined*-bones." to quote that fine 'll' we all've known all our lives, *maybe but oh so close enough* So, "spawned up within them the seed of someday finding important for mental health ***some larger purpose for their lives***." sub reference reference get it get it wink wink nudge nudge do you get it hey we do we do-o we—do (cowling) Thus, without full u{cat-*purr*} nderstanding of the need 'rr the thee those back of them yes yes those too two there came the echo *{sludge}* : big echo; *knw 'd prbbly ndrstnd wht thy'r siyang* ; end big echo: {this is familiar (*back up*) so familiar like as-was'wise do right now, n' ***Know*: 1.** Th' there was way back in four of your times a great funeral home in that corner out there, *BackWhang!* that hosted in many o'er many a fine viewing, but got too big and too comfortable, just like you. Do also ***Know*: 2.** Th' yon funeral home ended up biting up more that it could chew down its last *swallow*-got's clogged and choked it to death slowly and miserably. Do also ***Know*: 3.** Th' b' all inside then got flat-smothered down, hard-spread out the' there big blaster-con shockwaye that rippled out o'er a virtualized *Spirit Lake* some hot volcano-blast swept over damned fast. *what the Helen y' want hennyplace?* And lastly not likely do also ***Know*: 4.** the' 'e whole 'tire main drag down there came into the onrushing big fat (speculum-tackulla) great-big "*bang-shockwave*" (as previously documented) Havana crumb'd down *a' Dondi* mash'd 'll together last Cuban *Last Cuban* down to its essential vapors sludges 'n solids *take this whacko* : *what the hell are these clowns talking about* : ; last flow-melted o'er the lowest possible impenetrable what got crumbed over by the passage of time, *illusory of course 's 'l's 'moah* bedrock; *hard bedrock* 'hm roll'd 'way unde' yards acres square miles and whole continents pity those who enter here under the pretext of "here merely to

mow—truzt uz" *sighhhhhhhhhh* ; anywrench's foah' 'ares the subhabitants round here thought this just another pretty green moisty loamy spectacle of a plain old lawn, teeming with hard-won life underneath all down and there you were " now there's a tourist attraction for ya' " hey ya ya have that fallen face saying here you have rung these b(r)ells b(r)efore? If yes then so. You're a candidate to work here. So come join us. Come join (so come join us [come join { So come join us. Come join (so come join us [come join])}}]) join come us join come so; ***us.***
     bang   *;'*   *;[-*

                    BackWhang!

    So it seemed so *meant to be so* Jan *get yer fresh pickle-jam here* and Jon joined the team

    (sd-s-s-s-s now scan the workers at the site (who are the resurrected gridlock victims) who are uneasy like "I somehow feel this is not who I am, *judge*" perhaps I should leave and take up something else. So, anywhoop = those ones three or four houses down who appeared in a local news story for and all that *crap* were not Jan/Jon's whole new world any more and yoicks, man, yuhhh—what you stinker, you guessed it - yes many moreovers did get very jealous
               very jealous   *yes*
  jealous   *jealous*
    b-b-b-b-u', bingo!!!!!   the hole in their pasts start to pull them.

    transferred off from being sigh-say you can spend your life seeming to know who you are without even knowing you seem to know who you are until you stop dead stand tracks think about it 1 2 3 4 and—when it's nearly (we hope) too late to use any new information you now seem to know that all along you've been wrong about who you thought seemingly you are.
    Oh?

Yes; 'nd dit dit dit dit dit dit and last they got there saying (say!) eh, Crockett. If Crockett's your name (we were sent here to work and in the process) we will start small but end up big after the trying of making a mark in the world (yah that's right) the whole world we're Jan-Jon who are you o o we just said we're Jan-Jon who are you o o we just said we're Jan-Jon who are you o o we just said we're Jan-Jon who are you o o we just said Oh!

Great. Well, well. I thought you two were gone for good. Anyone spends several days crabbing out loud about this place and then leaves in a huff after finding their petty complaints ignored {what we're doing here, you know, in case you don't know's bigger than anyone's petty bitch-moans you know so much bigger} isn't really expected to come right back : but hold it no wait we've n' been here : oh sure you have. You're the same other two quit down on us last week.

No.

Yes!

rrrrrrrrrrrrrrrrrrrrr

We have not been here before.

Sure you have, you're *the same*!

The same as—as who? Don't say that it's wrong!

No its not!

Yes it is!

No its not no its not no its not **YES IT IS!**

After several weeks of this back-and-forth Jan and Jon began to wear down, this was not, was not good, as, they were new off the line in their first attempt at putting away childish things not gone through positively will have *consequences* s-so this had not been a wisely chosen first step, but their green raw barely solidified faces got pounded with the following; pounded, and pounded *jazz music pink towels cement mixer putti-putti* why can not anyone else but me see that we are all the same person *jazz music pink towels cement mixer putti-putti* how

can that be et et how can that be well well ***SHUT THE
HELL UP LET ME TELL 'YA—***

Jan and Jon slanted back in that wind a
"millimetrionne" or two from that wind and though it flowed
over them steadily they struggled back to verticality listening
hard pushing against it.

—we're all one and the same its just we can't see—

Jan's hand went up and, when Jon saw that then, their
hand went up, arms up and stretched out and the surprise of
the sight of this pushback shut up Crockett one munsa-
mummette enough for a strong reply to be forced through
even though it needed to be turned around sideways and
pushed 'bou' 10=ten=5x2={not equal to zero} saying
SHRIEK shut up that is nonsense you know it is push back
SHRIEK no its not hey her haw hem and hoomie! If I
brought here a freshly harvested chest heart {human} ||+still
beating reflexively+A: yes yes yes why's that important+A:
just is just trust us yes trust yes yes trust|| and slapped it on
the table could you say that this sight'd say anything at all to
you leading to a "know" in you of who this is as opposed to
others at all? I say you ***CAN'T***||well yes of course we can't
but that example's extreme |||| oh oh how it is extreme I think
it quite common as I got one in my chest right ***HERE***
[pounds chest] and you two each got one in you there + but
no wait that doesn't + so ***HOW*** on earth is a fresh cut out
heart beating reflexively on the table extreme in any way
they're all around it hundreds and thousands dozens and tens
uh uh | | | yeh but the extreme parts' not the heart but that it's
CUT OUT of an obviously live human who probably died
seconds after having no heart ***HA*** that's ridiculous ***HA HA***
that's so damned pedestrian ***HA HA HA*** that logic's so holy
it ought never have left church {what?} okay smartie-pants here
you go here's a long table in a super-secure place with lined
up cooled down washed over and impeccably arranged
complete human organ sets ***cooling*** which had required
rough' ten or more squads of certified registered white

coated white gloved pathologically oriented bright-shiny greenminted spit-young technicians fresh from the campus packed full of beans perfectly able to dissect out the specimens wash and dry cleanly and impeccably arrange o'er these gleaming steel tables all cleanly sanely w' no gore there at all. So do we see why this all equals the truth being that every single person on Earth is exactly the same as every other single person on Earth? So. Do you see that?

No not really, but—

Good. Am glad you can see that. Okay so you claim to not be the two I know you are. Tell me why do you have such a problem just admitting who you really are?

In Crockett's eye—back past the surface. Way down inside. Looking through there and straining to see as far in there as Jon possibly could Jan {J. also looking was deep in there as J. also looked deeper way in there past the furthest J. could look back in there actually} they both knew right there {*left slam to the right*} they were dealing with a hundred % {*right slam to the left*} totally honest Mm. Sincere of a person *so* stepping back as Cr. spoke they pulled back out what they'd shot deep into him and, as they stepped to the side so as to not self-repunch deep holes right through both themselves (this having pulled the drain out from Crockett in fact though not *totally intentionally;* they let Crockett go on, foolishly thinking they had the power of such "letting" with such a downrolling gravity of nature as d' Crockett did appear to be—oh no no no stronger to be truth say it stronger do not be afraid to say something one two three times stronger than might seem proper this is not a cocktail party this is not a popularity contest this is not a race to some imaginary super-successful brag brag brag metaphorical social and/or career *summit,* stabbing down to the left and to the right to force the competition back after all in the wild being wild's not hate jealously and rage fuels the race to be first bird to that seed-pile first bear to that h-put first predator to the prey it's just honest striving for survival in the wild the term "predator" does not hold evil water the animals are pure do you not can't you not why don't you want to see? Hey?

Ah—oh—we—

Ay oh we nothing its always ah oh we this and ah oh we that! Why can no one just shoot me with this = yes you are right Crockett yes you are right okay okay I do see = you are good people yes yes = = = = a right and good people people falling to their knees saying yes you are right, and you know it might see very foolish, but we do see through you yes.

(^ :::::   . . . . you and all what we thought were . . . .

lies but know now still are were and always will be . . . . lies you are a devil of an evil person not just up there but all the way down there toi toi toi yes but – [- - - - - - -

(*Jan/Jon in the meanwise stood stock-still taking in the bombardment*)

66 s;cgg /...[but even though knowing <u>ME</u> Crockett yes <u>ME</u> gatekeeper of this funeralalian archeaologistillsticklianne sight, may or may not be a lying page of evil, we still want the job!   (WAKE)

Do you two still want the job?

Uh—yes so, good—okay we want the job.

Jan to Jon = we? what do you mean we?

So?

Jon to Jan = isn't it true but = yes maybe but hey but = will you join me in taking this job = yes = Crockett said, Great—so. Glad to have you re-onboard, Eh.

<u>Re</u>? But we're not—

Are you really going to ask me to repeat every word I have said over you for the past more than several precious wasted days I've invested in *you*?

Uh. No, but—

But nothing!
But nothing!

But nothing—okay there's the brushes take two then go tango out to the end of the sweep cleaning line over there see see archaeology's not a big glamor job but on your knees brushing shit off and away only slowly and over a long, slow, time does the true past emerge what the hell'd you expect, eh—*serenade and flowers* GREAT BIG MEAL followed by *serenade and flowers* GREAT BIG MEAL followed by *serenade and flowers* GREAT BIG MEAL followed by *serenade and flowers* GREAT BIG MEAL followed by *serenade and flowers* tasty all the way like that NO no no you do the green behind your ears, mucus-mouth? How long's that green been behind your ears there, eh PAT behind your ears there mucus-mouth e PA behind you ear ther mucu-mout P behi yo ea the muc-mou beh y e th mu-mo be t m-m b see all does wear away in time does show t *spare me a few dollars, Meester?* he truth se al doe wea way n tim oes sho he trut e a oe we ay ti es sh e tru o e ay t s s tr y t = see it wear yes no wear see it or not wear all away given 'nuff time?

    *Any questions? **WEEN! WEEN! WEEN!***
No!
Good. DS sss   s   s   fffff
Party!
Party!   *spare me a few dollars, Meester?*
Pyrta!
Pyrta = Wons-derful!

    S T-m = भ्रम से पैदा हुई भव्यता में हम शुरुआत करते हैं। यहाँ इसकी टिप है. दल । दल । दल । दल **[there's always a way out *let me through*]** dig dig dig under supervision from beside Ho^1 = I k one sort of the of wher 'tis hi on to dig for or a HisLLW' ugh Ho^2 = I ink one mus sort of kw the oo of whver 'tis oes red on to dig don for or out Hisso-LAL ugh ugh Ho^3 = I tink one must sort of kow the *please go buy me a better shovel Daddy* ook of whaver 'tis ones ired on to dig down for or aout *spare me a few dollars, Meester?* Hisso-LALW' ugh ugh ugh Ho^4 = I think one must sort of know the look of whatever 'tis ones hired on to dig down for or about this sort of thing or things don't you think *Meester* Hisso-LALLW' ugh **[there's always a way through *let me out*]** ugh ugh ugh *I could dig much faster if I had a better one* ugh Do you not think that makes sense or once more are we yelling simply ugh ugh ugh ugh ugh *Up against the wall?* ugh ugh ugh ugh *Up against the wall?* ugh ugh ugh *Up against the wall?* ugh ugh *Up against the wall?* *please go buy me a better shovel Daddy* ugh *Up against the wall* **[there's always a way out *let me through*]** ||*help* the dam upstream's burst again so ***Get Out!*** || *I could dig much faster if I had a better one* *Up aganst the wall* ||*help* the dam upstream's burst again so ***Get Out!*** in una magnificenza nata dalla confusione iniziamo. ecco la punta di esso. festa . festa . festa . festa || *Up agst the wl* ||*help* the dam upstream's burst again so ***Get Out!*** || *Up at th wl* ||*help* the dam upstream's burst again **[there's always a way through *let me out*]** so ***Get Out!*** || *Up at th w'l* ||*help* the dam upstream's *spare me a few dollars, Meester?* burst again so ***Get Out!*** || *p t* ||*help* the *please go buy me a better shovel Daddy* dam upstream's burst again so ***Get Out!*** || *help* the dam **[*let me out*]** burst again so ***Get Out!*** || *help* the dam so ***Get Out!*** || *help* the so ***Get Out!*** || *help* the ***Get Out!*** || *help* th *et Out!* || help *Out!* || **[*let me through*]** he *ut!* | he *ut!* he *ut* he$_1$ *ut* he$_2$ *ut* he$_3$ *ut* he$_4$ *ut* he$_5$ *ut* he$_6$ *ut* he$_7$ *ut* he$_8$ *ut* he$_9$ *ut* he$_{10}$ *I could dig much faster if I had a better one* *ut* he$_{11}$ *ut* let me out there's always a way **[*let me out*]** out let me *through if I knew the look* there's *spare me a few dollars, Meester?* always a way through let me *out* you should **[*let me through*]**not be holding me back like *please go buy me a better shovel Daddy* this there's the door over there let me *through* it let me *through*{let me *through* it let me *through*}^{100} let out there's always *I could dig much faster if I had a better one* way out let *through* *it'd help a lot* you should not holding back like this there's door over there *through through if I knew the look* **[*let me out*]** {let me *through* it let me *through*} ^{90} let out always way let *through* should not back like there's door there *through it'd help a lot* {let me *please go buy me a better shovel Daddy through* it let me *through*} ^{80} let always let should **[*let me through*]**back there's there {let me *through* it let me *through*} ⁷⁰ *spare me a few dollars, Meester?* **if I knew the look** It always *party . party . party . party I could dig much faster if I had a better one* It should back thr's thr {let me *through* it let me *through*} ⁶⁰ **it'd help a lot if I knew the look** t[***let me out***] lwys t should bck t's t its really hard to dig here *please go buy me a better shovel Daddy* wow {let me *through* it let me *through*} ⁵⁰ t ls t shld bk t's t **of what it iz I'm digging for** itsz not eazy ++ *when the traffic flow blockage to one whole "lobe" of the city'sz vitrulariannesz wasz bought before him wasz thisz* ++ no itsz not eazy {let me [***let me through***] *through* it let me *through*} ⁴⁰ t l t szhd k t' *szpare me a few dollarsz, Meester?* t {let me *through* it let me *through*} ³⁰ l t hd t' {let me *through* it let me *through*} ²⁰ *I could dig much faster if I had a better one* l ++ the Jai alai sports complex must be completed ++ t' ***I know these are some kind of graves*** *please go buy me a better shovel Daddy* **but [*let me out*]** we've been digging for two hours now {let me *through* it let me *through*} ¹⁰ {let me *through* it let me *through*} ⁰ [***through***] the sun's up in the s(x   )y [***out***] **what's down here can't be what you'd reasonably expect** {let me *through* me *through*} ⁻¹ *in a magnificence born of confusion we begin . here is the tip of it . party . party . party . party* {me *spare me a few dollars, Meester? through through*} ⁻² *I could dig much faster if I had a better one* [***through***] how 'bout some water? {me *through* } ⁻³ { *through* } ⁻⁴ {}⁻⁵ -4 -3 ++ "forthwith *yes* it must be done forthwith ++ -2 -1 0 1 2 3 4 5 6 how 'bout a [***out***] break **given what caused them to show up here. Can you tell me?** [***through***]

Oh sure, I'll give you the spiel. *party . party . party . party* Here grab my hand I'll pull you up.

[***through***]

[***through***]

[***out***]

spare me a few dollars, Meester?

We figured all one of us, seeing as you seem to be a hard worker at the core, thought up to know well let me say—*deluded*? That fair? *Deluded*? Okay, sure, glad you can live with that, because we don't want to shut you off. You're running on surprise now you know. Or at least we know. Think a thing's running at full blast cares what it's running on {*do ya? **Esso** do ya?*} we do not think it so. Not to bore with that take whatever breaks you need quaff whatever liquids we go the box do you care what brand you drink? Akka? Akka? We said oo ah akka d'yacare what brand ye drink no. We thought not we knew you'd say no so so so. Say what length of story you're up to hearing now Top-mayor :: any length of story you care to ask let it go B.:: I do not think you should give up all control like that, Top-mayor. :: Its not giving up control as I've only got control down in those holes, digging. What you say and/or how long you say it, well, I got none :: yes you do :: no :: yes :: okay how is that then clue me in : when you're tired of what I' telling you you can just turn away and walk off ::oh yah? :: Oh yah, eh, oh yah? Well sorry, no. : why no? :: half control is not control :: half control what the hell is *half control* :: given that the story you tell has a beginning middle and end *ain't that right*? :: sure, but so— :: Here's so if there's only control of when to walk away from the story that's half the control wouldn't you agree? :: okay but what's that that's not any :: Shut up I am only half done, so—and it is similarly true that if I've control to step up and start to listen to a story in progress **OR** if I am lucky enough to be within earshot (either from serendipitously being there at the actual start of the story **OR** I walk up and remain idle waiting for the sto

• 101 Game 4

WEEN! ry to start **OR** : *get to the point* already I am bored to shit with this now *get to the point* :: don't interrupt that is <u>rude</u> so very <u>rude</u> **OR** I walk up on the story in progress *meaning* that the first sentence I hear may be incomplete and meaningless *worse yet* the first word I hear may be incomplete this/so meaninglessly garbled :: get to the point please I am bored with the two of you : hit shake and roll 'round the ground here/there *two of you*? What the hell's *two* there's just one of me—*two* of us—you got us and me tangly-whooped up your brain *gag* <u>go</u> *gag* <u>go</u> *gag*? <u>Go</u>. *Gag? Two of us what **two**?* :: (0)

Noah-*mine*
HOT!

Re-**Go**! = Then by all's snot sizzle you gained a few there Doc but you are so easy to catch up to why bother actually why; *why*; <u>*why-y-y-y*</u>; ***Bother?*** At all. Sizzle.

pain   pain and re-pain   pain and re-pain and

PAIN!
Great Big unfinished Cabin Cruiser Model O'er There On That Console TV Chris-Craft what? Chris-

Craft **WHAT?** ooooooo *Chris-Craft Chris-Craft Chris-Craft Chris-Craft Chris-Craft I like Chris-Craft's why Chris-Craft I like Chris-Craft very much yah yah the Chris and the Craft of it separately 'nuff,* **BUT** *I like Chris-Craft's why Chris-Craft I like Chris-Craft very much yah yah hence o'er hence this's the God-damn whole reason* there's a **Great unfinished Big Cabin Cruiser Model O'er There On That Console TV** all these bulldozers and shit came out of nowhere and started digging this gigantic hole in the ground. There ended up being a half dozen machines digging out this hole and maybe a whole dozen hardhats in orange milling around watching them digging and—I went up and asked what was going on and—

I swear to God, every single one of them ignored me. That pissed me off. Pissed me off good. I went back to the tent and called the cops and said I need to know what's going on, but they tossed me off. Said yes they knew what was going on, but said I'd need to "talk to city hall"—that's your office, Toppie. Right—that's your office. Right? :: yes it is but no one told me :: wait wait wait with the no one told me and all that crap. *Why no one told you's a whole separate great big problem.* But anyway when I found out what was going on I **really** saw red. So I just shot right down there, and what happened then rammed it home to the heart of me that those truck and that digging and all I saw—ohh, hey, what happened when I got down to city hall just—well, long story short, short and sweet, I mean—a couple 'a ones dressed kind of, like, deputies or something got me right when I got to the door, told me I was under arrest, and threw me in the jail over there, you know, that little one just a few feet down and to the left and :: Wait—*arrested* you? **No!** That can't be. I was told of nothing untoward worthy of anyone getting arrested let alone jailed relative to that particular project. :: HOLD, gotcha! *That project*, eh? I found out about that project. And you just nailed it down that there was a project nobody was supposed to know about to bury every trace of that gridlock incident (Gridlock incident? What the hell kind of a–*gridlock incident*?) everybody in charge's so hazy about—I mean, I had to be real careful when I went about digging up facts on that project, you know-after I got out of jail. But anyway, after I :: yah yah yah tell me what they said you got put in jail for :: okay here; when I said I was from out back the hills there and I wanted to know what the hell was going on with the trucks and the digging and the ruining of my neighborhood, the fat one stopped me there. Neighborhood? they said—you're living up there? No one's 'posed to be living up there. The borough owns that land and it's never been zoned for human habitation—and naturally push came to shove and you know by now you probably know my fuse is quite short and **WEEN!** my charge is gigantic—those two lit it and I went off and they pushed and shoved and I fought them but then its all a blur now you know after all—I woke up in a little six foot square cast concrete and stainless steel cell, and, well, yes by God, I did yell my head off until my voice shut down and my charge was all blown out and dead and—well not to bore you with a three-day rip o' big shot o'er it—it turned out I spent a long time in there :: hold it, *wait*. You didn't say why they told you you were arrested. What's they tell you? :: Nothing. They just said you're under arrest and I said what for and they said never mind what for just come with us, and they threw me in a cell. :: Hold it they must have brought you before a judge the next day or something didn't they? :: Nope. No judge. :: **What?** :: what I said. No judge. No lawyer. No nothing. I never got to see a single person's face for the whole sixteen days they had me locked up there :: Hold it, wait—what? How many days? :: *sixteen days* :: My **GOD** no no no that can't have happened—no charges no judge no lawyers no *nothing*? For sixteen *whole days*? :: That's right. The only thing was somebody shoved a tray of food at me through a slot twice a day and that was that. :: What'd they tell you when they let you out at the end of the sixteen days? :: Nothing. :: What? Didn't whoever came to let you out say anything to you? :: No, because nobody ever came to let me out. :: What? Come on, don't joke around, this isn't funny. :: I'm not joking around. Once in a while when I was in there I'd push at the door for something to do, like I'd touch the walls, pick my nose, kick the bunk, lay down, take a nap; you know, the little things you do to keep going when you're locked in a place you don't want to be with no one to talk to and nothing to do and you're ready to scream, and once in a while you really do scream but nobody comes 'cause they didn't hear you or they heard you and simply didn't give a shit—I idly pushed at the door once in a while and the last time I pushed it, it cracked open you know :: wait :: like its funny when something's lost you always find it in the last place you looked you know :: hold it, wait :: and *[Carmen Basilio]* when the car won't start it always starts the last time you try to start it you know :: hold it, wait, listen :: so it seemed only normal, and only right, in the greater cosmic scheme of things, that the cell door would open the last time I tried i   i t ii ttt   tried

                it   *tttrrrieeed* it

                                      ^pooliefloosh it out keep it clean bandage it well and
*you'll^*

      yup

                                              yip

yup

                yup yip   sssss sssss ssssss
*^pooliefloosh it out keep it clean bandage it well and you'll^* DO AS TOLD DO AS TOLD
WHY YOU INSIST GIMI ON NEVER DOING EXACTLY AS TOLD

      :: hold it stop, so—what did you do then : *hoops* <---> *hoops* <------>*hoops* <-----------> **hoops** ([{ **Uh, 'TENSION!** : *these here broke off your sergeant since* and because your **,** feels their need to intervene. As we've been known to *sit way above watching all the platters turn over above through and past one's* ten others (and most of it with a quite strained indifference), though something else not at all actually **God** but really quite something knowledgeable enough stated plain t' that what's just passed *to extract yourself from the game at this time press the Q-bird Icon un da zeensieseester river (hot bang SNAP and)* before you may seem nothing to you B-but eh, everything's a piece of a bigger puzzle which also is a piece of an even bigger puzzle wha' everything fits into God's great big puzzle book hey me and you and everything else too Ma Ma so shut down the bitch-moans they bore us *!NOISNET'* , *hU* }]) **spooh** <----------> *spooh* <-----> *spooh* <---> spooh |@|
and hey you don't look so bad here's another तुमने मुझे बोर किया, तुमने मुझे

बोर किया, सोचो मैंने तुम्हें अच्छे से बोर किया, तुम्हें मेरे जैसा होना चाहिए |@| <u>carry on</u>:   yes |@ | c a rrr y *on*

on   *o*   *o*

n   *nnnnn*   *n* (on)   : {anyway, *thanks for nothing for the interruption*} My God, but, yes, as I was saying. I got real warm as I went deeper and deeper in the strength of now knowing that at least some "God of the cosmos" cared about me anyway, made the cell door open, and then I thought that through a little deeper, a little but, and it came to me that it was more than just somewhat possibly true that this same "God of the cosmos" had been sitting watching me push at the door time after time all through the whole sixteen days, waiting to see the last push coming; and they knew, and it came, and right there that instant the "God of the cosmos" let the lock slip the bolt shoot off aside, causing my push to swing the door open. Y' know? :: uh yes but hold it there is one thing I— :: Okay and so then I went down a hall to a door with a red bar across w' said **EMERGENCY EXIT ONLY** in real loud red lettering, and, well, I wanted to go through, but I was afraid I might set off some alarm, but then, *Hey*, I said—*what the hell could they do to me*, like, *hey, put me in jail for another sixteen days or however many days the* "God of the cosmos" *would decide it'd take for my next call door to open the last time I pushed it,* and, then it all got all tangled up all complicated and I said *the hell with it*, put my head down and pushed through, but, you know, there was one little thing I did when I pushed the door bar, t'was I pushed it in a way that I didn't really believe it was really me pushing it k'now, k'now, k'now like I sort of stepped left and walked next to myself watching some kind of "other myself" pushing it, y'know—like if I saw it happening sort of that way, that if an alarm did go off and deputies came, I could honestly tell them it wasn't me pushed the bar, officer, it was someone else I didn't know whack whack someone else I never saw before and who disappeared to someplace I have no idea which of the *at a minimum* six possible available directions they'd just run away off to, I just happened to be here you know, you know, and like that—*got me so far?* :: I suppose maybe, but it's :: Yes, I know, it's sort of hard to believe but y'know it was really so simple even if I'd actually done it I could honestly tell the officers, Hey, sure, you know, like I told you I didn't do it, but even if I did, I didn't see it as wrong or unlawful in any way, since I never should have been arrested and locked up at all anyway, plus—just like in school the nuns taught me *that if you really don't know something's a sin when you do it then you're not committing a sin* if you do it you know officer something along those lines say you really can't legally arrest me again for anything at all, so, what the hell—buoyed by this, I pushed the bar, the door fel *WEEN!* l open, with nothing. Nothing! No alarm, no officers, nothing of a negative nature at all, the sky was blue, the sun was shining and so on and so forth and I came back up here and there you go. That's what happened.

So?

This:: t-this can't possibly be

Well:: it is t   Rennie across the brook by the dam valve nearby to a really big bullfrog

This:: can't possibly ever have happene e *ed* **2**

Well:: it did (((((end o- what the hell *Johnny* what if somebody said to you *Johnny* sit down here and write down everything you know, how long would it take you take you how long everything you know how long *that if you really don't know something's a sin when you do it then you're not committing a sin* would it take long it would take it for you great big *Johnny* eh Johnny eh eh Johnny eh eh eh no hold it eh eh hold it that's enough eh enough this is *crap* eh this is eh eh *crap* nobody'll ever appreciate this kind of *crap*   *oh* slash-down   who cares little poochie   who cares big poochie too this is *crap* but its *crap uh oh* slash-up *(8)* slash-down and oh yah 'bout the, trays I don't fucking remember if how or when they took away the trays but its not important anyway no but tell you what hunker-

down s''nce you can't believe nothing *bend over how 'bout*
I smack you with with this big board instead   *eh*
eh

          eh   eh
       Party!   crap how do you like
that what 's   with th
       Party!
       Party!   e   m,   I mean, everybody's whole day
is screwed and here w e   ar   e
       B' so eck ack cones-sizzle = *everything ends up*
applying someway to something somehow you know trying
to   he   lp pe   ople out a n d t-h-e-re   they
go
                        I mean those gym bags   sn
    blue

eakers and those   shi   t-faced grins and   *not even a*
thank you for us checking if they're okay
       spit
         and even after finding their power's out as well I
mean (we) mean, <u>really</u> losing power is a great big deal even
if its just one blue house or even part of one house {*it's*
unsettling to be someplace forced to be there doing
something else like it's the most important thing } well yes
but after all, isn't what you're doing at any particular
moment the most important thing in that particular moment?
And, isn't it also true that any possible thing big or small one
might be doing in any single particular moment is equally
(not more nor no less) important even if; its a moment spent
rubbing an itch at the corner of one's eye (which is a very
small thing in the greater scheme but in its moment its the
most important thing) or, if it's a moment-sized slice off
some   gargantuan   years-long   communal   effort   with
astronomical levels of effort and money making up the entire

thing. That momentary itch and that hammer-blow instant—both are the most important things at that single moment of time. *sookrahelde*   blast   please hand me a "banana" please   yeah I know there they went without a care in the world   damn them and how dare they how dare they damn   how dare

they   and that building 'cause two big mouth prettypeople want to play Jai alai—oh, yes, TWO people that's all, that tiny number of 2 people want to play Jai alai the whole damn town jumps up'n WHOOPS and hollers and HOLLERS and whoops and long story short just for these TWO they kick off a project the working of which makes the entire business district go from the initial very difficult to use due to the construction work on the gigantic and totally unnecessary Court Game Sports Complex (you got that right it indeed was quite complex even so quietly blue over-complex as to be IMPOSSIBLE to ever make work) to the impossible to use business district, and, we mean, and you and you would also be meaning if it were you and not I saying it {you know}

carmen basilio approacheth here/now to a serenade of a pretty-tune bearing morbidly over-gigantic bouquets bundles and in short way too many FLOWERS for any occasion at all but PUT SOME CLOTHES ON BEFORE APPEARING IN PUBLIC {please and thank you}   yah for just two people they have destroyed our town   which might even be accepted as the culmination of an important to everyone but hey-hell, we faileed what the hell it happens ahhhhhhhhhhhhhhhhhhhhhh if it had been attempted for the end benefit of the majority of the taxpayers of the town, but Noooooo, no; its for two simple losers   oh yah, oh yah, when taken to task that can always claim that work on the construction of the complex wherein lay their first Jai alai sports-court oooo yak

go on you can bray that unto the judge's face all you want that you never asked for it to be put up, it'd been put up already, huh ah yes yes yo yo (yawn yawn fizz fizz [pick hangnail pick hangnail (yah right in there *"Bucky"*, that

• 109 Game 4

was great can you tell us another) Bang-CHARLIE BANG
Charlie)   uh we're here because
we both need booster injections   its the law you know.
the law   SO THESE TWO ASK FOR SOMETHING
and who are they everybody jumps and well------

I mean out the ins your daily morning's wakeup peer
out o' an' see that the town's still standing great now I can
have my daily coffee quite calmy *very calmly* but hey—
during that time anybody see at any time from any vantage
point has anybody seen where those two go 9 to 5 I mean
what do they do? I mean do anything at all all day, and if so,
is the product of whatever they'd been brought on board to
do wellllllllllllll, what can I say. There's no sign of that. I
mean is there anything anywhere in the physical landscape
of the town anything the two Jai alai nutcrackers can claim
as a town improvement of some kind? Like Gregor that
whizzer—where'd the money come from paid for to put
together the community pool which we all love and enjoy?
Why, from *Gregor that whizzer is who*! Or Max Ganges
there—donated some wing off the hospital—and, eh,
{thanks loads, Max Ganges} if I may wax too small, me! Me
and mine two others (which = three) we overcame being just
three blank polesitters to ones lauded in that local news story
m'member? m'member? you got to m'member? for having
secured a high-level post in a theoretical experimental
mathematics department of a major {*bright lights*} Big City
university - |||[there see the difference they're nothing
compared to Gregor that whizzer, Old Ganges out there, or,
]|||| us. Or rather-sat *Me!*   Yes me.   y' big me
   and with this gran' degree under my belt I can
guarantee the town that-that {'s that-that like Jon-boy? }
who's Jon-boy?
      g   r?
m'member? y
      WHO'S JON-BOY?   okay we're here   no

around   w   peek

        l mathema   fling fly pop   *my God*
look what a travesty

        WHO'S JON-BOY? all the time? I mean,   fly pop
step, echo;   *God*   (r e a l l y)   blue   fly
pop step, echo; ball, bounce   *shameless these are totally*
recklessly shameless bounce, step, pop, and—sweat— and
they don't even try to hide it   the *balls* of them!

        God! *God* look at the damn (NW)   —
sweat—fling fly pop   the *balls* of them I mean really—the *balls*! b'no naggna
buck up pay attention get it **_all_** fling fly pop step, echo; fling
fly pop step, echo; ball, bounce, step, pop, and—*sweat*—
with the town in this shape they so shamelessly— *fling fly*
*pop; fling fly pop **no*** there are no words for it *step, echo* nail
them on something lock them up throw the key my oh my
s*tep, echo; fling fly pop step, echo; fling fly pop step,* so hard
my so hard to watch this over watch run right out 'nd ***nail***
'em *echo; ball, bounce, step, pop, and—sweat—fling fly pop*
step if we could you |*get this on camera and keep this on*
camera| know hey hey hey || Really? ***Them?*** || nobody's
here watching right now *ball, bounce, step, pop, and—*
sweat—nail the bastards down no but wait get the evidence
|we are going to need heavy set proof so kick yer damn
camera down all o'er them ***there see*** right the hell now *echo;*
echo; echo; fling fly pop step, echo; and| get the truth steer
the town over them |*keep it there keep it*| yah steer the down
bear down heavy with evidence and ***nail*** them down y' nail
them good crush their bones powdery ***nail*** them || Now that
you say it *yes **those two are pretty odd.*** || |*and keep it there*
and keep it| and crush them who would know ***WEEN!*** who
would care after the truth's got out the town 'ld be all
thanking us thanking us yes yes yes shit **THE GENERAL-**
MANAGER says this you say then **THE GENERAL-**
MANAGER says that you say so what, so what, they're in
the bed with them |*we three sat there/that log too many years*

letting this happen just my God oh my God simply| those three are of a kind all together they get dumped and/or sacked 'd be best for all y'know——|| I mean—***Jai alai?*** Who hereabouts cares to take up ***Jai alai?*** || *fling fly pop step, echo; fling fly pop step, echo play wildly circling 'round the long ago graves of the dead*—and the first to nail those two [look at them playing there all smiles & sweat (so much better than you {so much better than ***Us***} so Walta' hey Walta' nail the suckas (spit sidewise)) I mean all smiles & all sweat while Rome burns |watching and letting it happen *here's to 'ya wildly and wildly circling a circlin' 'roundy-bout the deep long wide way back past graves of the dead* that ***YOU*** caused yes that ***YOU*** did and ***YOU*** *here's to 'ya 'ya ess-so-****Sass*** that/this is why ***Rome*** burned yes| plus they're the cause || ***Jai alai?*** What's that? How do you say it again—***Jai alai?*** Is it a sport, a food, a disease, or—***what?*** But you say it's—it's ***what destroyed our town***? || oh don't let nobody tell you the cause they are _{not} ***or*** they are not the cause ^too many ways to say it but just ***one*** way do ***do*** it |for lack of attention oh yes yes gee whiz *wildly and wildly circling a circlin' 'roundnin' na bout-nin charged with gas blown up* Rome burned because someone was so simply just not paying attention| || ***Jai alai's*** what's destroyed our town? || we mean can-do sweep out the jail cells downtown there'll keepa' they be swifter than swifties but we'll ***nail*** them yes I *will* || How can something like--***Jai alai*** destroy a whole town? || |well say what kids know *we do know what's best fo' y'all* now kids somebody's *fling* paying attention real heavy attention and| *the world will end up seeing we are* yes we did we didn' sit on that long log all those years *fly flow pop* w/o feeling it ***come*** up in us yes the wisdom *the squeak of the sneakers* to know yes exactly yah 'xactly what needs to be done || ***Somebody*** had to be ***behind*** it! || ***So*** enjoy your silly Jai alai game *'n the glossed-up high court* will be over soon *so enjoy your last few moments son* children playtime is over || Who was ***behind*** it? || the adults are coming for you

• 112 Game 4

coming yes coming the adults are coming for you children ||
What? *Those two* were *behind* it? || *finish that smoke quickly
please now*|| *Those two?* || *it's time* so wise up cut down
your game || Are you sure you mean *those two?* || now
hands up *come along now it's time* turn around the pages
over t' next few chapters and a few next ones after that which
pages will exclude you both || *No.* || || *No.* || stop the game
now *it's time* put the toys down *it's time* come with us please
it's time and ||Come with us NOW, and nobody else needs
to get hurt.|| || *No.* || || *No.* || || *No.* || *it's time a stop has
been put on this the only way for this town is up you know,
up—but first you two—well—it's over for you two*|| My
God—*those two?* You're sure about—*those two?* || *you're
out of the way now here comes the new day God why is it
that one never knows how ugly it is until one steps away
and looks back dear God* || Well then—*we got to __make them
pay__!* || *why it that why is that too many maybes not enough
yes's and way too many nos you know come on its time its
time its* = *way back past-a-go* graves of the dead *here's to
'ya 'ya* ess-so-_Sass_ **ASK YOUR DOCTOR IF
EXPERIMENTAL MATHEMATICS IS RIGHT FOR
YOU** || *Is somebody going to make them pay?* || *see I did
yes we did and look where we 'nded 'p* **ASK YOUR
DOCTOR IF EXPERIMENTAL MATHEMATICS IS
RIGHT FOR YOU** *palla gesunda'* **DOCTOR IF
EXPERIMENTAL MATHEMATICS IS RIGHT** *palla
gesunda'* **EXPERIMENTAL MATHEMATICS** ||
*Somebody damn well better jump in there and make the
bastards pay!!* || *palla gesunda'* **ERIMENTAL
MATHEMAT** *palla gesunda'* **ENTAL MATH** *palla
gesunda'***AL M** *palla gesunda'* Isn' *'lla gesun'* 't this *'a ges'
'es'* game great, great fun? ||Come with us NOW, and
nobody else needs to get hurt.||

"Yes it's fun"　　　　　||Come with us NOW, and
nobody else needs to get hurt.||

okay   okay   okay   pull   that   switch   *NOW*
||Come with us NOW, and nobody else needs to get hurt.||
   Wonderful!

   BANG drop fall hit – go stay go stay go-go fling fly
pop   step, echo; fling   fly pop step,   echo;
fling fly   pop   step,
echo; fling   fly
pop   step,   echo;   ball,   bounce,   step,   pop,   and
sweat and blown out of the deep long wide circlin' down b
hiding deeper *bu* and deeper *nk arou* circlin' back *d the woodgrained*
bo down harder okstacks surroundi deeper ng them leaned in at
the two sitting at the library reading table in the university
library's *deeply-set* quiet. Silence was mandatory, an
unspoken rule in every library either of the two had ever
experienced, but—they maintained a casually fairly loud
conversation, this being allowed by the staff on duty for most
probably two reasons. The first being, that it was the dead
center of the semester break, and there may not have been
another single soul in the library within earshot; and, the
second being, their status as senior tenured faculty
professors carried some weight toward being able to
routinely bend and/or break most of the more trivial rules
across campus. They probably could get away with
conducting any kind of conversation up to and including an
all-out shouting match, and not be approached about it. Such
was their stature. But they spoke softly and evenly. As
though worn from hard work. The taller fingered the brown
leather clad binder zipped shut on the tabletop in time with
their words.

   Funny, you know, when it's time to leave a job, it
comes around to feel like you just started yesterday. Like
you've just been here an instant.

   Yeah, I—yeah. I don't know, I—I wonder why that is?

   Who knows why? The workings of the mind's not my
department.   *pork*

   Yes. Or mine either.

The one lightly tapped a fingernail to the table.

I don't think you ever said what got you started in mathematics. Or maybe you did, and I forgot. How did you?

I don't know. I—I think I've always been drawn to solving puzzles.

Puzzles?

Yeah. Puzzles—and for some reason the weirder and more complicated the puzzle, the better.

Oh. How is math a—well I suppose it does seem like a sort of puzzle. I don't know—how did you see it as a—a puzzle?

I may have not said that right. It's more like—you can solve puzzles using math. And the bigger and more complicated the puzzle, you can still solve it by math—even though the math to solve a big complicated puzzle needs to be big and complicated also—you still end up with the answer. You know? Like that.

Okay, but—do you come up with *the* answer? Or just—*an* answer?

Heh. Funny.

Funny? Why's that?

Every answer you get is both *the* answer and *an* answer—and as they said this, the taller felt most satisfyingly that at the instant they said this there must have been a brilliant twinkle in their eyes, sufficient to overwhelm onlookers, but—the other across the way merely smiled slightly and breathed, Heh. Very clever answer. Heh.

Why heh? Funny?

Funny, yes—*and* clever. But every answer you give to questions like that comes out that way.

Oh. Funny and clever?

Yes—and you know, that kind of answer seems to me to be very hard to not believe in.

Believe in?

Yes. To not believe its true. You know?

As the sentence cleared their lips, it pulled into sight behind it, a slight smile of the lips, and—the kind of smile it was drove an invisible wedge between them—manifesting in the other as a sense of wait, hold—*what did that mean*—what you said seemed so simple, but—yes there is definitely something much clearer and more basic that you want to say, but—you can't. You just can't, but—*no; let that go, shift* in the chair, that's just—just *nothing*, don't be silly, that means **nothing**, so—leaning forward a bit, they moved the binder a bit to the left, and spoke in an entirely different tone, which in and of itself said clearly, no matter, not important, *this* is what's important now, *which is*—Hey, wait, hey, listen—I clear forgot I got a meeting to get to *right now*—yes—*sorry*, we'll pick this up next time, don't dare leave without seeing me one more time because—well, just don't. Okay?

Oh sure. Okay.

Good! and in just a few fast moments, there they sat *alone.*

8 (9)   (4)   the finger down on the *empty and tired* and one of those moments they feel it filtering up from unknown {unknown usually being, unfelt and—unknown} what else is unknown but unknown I am tired and in the flip-o'er's what's known to all totally other than yes yes yes yes that fact's known to all totally buh how to be sure unless asked every single a large part o *WEEN!* f them wished to stay at the college forever *after all you're a big shot at the college* no no kind of big shot just *respected* is all buh respected is something most nobody achieves who can you name who's respected (say a name) okay there you go lets take that example up for some questions be you {burp} up for some questions sur' 'nuff go on shoot why do you say that person's respected 'cause that happens to be the general consensus no no no no never mind the general consensus you how about you do you respect that person of course why not...hold it! Why not? Why not? What kind of an answer is--"why not"? why not was not the whole answer were you not listening of course there you go see you were not listening yes I was now was I not see there there you go again what the hell is that supposed to mean? what the hell you think it means it means your probably stupid no I'm not of course you are there you go see see see what're you spoiling for some big sort of tangle maybe yes maybe no maybe yes more likely no there you go already changing your story how the hell what'd you mean change the story you changed maybe no to more likely no Hey there, pal—dozing in the library's sort of—not allowed, you know what I mean?

Long term *{golf}* colleague loomed over an instant as their large loose bulk swung that way, then rolled back this way, try*ing* an' *try to get awake try to get alert* oh hey hi there Pop, what's the story? I was hoping to see you before I shipped out *respect resp* "shipped out"? *Shipped out?* Strange way of putting it—*Shipped out.* And it can mean so many lots of things actually the number of lots of things it means is probably *endless* doesn't this sound so very formal an "infinite" number of lots of things but what's a "lots of things"? sounds wrong sounds defective what'd you bring infected defected and/or j.p. wring la-things in this store for plus there's nothing I can claim to respect about them they're now even bound in leather 'vrybody knows the bests 're bound in leather so what do you have to say in your defense huh they beheld the back of the colleague receding like *no no God God* how rude was I anyplace just how bad had that hypnogogical attack been *god* ought to see someone about that *god* but hi ho hey ho who the hell to see anyplace it is after all just a style factory mistake that its the sleeping pills *I use one third too many over the recommended dose* therefore = it's just a bit of brain fog or a lack of spatial awareness know up the no-no like every doctor *of your kind* "of your kind" what kind is that what the hell's that s'posed to mean *so we guess we better get out and up and somewhere walking around* then into the raised up face of the watch no-name watch no-name no no vanity in this watch hey look hey hey it is very important all see wh' watch we're wearing *no* not the precise keeping of the time of it *no no {there's four hours now before the flight (*yes there's time*)}* nor the look of it, actually—well, you know, I don't know about you, but as for me, I really can't tell one watch from another number *one* hey that's stupid *each brand's very different* = htsebvd they all have straps or bands of some kind but the damned thing cost thousands that ought to cut some slack in *quite neatly* don't you think no not actually because also number *two* htsebvd they all have faces of some definitely well-defined shape what does the shape of your watch face say about you dear consumer what does the shape say of you 'f you be round type you may be very, very common {which poor word, pity pity on common, it is a grey word neither sunny day stormy 'r hurricaneodde day tipsta-stupnammy flood it all down day word or pitch black at midnight word = common's not extreme but really really unfortunate's the fact you've a round faced common looking watch see, eh ah oh, oh yes, they said, looking back at the stranger from their watch—it's about two-forty five.

Thanks.

On no problem *face back in the book* but I'm sorry, there's one thing more {from the "stranger"} *face up from the book* Oh yeah, what's that look into the blank hung over the face of the stranger *who the hell is this anyway* which what-say-says, Oh, never mind, I—I'll ask at the desk over there. Don't want to be a bother [B-b-b, *why did my reaction need to be judged* I never said I will not answer the question why does this person assume what's inside me *unless*, of course, they're trying to read my mind but *indirectly* Oh no no no no problem what's the question?(?) see what kind of watch I wear don't say it don't matter I saw you peeking peeking I saw you I did *how the hell's one read the mind of another indirectly* like this to say to the subject the mind's being read from here is what is in your mind [1 2 3 a b c 4 5 6 d e f 7 8 9 g h i i h g 9 8 7 f e d 6 5 4 c b a 3 2 {repititioned up down n' down up o'er on' *oof!* times required to gain a reaction}] that being **why** are you assuming what's inside me **why** are you trying to read my mind **no no** I am not yes yes, **yes** you are *darn-tootin'* no I'm not are you saying that *1 2 3 a b c 4 5 6 d e f 7 8 9 g h i i h g 9 8 7 f e d 6 5 4 c b a 3 2* is not in your mind, Yes, *yes* that is not yes that is what I'm saying, and, *voila!* there you go that's how to read a mind okay back to the tax of it] oh no no no, no bother at all, *what's the question?* ^wait a minute *what* (we said wait a minute {so why what's so for?} that was not reading minds not even close) *oh yes it was* Before when I asked you the time you said it's "about" two forty-five, not about, but "about" oh you mean there's a difference yes of course there's a difference why did you lie about how to read a mind and then try to just quietly slip away huh huh that was a mind-read as it did reveal something you are not thinking about which is *1 2 3 a b c 4 5 6 d e f 7 8 9 g h i i h g 9 8 7 f e d 6 5 4 c b a 3 2* how do you know I'm not thinking of that 'cause you **told** me you *said* it oh oh oh *flustertentacioning alla-ovelly's broad dark curved skullback* I know but that was only a (only a *what?*) only, I *WEEN!* said, you know, something I said not what was really in my head then you're just another *stinking low-life liar* **What?** Me, a **liar**? That' low why you *sayin'* that I asked you "pointy blank" = **were you *thinking*** *1 2 3 a b c 4 5 6 d e f 7 8 9 g h i i h g 9 8 7 f e d 6 5 4 c b a 3 2* and you said *No!* So- are you now saying that you are *thinking that?*

No! Of course not!

Then—what are you *saying?*

That I'm not thinking that!

Then—*that is what you're thinking!*

HOW?

Do Not Yell at Me! the statement of what you were thinking when asked that is I am thinking of anything other than *1 2 3 a b c 4 5 6 d e f 7 8 9 g h i i h g 9 8 7 f e d 6 5 4 c b a 3 2* – and so, therefore I know what's going on in your mind, and to close this case entirely, class—*that does mean I've successfully read your mind!* so then now th' that barf's out of the way, how 'bout we tackle this other problem?

What other problem?

The difference between *it's* **about** *two forty-five*, and *it's* "**about**" two forty-five, and then, based on the difference, what does that say about the attitude of the person giving the time in each of those ways and then—why was the "about" time given instead of the ***exact*** time? This all needs to be analyzed, and <u>call they were ready a</u> the truth chiseled down hard, before there can be true mutual respect between us. Okay? So let's ı   *j'***mp** *in.*   {0} <u>L</u>et me start this off by saying—*p wait*   wha   t   *opw   we*   ll hello   *I got a*   send in   Profe   *yes*
the   **there's**   *fire here*

"ssor *swift ships*   hi there *doc*   ,*k476*

po   *tor?*   *Poe!"*

]   *beans*   *doctor!*

DOCTOR!

wpl   *1*   *2*   *3*   *kks*   *4*   *6*   *5*   *1*

Here you   b

are,   ow

\]l

%%%   *Doctor.* Your tickets an

for this afternoon. ___ **w** *w* w **w** *w* -*W*ant to look them over and confirm that the date and time of your flight are correct? Also to be sure there are no other types of problems with the arrangements I made for you?

Oh I am sure it's all fine.

Yes, but—can't hurt to be doubly sure. Check over the details. I insist.

Smilingly, the professor checked over the tickets, then slid them away in a pocket. The clerk said, How's it feel to be moving on to something new?

It—it feels good—say, how long have you worked in the office here?

Why?

Oh—I don't know, it—it just seems this whole campus has been the same way forever.

I know what you mean—I've worked here eleven years—oh, no—it'll be eleven years the end of the summer. How many years have you got in?

I do not want to think about it, chuckled the professor—but, since you asked, its been twenty two years.

Wow.

Way back in the stone age, eh. I remember when I started I was disturbed to be among all the *Neanderthals* (eye look of clerk—backed off the giggly-glint now saying Eh I do not get that but I liked how I felt before you said that maybe you're trying to show how bright you are what am I supposed to do now say even though I don't get it or am I supposed to say *Sorry, I don't get it* which would **stall** this whole non-conversation <small>what the hell is that supposed to mean</small> that means that's what the conversation is headed for that brick **wall** speeding at us which will only stop when you've been sent a **reply** but what oh what is the right **reply** uh uh uh no more time here's the wall say something blu-lurt-blurt out no oh not so much s a reply but a laugh and grin and an *eye-twinkle* which the professor can take to have any meaning desired, *and* push past it fast with *are bananas in season* **no not that** *are bananas even a seasonal item* **no no not that either let me help let me help see see what's said next must not be a question or even really a statement referring to the conversational partner but just a general statement of fact examples;** ocean liners are generally huge, all holes are not deep some are very, very shallow, a given number of beers will intoxicate some, but not others, the sun is very very far away, and every human with feet on the planet must periodically clip their nails—s*low down* nuff nuff you've now enough examples so the answer turned out to be yeah I know I actually thought they were *Cro-Magnons*, **myself** ah ah ah ho ho ho hee hee hee tee tee tee but the professor was already clear of the office when it also occurred to them that the neanderthal/cro-magnon joke was not the best possible joke for the mood of the moment SO understand, *class*, all jokes must be appropriate to the mood of the moment and if not as sprach the beasts inside the ole IBM manual-sets, *results may be unpredictable*, and the experimental mathematical doctor reached door realizing that in the morning they will be up and away and never back here again never see that office clerk again so God they wished they'd made a better joke they wished they'd actually said goodbye in the manner befitting *they are going to miss this place* why why they don't have to go but they must, *all's been arranged,* but, no no no no let go tired, too tired, go to bed on the last day *the last* but tomorrow's the first again **God** no sw   ellllll   w   e   jdt don't   real;lt   reallyt

get it cro   magnon   netah   anderthal
bruce-cap s e s ,l s e l s e ee l; slelepp sleeep
seeeeeeeeeeeeeeep   sleep sleep sleep sleep party party
party ! ! !   Piltdown   *blessed be!*

    Wonderful!

    Spit!

    *I will miss that person I don't even know why ahhhhhh they   pain   butanday-
dane's Winckle* the great big round fuselage machine
smoothly, all packed up with correctly ticketed-in Jeannies
& Johnnies, all assignedly seated n' in-strapped ready to ***dog
it*** out up 'ta one's end destinations, prepared to spend some
number of hours in this temporary transportation device with
sufficient life support for some thousands or tens even of
feet/meters/miles and—the school shot away into the past
behind n' below and {*why* are you quitting this tenured for
good "**capfeathered snoozer**" for some ahem ahem did you
say *planetary research* but not intraplanetary research or
extraplanetary or or or rrrrrr} and all such nonsense as the
great big smooth silent fuselage whisked them all up and
way, 'he mem-membered will you really throw down the
ease of each morning being exactly the same [had said what
in *not to repeat but it must be repeated that* most situations be termed the
"boss" or the "department head" or whatever who shit now I got
to go dig up another shit I think you have it made here, after all think
of how far you have come in your years here shit now I got to go
dig up another shit if you change your mind about leaving I am sure
[*ahem*] something nice could be {*ahem ahem*} arranged for
you to take that next step up the ladder {***get*** it ah ***get*** it up the
ladder +**wink wink**+ you know, +***nudge nudge***+ if you know
what I mean shit now I got to go dig up another shit yes that is what this is really
means who cares about m surely no this one, but (up at cruise
level in tha calm all placid places which much be got through
in the process of getting from some place to its next the what
they'd ge'en out 'ad been intrigeeging *you got it yup that's
what I mean that is damned **straight** sure as sh*t what I
mean* we suspect the planet (which one? ***This one!***) shit now I

got to go dig up another shit *hips'la tango!* we call home's *days are numbered* soon to be stripped of its garments and they did count all its bones (its? Their? (h)is? (h)ers? who's da blammo? ***WEEN! WEEN!*** who's da blammo la *WEEN* lala ***WEEN!*** anysense *hoinck* b-but, we have been in the air for quite some time now*hips'la tango!*, so—cobwebs being shook-shaken (either/or your choice Ganges) **we must be** pretty far out by now there look over, skim stranger's profile (who's reading a small book from their lap), and the half-window shade's halfway down (supposing said strange fellow traveler pulled it down to be rid of some glare {w *not to repeat but it must be repeated that* ithin which's eyeshot'd be harder to read that thin, tiny book *river Ganges*} the light in the window's so what and so bright I know where we're going's someplace far north*hips'la tango!* +they said they chose their research location {pillo} to obtain the necessary solitude required for this particular type of research {no no no won't do it do not presume to edit the words of another for clarity if the other is one o' the ring'd facets *bed turned down chocolates on the pillow* down und' yourself (and sometimes me and myself ha ha ha, *too*) *Hips'la tango!* Metaluna ^head of the gorgon^ ~~swagger~~ but how far north *ought to have asked* but; wished suddenly to have selected a window seat &how deep into that book is this neighbor *like a good neighbor....* {no TV up there no satellite short wave or pianola concertos way up there, *too*} I mean weren't we supposed to go there, *too*? Perhaps there is snow below we really have to see if thats true we did not book a window seat *Hips'la tango!* when we ought to *Hips'la tango! Hips'la tango!* we do know that too but—the book how hot is the read and what kind of a person's profile is this "as a boy little Johnson always claimed the window seat as a child little Johnson always Johnson always claimed always claimed the window claimed the window seat window seat as a child a child little child little Johnson always claimed the window seat *Hips'la tango!* the window seat *Hips'la tango!* yes yes yes the *it seems its time* window seat yes yes *for your next injection* yes yes the window *pull* *'em down and* seaaaaaaay may I please *roll over* thank you doctor *its time for your* you know *next injection* so, **roll over** and all at once, there's this face what face is this and what is this wide wooden carving of a wise doctor's face going to say going to say going to say to say going to say *you're going to feel a little pressure* why well, of course I'll switch seats with you, I know, I know, you're one of those always needs a window seat *Hips'la tango!* yes yes yes, that's to be expected. *As a child*, I used to require ***absolutely require*** a window seat *Hips'la tango!* but now well eh ah, I can take it or leave it {what b-b-b-b was I just told [on top of that I actually asked a total stranger busy reading a book to change seats oh, yah, oh yah I get it now they're saying as I child they wanted one too but now that (I am grown up so unlike *you!*) but I think that to do this we're all going to have to get up could you ask the person other side of you to please get up and let us out (*Me?* I have to ask the aisle seat occupant to get up and get out? *Why?* No no no, *you* ought to do that *you* said yes to switching with me thus **who** using the legalistic fiction of what the *ahem* **"reasonable man"** might d *not to repeat but it must be repeated that* ecide is right to do here I think you ought to ask no no no YOU you're the ones wants the window seat you started this is was YOU so YOU ask no no no no YOUr decision was the last to be made we should go on the theory that the LAST level of approval in ANY chain of approvals required up the chain is the approval level who's approving person needs to do an ask of this kind therefore YOU no no YOU yes yes YOU no no YOU yes yes YOU no no YOU yes yes YOU *flight attendant please to aisle twenty-three* no no YOU yes yes YOU no no YOU yes yes YOU no no *please to aisle* YOU yes yes YOU I can't do it I am getting the ***fucking drink*** *is there a disruption here* here *Hips'la tango!* ***service ready*** *no there's no disruption here* remember what we were told all meals on *twenty-three* TIME no no YOU yes yes YOU no no YOU yes yes YOU no no YOU yes yes YOU all meals on TIME no no YOU yes yes YOU all meals ||said senior flight attendant *Jan* what seems to be the problem here?|| on TIME *stewardess?*

problem *eh no no, no problem at all Hips'la tango!* I can see you're one of those always needs a window seat *Hips'la tango!* yes yes yes, that's to be expected; as a child I also **_absolutely required_** a window seat but not now, no more we have grown past that, thus what this proves *ahhhhhhhhhhhhhh* is that some of us want to remain *"children forever"* like that one positioned behind you such that *if there be* an imaginary line drawn from *here* direct to those three back there on that weedy-rotting log ‖‖*which was actually a utility Experimental Heemio pole-trilliac pole, c'est other wise known as a rotting heeliog of'f a trilliac'd down Experimental Mathematical quite long t'phone pole‖‖* **what?** *And,* thus enticed to whirl-round *about yes to see,* all'd been nicely down'd do ‖said senior flight attendant *Jan* what seems to be the problem here?‖ wn under in perfect unison with up over and head turn *swivel down* having put everyone in a great big frenzy just to the get this God-damned window seat, then you better well spend the rest of the flight face glued in tight to the glass of the so damne' *not to repeat but it must be repeated that* 'd important oh-so precious *great big* **window-seat!** *hoinck* b-but, we have been in the air for quite some time now, so—

B-*boom*! b- Party!

B-*boom*! b-b- Party!

B-*boom*! b-b-b-b- Party!

S-splat! —b-but the steady subliminal fuselagical vibration put 'vryone's whose anybody't concentration back on track since = due to = because *take your pick* the time hast passed th' doth heal all wounds so and it did yes no not become that the staring out the hard-won fuselage window into and down at the ground slowly drifting by there being *as so many'r wont to say* not a God-damned cloud down there under the sky below and the no doubt-suspected to be mud under that that is it we weren't **Blessed With this Beautiful Day With Not a Single Cloud Lying Atop the Sky** down below us asssss, *ferp* it's all meaningless/Susan as I am curious/yellow and/or the flung-down beach ball bounces

first that-a-way then th' this-a-way and on and on on first that-a-way then th' this-a-way then that-a-way then th' this-a-way and'a and'a and'a cannot look away *because* = a God damned big deal was made to get here so calm down and *live with it* cut-down and *deal with it* okay so what ***it's a show.***
||said senior flight attendant *Jan* what seems to be the problem here?||

A show push the face hard you *Party!*

Show the face hard you asked *Arty!*

How face hard you asked for it *Arty.*   *push harder   you asked for it*

                push   harder   push   push   harder   PUSH
harder PUSH **PUSH!**

                        okay here's what you asked for

get ready set

GOD!

GO! wow *rty rtt ry rtty what's that spell* bi flat radioteletype [*Really,* oh *really,* how bad can it <u>*be*</u>?] Ga *No thank spells   spells* bi rdioteletype *No thank* I do think I've got someone capable of this' *spells* decipherment *spells* bi radioteletye? *No thank* I think got capable this' *spells* decipherment there will be well-known **rap bands** attending bi raioteletype , as well.

Great! I got to make the best of it *No thank* think capable *spells* decipherment bi radioteletpe *No thank* think *spells* decipherment bi radoteletype *No thank* hink *spells* bideciphermen radioteleype *No thank* *spells* bihk decirmen raditeletype *No thank* *spells* bidecimen radioteltype   *No thank spells* bi Desimen radioeletype
                step   back
Okay   So, now I got myself inside this predicament of having to seem totally crazy obsessed with, preoccupied by, and addicted to gaining a *"window seat"* each and every time I fly *No thank spells* bi Desimen ra *not to repeat but it must be repeated* diote [*Really,* oh *really,* how bad can it <u>*be*</u>?] etype *No thank—*

As making the best of something's always the wisdom—how 'bout it? *Believe?* Come clean. *Who are ? Believe?* Taste *spells* bi radioeletype *r vengeance, so—*believe?

Since most everything encountered in life ends up temporary— *oooooooooooooooo, not to repeat but it might need to be repeated shut up/back up* stay up be up

OH!

Silly me, I nearly said "more or less" temporary when such as that's a lie *No thanks no dice toss 'em there'll be* **No Quarter! Make r move!** *spells* bi rad! |||||Turok, Son of Stone||||| **Taste r vengeance!** *spells* now in use danger danger danger *spells* are now in use ||||||

in-tuck'd red sphincters |||||| **DO NOT USE**

Every single something's either temporary or not so what? *so what? Taste r vengeance! Give No Quarter! spells* bi radioteleype **Desimen! Make r move!** tuck! co!   **Make r move!**

Much like the notion of being above = There's no "more or less above" **SO Make r move! Taste r vengeance! Give No Quarter!** ecom? a, no, thanks anyway **OK! Make r move! Taste r spells** bi radoteletype **venspells** bi radioteletpe **eance! Give No Quarter!** ||said senior flight attendant **Jan** what seems to be the problem here?||

There's either above or below. *Whack? Then—***Desimen!** *Desimen! Make r* bi raioteletype!

Push!   Give No Quarter!

Which, actually, is a lie also. *No? Move! Taste r vengeance!* **Desimen!**

Desimen?

Yes! **Desimen!**

W-Whoah!   *Desimen!*

There's either above or at the same level as *Desimen!* **Desimen! Make r move!** No thanks to Ms. *Desimen!* Plus, Ms, *Desimen! spells* **Desimen!** *spells* bi **Desimen!** not some **rdioteletype!** **You silly fool!**

Fool? Okay—though it does not really "feel right", *actually No thanks? No, no thanks. Sh-eeer cries of "imen! Desim-Simen! Desimen!"* began to *become very tiresome.*

No no *No spells* bi*flatthank;* **Desime** *spells **bi*** [It's just a little *skinny* of a thing how bad can spelling it wrong actually *be*?] **De-men! Desimen!** *No thank you, but; not to repeat but it* must be repeated; *No thank you spells more than just* **"Desi**me-es**imen"! but how much more you need not know as a matter of fact before we go any further** *please produce* three forms of government-issued unexpired identification *please, please 'n thank you ess then* it began to become very *"tirinto iotelety"* in their 'eads.   be   cause   ::said junior flight attendant **Jon** what seems to be the problem here?::   because   cause be = *boom*

Think; above or below's fast 'nd snappy *No thank* **mushi-***spells* bi E*sime-es***ime!**

Quite taut, and very crisp, **-m** [*Really*, oh *really*, if not so good how "bad can" the outcome *be*?] **oo** iotelet *Ga* become very *"tirinto"* face-flattened tight to th' *No thanks spells.* ||said senior flight attendant **Jan** what seems to be the problem here?||

And, oh so elegant bi mushi- -moo otelet Ga *No thank* **mushimoo** keep face *spells* biflattened tight to **konck. (.).**

Which in and of itself, is quite the fine word, la *la spells* bimushimoo-tele, buh, *No thank you* **SPLAT** tight to the windowglass (shatterproof plate grade glass only)

As is luggage = s'specially since the glass *spells* biwasn't glass musmoo ele *what's that spell?*

As is fuselage = *No thank* mu-oo el Ga *No thank* ^ u-o the ^^^

As is *spirit level* = spirit level sgpliarsist wlaesvne't glass some flexible plexi sort of see-through plate glass stock.

As is T-square or *spells* somethin-like uh off topped roman cross **stood straight up**! (!{????[G-g-g-g-{1 2 3 4 5 4 3 2 1 }g-g-g-g]????}!!!!!!!!!!!!!!!!!!!!!!!!!!! like that like that) *stood right straight up.*

WOW!

Doth thou *see*? no God doth you? Eck, Hans said {off the record} No *thank, in a way like,* like much lighter than glass.

Enter here if you want to believe, said the ***past-master,*** ***{what the hell is a "past-master"?}*** but thousands of times stronger **HUH?**

Do you want to believe? stronger eek ack ***swoo-oo-on!***

Yes I want to believe [*Really*, oh *really*, how bad can it *be*?]

Esperanto *yes* spells bi hank? No no no, spells "radioteletype"

YAK!

Quiver *NO* no no r-a-d-i- **output of the battle** *yea* ::said junior flight attendant *Jon* what seems to be the problem here?::

Sheath *yea* not to repeat, okay oke, CHECK!   o-t-e-l-e-t-y-p-e does not spell radio.

Deep is the word to remember, assemble, disassemble, and—then assemble ***again*** have to pull the face back, see the rest *first*, down there's the sk' Autotopskipy, eh? *NO!* NO not *no!* /big r-a-d-i-o sez big sharp knife not *included buzzzzzzzzzzzzzzzzzzzzzzzzzzzzzzzzzzzzzzzzzzzzzzzzzzzzz/*

Parts left over? -o-l-e-t-y-p-e spells radioletype (Huh?) *NO* *the rest of the world's a no, too* zzzzzzzzzzzzzzzzzzzz

Left over? *yea* How 'bout it? Come clean. *Who are you*
? t r-a-d-i-son y' know and y' know an'y' (0)

Parts left over means (0) 're screwed (?) *NO* not *no, no.*
zzzzzzzzzzzzzzzzzzzzzzzzz

If 're a manned moon rocket 're *screwed* (an' y' must yes
really know for if not then it's *spazzzz...*)

Or a fully packed luxury liner—also, *screwed* as b. *r-y-p-e*
too, + **anybody anyplace hereabouts had left** {Danger! Sharp Scissors!}   Come
clean. *Who are you ?*   ‖said junior flight attendant *Jan* I can't help you
until you *stop* and *say* the problem‖   *loose tooth*

Anything man-made, high in the sky, like this here, is
screwed, face flattened tight to the windowglass s'specially since the glass *not to*
repeat but it must be repeated wasn't meant to save lives *any lives. Come clean.*
Who are you ?

And there, and those, well—yes they are all screwed t
glass some flexible plexi or something much lighter than glass [It's just a little *skinny*
of a thing how much bad can it actually *be*?] but thousands of times stronger
{eek! ack!}

And this very fuselage ***estamos atirando em algum***
lugar, high, wide, and loud, fast and gone—yes it's
screwed! So—son, dear son, y'kno *not to repeat,* but: *it must be repeated* y' know
y' *have not* **been listening 'fter all's swanne d' all's of it tell**
us now tell Who the hell are   anyway eh Who are ? Who
are ? Who are ? <u>**Come clean!**</u> *Who are you ?*
—what what what what what—

GOD!

Turn away from the window, push back in the seat, and
dig for something mindless to read in the seatback pocket
slanting itself at you and—barely touching {*and maybe not*
even actually touching }whacks a hard voice from the left
saying, Well, God damn now. ::said junior flight attendant *Jon* what seems
to be the problem here?:: You—aren't you going to look out the
window after putting us all out this way [and hi-tone says we
only gave in to shut you up you were *so* obnoxious we'd had
enough of you so God-damn yes, *pillo,* we said okay fine have
a blast go on have the seat here's the seat and, I, I'm not
really telling this *{fart}* this hint hint wink wink nudge nudge, but, my
partner's legs are half crippled from, excessive youthful
ballroom dancing[well actually not "*ballroom*" dancing(s'
just the word "dancing" sounds too weak standing there *so*

very naked, and *so*, 'll, *nothing so ı'* it had to have some sort of two-syllable adjective preceding it, which one, ah well, I right off didn't know, so {before settling on *ballroom* dancing, we considered several other words such as, tap line break disco Spanish modern belly swing mambo folk quickstep ballet jazz contemporary hip-hop Irish swing and **ballroom** + *dat's stagga'* ‖said senior flight attendant *Jan* I can't help you until you *stop* and *say* the problem‖ *rungelette* + s' we snagged that key out flume 'ehind ∷said junior flight attendant *Jon* I can't help you until you *stop* and *say* the problem∷ the hotel front desk : and were <u>surprised</u> and <u>dismayed</u> by the ease of it at the same time, as that you'd think that when giving up such data slots right into a standard pack o' dancenames, like; tap line break disco Spanish modern belly swing mambo folk quickstep bal {fart} let jazz contemporary hip-hop Irish swing and **ballroom** ‖*ita sis-lacticized in the event ot the offended herebye never requiring a general election HAH HAH HAH HAH HAH* and that since that's so it could fall into the hands of modern-day identity thieves tip they to ave-hacktually asked for some form of government issued unexpired identification ‖said junior flight attendant *Jan* I can't help you until you *stop* and *say* the problem‖ (as they would have if I/we were "<u>running the place</u>" you can betcha') {groin} but tennie's plave'ee t'was_*gas* and so th' the nickname big-Ballroom was decided upon, ssssssssssssssss-ay it to yourself *Ballroom* then add it to to *Dancing* there you go *Ballroom Dancing* yas yah and hell **straight down the middle** who I didn't know from craw's dad 'fore this need to travel (yuup yup yup we do gots the right to **travel** right to **freely and safely travel** and so down-butt number five ah ha look look look how big c ‖said senior flight attendant *Jan* I can't help you until you *stop* and *say* the problem‖ hief we're off kilter eh sonny eh pal e'en tho ‖said senior flight attendant *Jan* I can't help you until you *stop* and *say* the problem‖ ugh you're too new to be officially sanitized hey there reach out open handed and whap the side of this terminal go on 'gain whap and whoop and whop ten gains and ten whhop whimps and woooosh's, there! Thank you the strain had got us but here you came to save the day which means that Mighty Mouse might be on ∷said junior flight attendant *Jon* I can't help you until you *stop* and *say* the problem:: the way ^{on the} _{sea or on the} ^{land he's got the} *situation* **well in ha-a-a-and!** Hey hey. Hi Dr. Flowers hi spaghetti broncos or but well stannieways, the excessive successive shocks to the system o'er the 50-60 well defined time periods they, themselves, and them consulted their time into the craft of ballroom dancing at the age of nine in the vast furnished downstairs of the **BON TON**'s Colonial Home and book depository /ripped free of all covers as // in that Len Woodlanian's **lost magazine trove-store**^{tm} down **Ziggurat City** void all stainglassery long ||said junior flight attendant *Jan* I can't help you until you *stop* and *say* the problem|| story short *which most do$^{(ue)}$ prefer* eh look look look look look class, there goes some **Baboons!** so 'he smashed up humm's salvers way way deep down, wick-twisted some tendons **and** at the meek age of a too-low number, pity pity pity *could no longer do dancing* mercy mercy mercy pity *Oh? What kind of dancing?* pity pity mercy mercy mercy *Oh ballroom style dancing and* pity mercy mercy mercy pity pity pity mercy *t'was **not only** the great great pain involved **but*** mercy pity pity pity mercy mercy mercy pity pity *the loss of an income* cry mercy mercy *whose income* mercy mercy ::said junior flight attendant *Jon* I can't ||said senior flight attendant *Jan* I can't help you until you *stop* and *say* the problem|| help you until you *stop* and *say* the problem:: pity pity pity mercy *Good God how thick are the majority of people* pity mercy mercy mercy pity pity pity mercy mercy **their** *income of course* mercy pity pity how could you have got that **all confused** (?) and lastly _{gesundheit} to cut to th' swee' t' 'it, <u>*I befriended this devil poor devil poor devil I befriended this devil this devil this poor*</u>. Hence, the *reason of this trip* _{which's fully on me,} ^{*of course*} was to provide my friend with a final fine vacation which I have timed out such that my friend will "pass" on the <u>*final*</u> day _ but we all do "pass" on a <u>*final*</u> day don't me what was to special and expensive to **set it up**_ I will not answer that as it is so so very arrogant of you to say such a snideness, b-b-b-b-bit, the point I an trying to make all over your face's that you put us out you got your window seat et al (***McKracken***) and then DO NOT HAVE THE COMMON DECENCY TO USE IT what the hell is the matter with you that you put us ::said junior flight attendant *Jon* I can't help you until you *stop* and *say* the problem:: out so thereby casting a pall over our very special very last vacation *How dare you!* ||said senior flight attendant *Jan* I can't help you until you *stop* and *say* the problem|| *and so forth* and so on and some may say why say nothing to this you absolutely did look out the window seat pressure of suddenly angry "teeth" down *yr* "*lip*" what the hell is harder bit harder the matter with you how can you harder reaches the right ||said junior flight attendant *Jan* I can't help you until you *stop* and *say* the problem|| fist just sit there like that will you say nothing fist clenches tight tighter rippling out to the other I mean you have just ruined no no no no its what the the start of our vacation hell is the matter with **you** ought to be shouted nothing to say for yourself, **good God** right in here right in good God you are really going to sit there all the way through this eleven-hour flight {hey no no its not an eleven-hour flight keep on *exaggerating* like that *pushing* just a bit too hard as you've got this ***inherent tendency to do***} no what is the matter with **you** is the ||said senior flight attendant *Jan* I can't help you until you *stop* and *say* the problem|| question here *lift teeth from lip before blood appears* uh, what did you say ||said senior flight attendant *Jan* I can't help you until you *stop* and *say* the problem|| ? It **speaks** look at it **speak** how entertaining it **speaks** I beg your pardon are you speaking to **me** in that tone? Yes I am! I was looking out the window after we switched! Where the hell are you getting I never looked out the window ok ok then what the hell'd you see out the window then no no no that doesn't **matter** oh yes it does what did you see it doesn't matter yes it does what did you see and again and on forward it rippled from front to back and all across the whole fuselage yes {this is very **disturbing** what are those passengers over there **screaming** about [no no no we are not screaming we are merely having a hot friendly conversation plus who asked you) nobody asked me but all in this cylinder ought to get their money back :or at least a bit-O chunk of it *just like candy* : what the hell + look at them over there ^louder and louder^ % ring for the attendant & in these cells they were locked for punishment @ something about a window seat O'@ I did too look out of it ||if so then what the hell'd you see|| and now here we enter a more "recently refurbished" wing of the hospital – done by mass plaster-boys assembled eating cake – round about the era ||said junior flight attendant *Jan* I can't help you until you *stop* and *say* the problem|| of the seventeenth century I did use it that is how damned old this state hospital is *kind sir* oh yah then what did you see? (one pound of those is the heaviest single pound-weight of a thing quite never been seen in this *century* } did too "And in this here area *mass showers* were taken" ventriquolee ventriquo*laaaa* oh, that? Oh yes. That's just two or three half-baked veterinary hospitals out that way (ha ha ha hee hee hee after a mere ten steps they'll praise God ||Please stop and say the problem *please*|| it's all the way downhill from there) gimme that magazine will you please :[[[*Country Squire*]]]: be not afraid to save me a piece – but it won't keep forever how the hell long ||said senior flight attendant *Jan* I can't help you until you *stop* and *say* the problem|| g might it be – not long :did too: okay but—no put it up there where the dog can't reach :did not: don't you ever feed that thing it's *skin and bones* mere *skin and* :did too: *bones b o n e s b o n e s* :did *NOT*: good morning passengers this is the captain speaking those of you on the right of the fuselage (as viewed from the rear of the cabin) :did not: are lucky today as you're (no that would be as viewed from the front not ||Please stop and say the problem *please*|| the rear) going to get a fine view of *Mount* :did too: *Skatello* in (hold we got to stop the captain first [yes yes but *how?*] full eruption :did not: +you figure it out, being as you're the biggest a-hole on this particular edition of a third-world workforce puddle jumper obsolete flyplane *today* :did too: yes *today* :did not: no its not yes it is its today all day every day and forever *it is not often mere humans see these great peaks in full eruptive fury* *as you souls have been gifted to behold this fine wonderful day* what the hell and who cares we are not on that side of the airplane anyway anyway it would have been possible to ask these idiots who they interpret *those of you on the right of the fuselage* to be but; *they hate you now* you got to face that don't you they do in fact *hate you now* and being this is a long enough flight it might be a *million* of some increment like *hours* but what does an *hour* contain at least a *million* of and you have *on the right of the fuselage* just screwed up this method of escaping their hatred <u>too</u> ::Oh? *Too? Really?* Really. What other method of escaping their hatred did I screw up, <u>too</u>? :: oh no no no please seal off that tone I meant nothing by that nothing by that :: No nothing? :: No no nothing :: Are you in the habit of just saying things you don't mean like its ha ha and no no this kind of place you can just lash out spasmodically and hurt the feelings of others? :: *this peak, being actually the oldest peak of the "**Stan Hansen**" Archipelago, had up 'til now been considered* :: I do not "lash out spasmodically"; but you are doing so right now by lashing out at me like this :: *perp?* :: an hour has a million millionths of an hour in it <u>*stupid*</u> so what other ***stupid*** question you got for me today <u>*stupid*</u> :: listen I meant nothing I meant nothing good God I simply desired the *window seat* and it has led to this:: *extinct having been so for centuries but **it's** sudden eruption has led volcanologists to* :: yah see here look how long God has gifted us to have no goal "but to torment you" :: but I did nothing and do not deserve this ***Gimi*** why you :: *revisit the yardsticks by which they determine a peaks* :: I must do something else out from under all this **ha ha** :: *dormancy vs. extinction the pursuit of which has led to many* :: have you no goal but to torment me ***Gimi*** :: oh **where** and **oh** well :: at this point it was noted the plummeting fuselage began finally and tortuously to break up completely :: *advancement in other areas of volcano science* ::   you will receive by parcel post some documentation we advise you to study before reporting here

:: as well as other areas of geological study which up until now have not seemed to be related to volcanology *Gimi* :: where is it it's *here in my bag* :: but why volcanology *Gimi* :: *all right now folks the "Stan Hansen" islands are receding off into the distance behind* :: shit no crap and ass where's that bag giddy-UP giddy-UP : what's **BLUE** wrong now *Gimi* what'd I do wrong now *Gimi* :: so what there's not nothing called "parcel post" no more *anyway* the stuff got here *anyway where the hell's it be uck uck hha ii* :: the first fragments to reach the sea were observed from a distance by Indonesian Fishermen who lucky for us had the presence of mind to :: why *Gimi* oh why :: just relax now we're just twain-ten-too hours from our final destination :: look her 're those *buzzard-birds* :: hey ma-ma *buzzard-birds* lets get a shot of that :: I could understand volcanology *Gimi* but ah ah geology as a whole why that also *too* :: shoot some footage of the incident which channel three thousandths has obtained just for you ha ha *hee hee* but be forewarned some may find the sounds and images in this clip *disturbing* :: excuse me :: **What!** :: I'm afraid my bag is under the aisle seats foot space will you get it? :: **NO NO NO** of course not *I will not get it* what what what so excited 'bout your precious *window seat* y' frogott t' get it *what's frogott eh ah* well I guess that's *your loss* :: [glare wince tight-lipped] "quasi angrily" *spat* I'm sorry but *I need it* give it over here— *please?* :: oh pussy big pussy hey get this off this fool heah' because 'e frogott his bag we're sp' to *put out again* for this ass yah yah *put out again* 'cause this a-hole frogott :: [spat-spit 'nuff spit spat-spit more than more than enough] Okay idiot I have *had it* :: had it? Eyy eww looky-head this greenball's the idiot – 'e's the one way *frogott it* :: chalk blackboard nail scrape *wince* ey what the 'ell's what dumbo what's up with *frogott it you stupid or something* :: **WHAT?** say **WHAT! OU KNOW** not the *meaning of one single word frogott it* oh yah I know words fine I reall know words fine eh eh what're you stupid use some babytalk word *frogott it* that's not a *word* that's **WORDS** what what what you can't see word one for the shadow of word two can't you count I can count dum-do *frogott it* not no words not nothing similar to you I see uh huh I see uh huh I see I see *Gimi* why you make fun this way *Gimi* :: out in the distance the last shards may be see falling idiot-stupido we can only hope and pray they suffered little of not at all God is wonderful *God is Great   and ana*   ord

                    mourn the loss   eh   a   n
d   mys tica   lly   ouogh   what're y   use
SOMe babytalk word *frogott it* that's not a *word*   **not the** *m*

what what you can'   the**se observations *made**

in the   ar   a   of the   hansen

geologi   *who passed that day*

            n hour has a million   :: *WHAT?*   say **WHA**
millio

            cal "plate"   led to the
unfor   tunate   ly for the souls
so we're ending this lecture with this short clip which goes a way toward transforming cosmological theory into documented fact   lights please there go here it is shut up *watch and listen   do you know how do you know how to work to work the machinery work the machinery answer us NOW do you know how to NOW how to work the machinery work the machinery work the machinery NOW work it NOW do it NOW Peter NOW Peter NOW*

            OK!

After mounting the closest available unoccupied high-horse, *Peter* plainly stated loud, Mickey-Mick Bar, McBarley, Sunroom, Stadium-Town, Crayolianne, Gas, and Twizzle (all sons termed esquire) within whatever particularly stylized parking garages they chose to use in those days (when such things actually existed) but yah yah please, **Old** Pop, we need someone well versed in exp*remin*tational mathematics (ideally with a minor in forthwithpical prosidy *jugular* gone wild with emotion as they fat-hand these facts and figures {ready set *go*}. The day of reckoning is fast approaching. We know this, well— here's how we know this. We know this since first, its a truth that's self-evident (with all companion beeves and beevies) strant-toodle that for heck's-sample, here I stand and there you stand (and in doing so we 'maticulously hassume we've been standing in all these kinds of heres and nows of Hic-spaces all the downs off our lives [as the poet says *O*, live your life as though it's just being in one place after a time (hollow out the hills you are going to need the spot you make, *Soncrafter*)] and for many this is hackstistupulously true as driven nails {rrr spacktangled tacks} [oh why oh why lords are we so far and forever out as though only copies of what—lost that one try again Willie sounds like it 'as about to be a good one (SOUND ALARMS grab a basket you've just got the +long-handled+ job of taking up a Sunday mass ten-o'clock strained down to a liquid kind of messy yet profitable general collection {grab MONEY grab MONEY need MONEY yes indeed yes indeed MONEY} *pop* but in many cases that is not true, they are just seeming to be face to face when—well let us just say if one or the other stepped up to touch the other that touching hand [pink whizzie!!!] would enter and pass through that to be reached into and passed on through pink belly of the other's kind to cut to the rat's tail of all this w' noodlin', what we see as one home planets really several many segma-planets linked together by an elaborate and rickety illusionary system of catwalks slim scaffolding mind/memory machine tools, error traps, run-off diverters and pap-*scagglia* la la pap-*scagglia*, *hooonley*, with the necessary vision generators belief drowners hoit-toit **Spangle!** Co-lock't **Spangle!** of a **Spangle!** and scads of other barely profitable jury-rigged illusion systems designed by the fathers for one purpose only to give the ***illusion*** to the ***Earthlings*** that they've safely at birth been onboarded to one safe sane stable and really really real ***Planet Earth*** but—

heavens to Betsy, it's all to too-soon a' crumble *We Know It* so this it why we need you *Gunnar* though *Gunnar*'s not your name wouldn't it come in handy once in a while as as— let me introduce you to our new "lowrider "*Gunnar*; or Here's whose been brought in to troubleshoot the legal department's problems their name's *–be praised*—Hans-Gretnel conk'd *Gunnar*; and so forth down the Dailt Whistle, SunBeam nightly new edition, size large info-machine, gas-guzzlin' long sticky pull-zipper with accompanying fresh painted blue toolbox into which all future flammables or quite nearly stowed after all this is doing the thing properly and according to *code* here-round down's bouncies all got to follow some *code* huh "some code" no *the code* uh, wait, hold it, and *Pop!* that there's a silly no it's *code* no no it's *The Code* no no it's *code* no no no it's *The Code* no no no it's *code* no no no no it's *The Code* my my my ain't they *swankie* no no no no it's *code* no no no no no it's *The Code* ask Gunnar they'll know ^magic be the machinery today^ no no no no no *code* no no no no no no *The Code* no no no no no no 'ode no no no no no no no *Code* no no no no no no 'o'e no no no no no no no *Co'e* no no no no no no no '*'e no no no no no no no no *Co''* no no no no no no no no''*e* no no no no no no no no no no '*o''* no no no no no no no no no no ''' no no all no no no new work no no no '''' no no no no work must be no no '' no no must be done according to no no '' no no no code no permits must be 'no no obtained as per no no no procedures '' no no all permits must be prominently displayed no no no no in

such a 'no   no no no manner that they are clearly visible s no no no no   no no and entirely legible to any no no no inspector no no no no *coming* by to check on the work no no to ensure it is proceeding no no according to all currently approved and documented *codes* no no no no *Gunnar* no no *Gunnar* didn't you listen can't you listen why can't you do as told do all work according to *Code? for this reason methinks you're as of now terminated off this position Gunnar please leave the property now take your dogs with you your pet dogs all pet dogs here and now PRESENTLY* hokay nokay HUP condo', HUP so: here stands the necessary to know great big history: all started at *Earth* conceived without sin a*nd as can be seen the leap-space was not 'cause it wasn't so-so* then th' next swung down off creation n' stopped short of a full *home-slam* up aqainst Earth this to be call-cued up as the   *Rstyj*   and as might be seen *the leap-space first appeared and the regimes at that time felt the people'd go MAD 'f they knew such huges could be coming so* they slender-lashed hypnosis-saturated lincolntown loggery style catwalks climb ladders lashed up faux realities and pulled down the exact same number of blindfolds as th' momentalized-nation gross fact-figure of people 'board both {in absolute totality HICCUP } so t' hey hey *What* what'dya mean *new-w* planets hey yah really well who cares that's so four o' clock's Friday by this time, *Y' know*? Batwennyway, *exile* all labored on, interconnected by the belief they all were atop the same place—too much to know for the simple people, *y' know*? Inhabiting hot-cored rocky spheres spinning 'cross space that that *y' know*? As God themself hand-formed hot from the wash machine muddy globulars meant to harden into said rocky spheres, *y' know*? Who the hell's to believe that, *y' know*? So the creator felt it more easy to manage the day-to-day of their creatures, *y' know*? *"Hap" Arnold* so it went until then came the   *Tdyuk* which took the engineers by some level of surprise, but— being hardened by having the experience of managing the *Earth-Rstyj* connection under their belts, they quickly lashed out simple extensions of the hardware and cabletry used to span that crisis and managed, before the simple inhabitants of *Earth-Rstyj* even rose the next morning, to have all squared off, cleaned, dry, sweet smelling, and 'gain one single still solid virtual planet in place *just like it never happened*. So. So. *But*—the increased width of void to be be bridged this time was way more than they were comfortable handling, using the same engineering practices and tools as when bridging the first gap, **but,** what could they do? There was nothing to be done Rome was not built in a day and the need to deal with the actual Romans was even further off than that Cuban missiles *Jack,* go deal with that *Jack* we got one too many rectalines to deal with hiss moment to give a flyin' crap o'er *that* which was especially true since nothing ends without some sort of funeral and most live their lives inside thick shells of impairment which no healer of any stripe could ever penetrate, **anyway.** *cliff-dwellers, primarily, ah, hey—you up there you; you got a question for me? Yes you! Yah you! Okay since you don't, please shut up and sit down just because you do not want to learn don't keep the whole class from learning anything today,* y' know? Oh yes we do—so there/then/anyway and, *they call the wind* **Mariah**. *hey pau-u-u-ul, Paul Bunyan! (Paul Bunyan!)* ---swowa hennyhooch---**big gizzards---n n n n n without belaboring the labor over and under all yer available attention spans yes it did so happen, eck ahhh**—Party!

Party!
Party!
Party!
Party!
Wonder spit! *ful!*

Take me Jesus = *so here goes how it went since—the plane is due to impact down very soon*—so take deep breaths *here we go* (**0**) platters that was just the beginning of the start of it, where we were's when there were just *Earth* and *Rstyj* *{the brain-bound connection's sass deep down d' Phillipines [yesso!]}* more came in breezy succession as........*Tdyuk*........then................

Yfuil................then....................*Ugioz*....................then........

.................*Ihopx*.........................and—here's where the inhabitants would begin to sense the reality surrounding them was somehow slipping as in as as in in *asin* and *asin*, DOS 360 Peach-Breeze and Patty VonSickle would have the following breakfast time conversation {it being Saturday morning with the usual stretch-out relaxing common conversational space available for open-ended expansion] **RO!** tilt tilt tilt tilt tilt eat egg eat egg eat egg eat eat eat egg egg egg 'nd hey I've been noticing something for quite some time *now*, and up until *now* have thought nothing of it, but there was an article in Sniffout Magazine last Sunday made me think. Y'know? egg egg egg eat egg eat egg eat and an eat and a eat eat eat egg no.

Explain it better. I sense you have left out a lot.

What do you mean?

You said you've been noticing something for a while and found an article about it in—what magazine?

Sniffout. Last Sunday.

Yah. Sniffout. And they you said y'know, like I, well, okay. You read something in a magazine. What's to know about that? egg egg egg egg eat egg eat egg way out <u>hen city</u> {NOTE: note that Peach-Breeze did not include in the information [as noted in page three copy ten of the information] we find the defendant—*not guilty* what exactly they had had on their mind—_{suss}—but what the thing was and why they didn't say it will be filled in for you later—let them continue}

What? I don't think you were listening to me at all. I said it! So—what do you think of it?

You said it? Said *what*?

What I been thinking about that I found finally confirmed in that *article in Sniffout magazine!* **BUY ESSO GAS**

That? Oh, I told you my opinion of that a while back.

_{stun} eat egg eat sausage sausage eat egg eat ea' <u>Opinion</u>? Hey—listen. Don't mess with my head its been a eat egg eat egg good morning so far let's not spoil eat egg potato potato egg egg sausage potato potato potato it, okay?

Spoil it? You asked me my opinion and I gave it. How's that eat egg spoiling eat sausage the day quaff coffee need more but too lazy too lazy too lazy hold it hold it *where's the dog?*

Okay. Enough. Now don't get mad. Humor me, okay? Promise you won't get mad?

No I don't think so. Never owned one of those. I think those people moved out that house down back that *really deep garage* with the radio shack drank "Ganges water" one time back and I swear to God I swear eat egg they damned near eat sausage eat egg finally and permanently passed—

Then; over the table went Peach-Breeze out-clutching for the *narrow* neck what Von-Patty Vanh'sSchnickle put on that morning to eat eggs and sausage in not to be attacked down by Peach-Breeze all either wanted was to calmly and cooly eat egg eat sausage eat eat eat egg sausage potato *egg n' sausage* **BUT** it ended with roughly ten uniforms three sergeants and veritable *scads* of heavy detectives milling round 'ar rebout the new-spawned quite complex crime scene and guess what you know why this all happened eh ha *you do* no I don't.

YES you do—the new planets. It's just one typical of the confusion caused by the need to span o'er such wide-spaced out new planets that they are not all being able to stay connected together all the time *Don't you Get It?*

No. *Sorry.*

Okay then. *Get out.* Hey Pap! *Next Airplane Please* but open my mouth and comes out *this shit* please prepare my spaghetti dinner immediately!! *fist* just sit there like *(What?)* that bursting through *to the next level of the warehouse* ||said senior flight attendant *Jan* what seems to be the problem here?|| *(What? What the hell's this now?)* eat egg sausage what's the matter why'd you bring those bullwhips *(What?)* here potatoes eat egg sausage potatoes eat egg sausage potatoes *(What?)* eat eat eat egg sausage pot {wash}[catfish!} atoetat e *(What?)* gg saat ps eg spaghetti dinner Earth, g e {who?} *(What? What the hell's this now?)* y eat egg sage potatoes eat [w we hung your bullwhip e ca Who are *you? n't hear you*] egg sausa *immediately!* stand by here until summoned *(What?)* if you do **NOT** your punishment will be both swift and severe so then there was that other time when another Peach-Breeze just like the first one {yas if you see them in person you'll know that they're different but here you can't see them so their difference's told you} *prosembulage* ge potat& ***Adam-5*** oat egg sausage p *Number 15²* egg salmighty} *e* pes eat *e* {Carmen Basilio} *a* [catfish!} t eat egoage pot egg eg *please prepare my spaghetti dinner immediately!* g s {pillo} ausa [*we can't heau*] gage potatoes[*G* in the crisis caused by the great big bang *od Willing!*] sage potatoes *lab* {"what life looks like inside to the math", *professor*?}]] *e* Nye-way this second Peach-Breeze said to yet a third {same thing 'bout this 'un's inside the curly brackets *up there before*} its funny but why/how can it be, my daily commute used to be 'bout twelve minutes *but now its twelve hours l no. 45* egg e {*Jesus* [pleas we resent having helped them and not getting even *a* thank you *e* speak up] *Christ* almighty} gg sausage at eggpotage eat potatoes *oh boy* egg eat egg *my spaghetti dinner* eat sa {*who?*} u *N*::said junior flight attendant *Jon* I can't help you until you *stop* and *say* the problem:: *umber 15¹* sa consists of metal st*ran*ds tightly why the hell'd they go and change it why the hell these things all got to change (no REASON of course t gush here's never no good reason) wound together wrapped in "goat" skin ge eat potatoes *oh boy* (*What?*) egg *Number 15¹* eat egg eat sausage eat *p* {Carmen Basilio} ot {pillo} atoes *oh boy* eat egg *prepar* spg *g* [*we can't hear you*] e s ea *please prepare my spaghetti dinner immediately!* t egg sae eat potatoes for it seems like just the hell of it |'nd then comes Peach-Breeze number three saying *really*, really *loud* that all's a buzz = le all stumble around with no choic where we hung your *e* but to contin *Who are you?* ously so [please *prosembulage* speak up] lv (two   no mention of *anything experienced* except   -   behave in th *where'd we hang your* bullwhip? We hung it over there *e* way you'd expect them to, given their past   *e* and then next what's the matter why'd you bring those *bull*whips here with you one *prosem Nu bulage* and next one and next and next *o* = *h boy* egg eage will you say nothing **fist** well mine changed also went from what felt like days to minutes and I wondered-down about all this *theirselves* clenches tight potatoes egg egg sausage potatoes {wash} egg eat {wash gg eat sausage eat pot [*God Willing!*] atoes *oh boy* egg eo where we hung your bullwhip over there There tat Earth, o{*Je*::said *sus Christ* almighty} esind/memory machine tools, error trap (*What?*) I took Wally to the park y'know, (*What?*) being that the park's just 'cross the street out the front door and Wally and me we went across and down the lawn (*What?*) and-and s, run-off diverters *oh boy* egg eat egg eat sa *Number 15* pace that that y' know? As God them² usage eat [pleas [catfish!} Rstyj, Tdyuk, Yfuil, *e* speak up *my spaghetti dinner*] yes it did just take seconds we walked down the slope of the grass toward the brook and potatoes *oh boy* *Who are you?* (Want a fast answer? Ask big *Gerald*!) eat your bullwhip

over there egg & *Adam-5* sausage potatoes eat egg sausage potatoes eat egg sausage *d*
Willin please prepare "my" *spaghetti dinner immediately!* *g* { *oh boy who?*} potatoes
oh boy eat eat eat egg snausage potg sausage potatoes egg [*God Willing!*] egg sauatoess =
Numb [p [*we can't hear you*] lease spe*spagh*ak up] er *15¹* {*Jesus Chris* [*God Willing!*] *t*
almighty} age *the winner of each point stay* and Wally just stopped me
turned around and looked amazed confused and concerned
all at once and *s on the court to meet the next team in rotation* potatoes egg eat *e*
{wash} gg eat *oh* ||||the ball is *now in play*|||| *boy* sausage & *Adam-5* eat po Ugioz, & Ihopx.
tatoes *oh boy* egg *e* hell is the matter with *you* at egg eat sau we hung your bullwhip *s label*
no. 45 age ge potato *(What?)* {*Jesus C& Adam-5 hrist* almighty} es ea Rstyj, **Tdy**uk,
Yfuil, *t* egg hell is the matter with *you* s Ug ti *please prep* and I turned around
and there it was the very damned sight changed my life *what*
life well my life of course what the hell else *are my spaghetti dinner*
immediately! ghter rip *my spaghetti dinner* pling out to the [please *prosembulage* speak
up] other I mean *oh boy* you have just ruined ioz, & Ihopx. big warehouse job looking fo
prosembulage r stuff "tight d" [please ***prosembulage*** speak up] eadines everything's
(What?) even in a differen ausage potatoes eat eat eat [*we can't hear you*] egg sausage
pota {*who* and he really wants to get the *((What?)* all in different languages *and*
formats *and* "et cetera"{**Carmen Basilio**}) re doesn't want to   will   won't eternal
all's eternal there's no end but *the* end   once that's destroyed, then
everything's **gone** *?*} toes egg egg saeat potatoes undertaking a study 'bout some
interplar *yo*netary "shit" there was no street *no house* just what—no
it couldn't damned **be** – felt strangely drawn – but with no idea why *oh boy* egg
eat egg *e oh boy* at sausage eat pot {Carmen Basili here a cafe materializes an *oh boy* d the
polesitter who got the top academic job "in *one fluid motion*" turned out it'd
turned over to a ten-mile *hike* *oh boy*'s chatting with a campus colleague
just nearly never got home scared to death *nearly died* *y oh*
boy ears later reminiscing a bit **meequatreenio** quiet *o*} ato [catfish!} es *oh boy* eat
{wash} egg saour bullwhip ovus everyone's got their death date across their forehead
{**Carmen Basilio**} *but they cant tell anybody they see it* or what it means and no one can
see their own not even in a mirror *age* potatoes [catfish!} oss their forehead but they cant
tell anybody and there is really no need to continue on in this
deep detailed manner they *please prepare my spaghetti dinner immediately!*
{**Carmen Basilio**} se I don't want *e* = *verything* in my life to be a clue to some puzzle I'll
never be allowed to *yikes!* oh boy oh boy you want to see what they're seeing *oh*
boy but you so here goes – v-v-v-v-BANG Voice 1: Hold it stop no come back don't bolt
out let's just say this p-planetary *ruck* disrupted so many over
town {God what enthusiasm we have "picked the *right ones*" {heeeere's *JOHNNY!*} =
now let's not go blasting off on your limbs the way you did way back in the first time no
no no *NO!* can't   want to   won't   have to   must   will   *oh boy*
can   *oh boy*   do (Lawrence, Lawrence! *You are such a card!*) know the answer to e
it eat egg s *N Number 15¹* umber *15¹* ausage each similarly stating just

nearly never got home scared to death *nearly died* **oh boy**
potatoes eat egg saus *Number 15²* age potatoes e *{who?}* at eat eat egg saus ||said senior
flight attendant *Ja**n*** what seems to be the problem here?|| ag Rstyj, Tdyuk, Yfuil, *e* p*are
my spaghetti*otato *{Jes {***Carmen Basilio*** *} us Christ* almighty*}* es egpotatoes & *A* ::said
junior flight atten the ***swirl*** inside the *"seemingly calm"* **shell** dant *Jon* I can't help hell is
the matter with ***you*** yo your bullwhip over there u until you ***stop*** *oh boy* oh boy and ***say***
the something terrible seemed to be happening problem:: *dam-5* egg
eusa *{pillo}* ge pe potatoat & *A* **prosembulage dam-5** & *at this juncture—all seems
apparently bonkers so many* saying just nearly never got home
scared to death *nearly died* egg eat sausage eat *t* sausag (held in place temp
we hung your bullwhip orarily by tightly specialized *"damage-strapping"*) *e* ea *Number
15² t* potatoes *oh boy* oh boy egg eat egg eat sausage [*God Willing!*] pootatooes there's
no God-damn reason for you to act *so tense oh boy* egg Earth, eat these sorts of extra-large
po *Who are you?* **Top-mayor**, after catching their breath after
catching their breath completely werful machines must *hey that looks like
Mauve Spititsultanian* be leveled usag *{**Jesus Christ** a-do* **Jai alai's played daily o'er
the grave of the dead rotted down** wn properly [*God Willing!*] [*God Willing!*] to a t
so-so many saying just nearly never got home scared to death
nearly died oleranc no no no no its what th loo*{exist}* ked down/*looked
over* at nearly *2000* white grave stone sockets *e* the start of our
vacation *e* of less than .00006 *mm* mmm mmmm (camera sound)   gasps
and spurts   of disgust and amazement   **great big clipper shippe**   where
nearly *2000* white grave stones previously stood*{exist}* and
mm egg eat sausag [*we can't hear you*] [please spe Rstyj, *please prepare my spaghetti
dinner immediately!* Tdyuk, Y **label no. 45** fuil, *} {pillo} e* ak up] *e* eat potatoes *oh bo* egg
egg sausage standing behind that same numbers o' unmanned
mini-graves w. heachie-lump's o' a***hh hunk-o-steel*** at *dinner
immediately!* oes egg atoes [catfish!*}* austatoes *{who?}* egg eat egg eat sausa losers go to
the end of the line to ***good-n-plenty*** await another turn on the court *why?* ge eat
potat hell is the matter with ***you*** oes [*God Willing!*] otato *oh boy* egg eat egg eat sausage
eat p *Num* Ugioz, & Ihopx *Number 15² ber 1* Earth, *5²* ota hell is the matter with ***you*** toes
o{Je --- prosperous to before the big bang wn scene & sounds *{exist}* ***bit-o-honey*** -
-- *sus Christ* alm *Who are you?* ighty *Nu* [list of things that have dates asso pulled
from the empty of the *nearly 2000* apparently empty ***slots-
n-the-DirtHole*** life in prison without possibility of parole ciated plea *my spaghetti
dinner* se speak up] *mber 15¹ } h* bausa [*Go!*] *t* egg eat sau junior flight at your bullwhip
over there tendant *Jon* I can't help you until you ***stop*** an hell hearing a say-out of
there's nobody here how in hell's ***this a cemetery*** when
there's ***no bodies*** here *spaghetti dinner* is the matter with *yo* we hung your
bullwhip *u* d ***say*** *please prepare my spaghetti dinner immediately!* the problem:: sage eat
potat *{wash}* o = ***prosembulage*** es **label no. 45** *oh boy* {Carmen Basilio} *mber 1& **Adam
Who are you?*** -5 *5¹* eat *{pillo* + the end game's to know wh whip over there at the *"**others**

are thinking" + *}* e how in hell's ***this a cemetery*** when there's ***no bodies*** gg [catfish!} atoes eat egg sausage potatoeusage potatoes eat *uve Spiti* eat eat egg *why?* sausag *because fruit cups don't boil over* e potatoes egg egg saus hell is the matter with *you* at these "2" are up to something = *we gotta find out w* (also hand crafted) *hat* egg eat sausage eat potatoes *oh boy* if you're going to tell me you ought to *do it now before I brain you* <u>Who</u> are <u>you</u>? <u>Who</u> are <u>you</u>? <u>Who</u> are <u>you</u>? <u>Who</u> are <u>you</u>? [not really said ***out*** but thought *in* really loudly] *please prepare my spag* everything's being moved crazily around t *why?* o all different places *who's the joker* *do it now before I brain you* *hetti dinner immediately! please prepare my spaghetti dinner immediately! please prepare my spaghetti dinner immediately! immediately! immediately! immediately!* Tucumcari Close my mouth and comes out this big, (**0**) ***do it now before I brain you*** this is sort of the manner and type of deep throated analysis *needed to solve this problem!*

Kevin Seltzer? *Who the hell is <u>Kevin Seltzer</u>?*

Just nearly never got home scared to death *<u>nearly died</u>* Party!

Party!

Party!

C'est crank c'est est'c *Crank* the ea{exist} rsplitting bang of surprise at finding where there's s'posed to be many ***finding nothing at all*** n' so Top-mayor had to turn from the memorial lawncutter n' overall yardmaster, find a quiet corner, sit down facing into it, and think through what started out being needing a *spend some time thinking of nothing at all* deep spend-of-some-time, bu *t* = the corner.

The corner.

The crease of the corner.

The crease up the corner makes the corner 'til reaching the top of the corner's the ***end***.

The ***end***. The end up past which the corner is not and nowhere like somewhere a ***dunce*** like Top-mayor's able to {exist} exist. But one can only be a ***dunce*** if a pointed cap and corner are available—plus a chair. And the chair the ***dunce*** sits in must be a very very uncomfortable chair [Isn't that right, ***Gimi***?] and the corner the dunce is sat down looking into must be a very uninteresting corner [that's right ***Gimi*** we are experts in corners you know, ***Gimi***.] with nothing to lessen the pain of the ***dunce***. *(yes that's right)* Long kareesey 'nd *shortnap* all this together forces the **dunce** in the pressure from all sides on the deeply descending **dunce** ₛwₐg *to spend some time thinking of nothing at all* deep spend-of-some-time, bu t = the corner and it came down in under and through to you, too **nudge nudge wink wink** ᵇˡᵃⁿᵈ better to sit right there and do nothing since what whoa &Kevin Seltzer& whack whack ,,, ... ;;;;;;; wait hold look see there see there [point one if you got one] Kevin Seltzer look there there's what is that lean in a bit squint a little if necessary since the light's inadequate Top-mayor did find = that there's no such thing as = uninteresting corner what what how do you know ho ho ho big shot, how do you know you've seen every current corner yes prize yes prize no but it's got to be true that if looked at long enough everything in creation's got its merits its points in its favor/cute little quirks bright side moody days big hair big hair big hair big hair big hair *hipsla-tango* see there Top reach touch and feel this slight irregularity deep in the corner crease see see and the light, where's the bulb, oh its shining Christopher Columbus and the smoke [smoke? There's—there's no smoke here what's your problem eh dead man no smoke here 'nd no smoke there either eh eh dead man what's your problem what's your problem want a problem eh I'll throw 'ya a problem a problem or two please oh oh a problem or thirty] *you can't swim your way out 'f this hole Bruno* Top-mayor tensed taking all this in forming it kneading fingering the idea spun on a potter's wheel it'd need to be if only the exactly perfect wheel were actually present in good working order smooth-laying a hum down the room which room this God-damned room which I swear to God **BLUE** [yes swear to God] 'll be the last room within which we sit **dunced** *all the way down* look deeper uh oh yah up the corner's crease Top'd go [as up we go or you go 'know] the purpose of **duncing** is coming slide up inch by inch might there be more such interesting things tucked in the close crease of this uninteresting **dunce's** corner there what's **hammer** what a **hammer** what is all this damned noise this is

• 147 Game 4

a *dunce's* corner, there must be silence in a *dunce's* corner but what's all this noise? And who are all these people this is a *dunce's* corner there's "can't be these people nor this person" [there's not s'pose to be other persons in the *dunce's* corner either sayin gush g = I don't know; I'm not sure; do you got = do you = got ==any other reasons we might want to *hire you on*? I—*uh*—no what the hell *kick yourself in the butt if at all possible please* there's nobody here but us *dunces* heh hah cannot believe you were going to gush actually answer straight into the wall's c gush orner-crease aren't you going to answer *hm* you must not want this job too badly, what? Oh, clear the haze please this-s could only be real within some thick choking haze when dying everything stops making sense yes of course I want the job we need food on the table the *dunce* angle works we feel as if somehow we're shedding ourselves eh *hammer* see we are qualified we know how to shake a *hammer* oh that will never do what else you got in desperation re-search the corner crease yeh yo *here's* a *clipboard* complete with *pad* and *pencil* plus a *hammer* what more do you need *mmmm mmmm* okay oh so you're—*management?* You're looking to join up and be *management?*

    Ha ha ha ha ha ha ha ha!

    Uh. Whatever. Whatever you got I, eh—yes yo just *whatever*.

    POP! bang Oh come on, hey, what's the matter can't you make up your mind *what you want*?

    What? Why do you say that?

    There you are—dressed as, well, M. "Mutual" *nothing*, with a hammer (used by the workstaff) in one hand and a clipboard with pad and pencil (used by management staff) in the other, and, hey your head? What's in your head when you come up displaying the feathers of both worker and management how can you expect to ever possibly mate up with your desired?

Too MUCH officially—ye y this has just been another o' them damned hypnogogical drift-states perk UP perk UP don't nod OFF don't nod off eh eh here what will best serve you for survival in the wild, hey; a clipboard wit' pencil and nails, or a hammer?

What?

What do you mean, *what*? Which will serve in the wild?

I don't know.

Yes, you do. Clipboard or hammer?

I don't know.

Yes, you do. Clipboard or hammer?

I don't know *yes you do* clipboard or hammer *I don't know* the first way in's a narrow rickety ladder to scale high yes you do *clipboard or hammer* I don't know and higher, followed by the need to walk three or four differently directionalized narrow thin plankways {requiring one "foot-put" before the "next-other"}yes you do *clipboard or hammer* I don't know arriving at the top of a comfortably wide really high wall the fourth of three others forming a rectangle 3-4 stories high +maybe perhaps all measured by eye+ where the tools were issued not one at a time but all put together in heavy blue steel boxes each unique to it's newbie {*which said kinds of boxes appeared up down the worksite some open some closed but all near one kind of toil being toiled at by one or more workers*} working building a building so - = eh? Ah! Yah still 's beev' Top-mayor *buh* erased of most *buh buh* most yet not of all pretense *buh buh buh* its a great picture-snap hurry and hurry <u>write the</u> <u>damned thing down</u> and there we were they and the others around all blue toolboxes clothing hard hands moving fast this-*n*-thating 'nd this-*n*-thating and this was where *T'* = no no no *who*? belonged way way back-but, being den in da handz off stupe-dumbos who felt baby one s'wash'd moah betta' than that, but—*in the end they were thwarted* does that word apply *captain* when their acts weren't intentional =

captain said = maybe no and maybe yes but it sounds best this way so *leave the damned thing alone* what's done is done *here we are*: **Eh,** Hello there. First day, ***eh***? Mine too, but—sort of, really—I got here yesterday—***HOW ABOUT YOU***? and they found out their name was ***Sweeney*** so there on this "nametag" {which when present provide those encountering the wearer with the first clue as to their public identity, but which should not be used to form deeper conclusions 'bout the wearer (beWARE all snap judgement be wary stay aWARE)} *brillo-hiss-sizzle gahhhh...* whoah-whoa *that be a close one* BUH *hey, Sweeney? I knew a Sweeney. I did— maybe you're—ah, eh, hey*—my manners are sometimes bad, forgive me—my names MahJohnglie-McBlanch ‖‖attn could not really hear it this one was so soft spoken but never needed to say the name again who cares, they let it go ‖‖‖yes stat son yes that's *so* from the "heady side of the clan" *ya know do ya know* wh' what being from the "heady side of the clan" really *means*? ‖‖‖‖like think this over somebody says {garbled} then you got a choice which is this to say, *1.* Hold it back up what did you say and/or, *2.* Let it go let it go‖‖‖ Really *means*? I mean do you really, really *really* totally know wh' what being from the "heady side of the clan" really *means*? ‖‖‖‖after deciding if that's wise *but*‖‖‖‖What's the matter why don't you answer what you can't answer hey ‖‖‖‖that can't be assessed without having heard the full message leaving it only‖‖‖ ***Doc*** this one here seems unable to answer should we give them the treatment ***Doc*** ‖‖‖‖a 50-50 proposition that not stopping and asking will not be a problem‖‖‖ should we treat them should we ***now***? *cantata* ‖‖‖‖later on when the rubber will have long since left the road and every play is played for keeps *gahhhhhhhhhh*‖‖‖‖

Okay Mah', show Sweeney here the ropes, they're new. Okay?

‖‖‖‖so the conclusion being's the only stupid question's the one that's never asked but‖‖‖‖

Yes. But—are you sure we need another hammer in my section? *cantata* We're keeping up pretty good here. There's no slabs waiting down there to be packed in.

||||but but but that's not true in every situation you understand ***DUMBO***||||

Yes. *cantata* And that's why I'm setting Sweeney up here. *cantata cantata* You got the time to show them the ropes. ||||oh yeah okay go on yell 'til Ur blue for clarification *gahhhhhhhhhhh*||||

Okay. But. How long do I got to show Sweeney the ropes?

||||there comes a time place and situation ***you're on your own***||||

Not sure. Depends. You know? Like most things 'round here tend to depend—*voice shaking down weaker down, then back up*—*go* —on other things. **BLUE** ||||shut up turn around go away ***you're on your own***|||| You know but—*again*— |||Ten free tickertz t' th' **CrinckLeeDiePappula** *Festival* for every tenth client wh' signs up ***Right Now!*||| *again no yes no got to sorry really sorry but got to getta 'way right now* **yes right now** —tell you what, you decide. Size things up and—*go*—let me know to—*go go go go!!*— let me know tomorrow—I got to *run* {and run they did 'round the b' blocky end of the scallop-wall partially erected getting higher every day and were *immediately gone*} leaving new Sweeney with Banger McRogers or Blustering Billy == *which/what used to be* "MahJohnglie" "McBlanch mahh jonggg" *or something's same way* == mahhh mahhhhh mahhhhhhh JONG! +ah **gash** hold it **gash** why's this whole damned room ***spinning***? + *kuck rattle-trap* !snap! stop. +hold it **gash** 'ole it **gash** why's this whole damned room ***down***? + [the following is something gone forgotten until years later] the job whistle steamed out ***Hey this is the end of the work day*** eh co-co *servants* eh co-co-co *servants* "so" a quite important *whistle of the day* at who's pipe **2000+** workers dropped tools got up left immediately for their homes and 'fter they'd been Sweeney here for some number of and interval you feel's reasonable that that where did they

• 151 Game 4

go what did they do th ᵍᵘˢʰ e *2000+* what did they daily get out and do the *2000+* until next/same forever *(?)* tomorrow depending on your personal mode of perceiving the passage of time go every day night holiday *swish* we'll be a damned Jordan's *Net* if we know damned Jordan's *Net* Jordan's *Net*
*brake-stomp screeeeeeeee e ee e ech. !   big tall b-ball player / Ginsu Knife / **Kazoo!***
      swipe
cooooooooooooooooooooooooooooooooooooooooooooooooooooooooooool !!   part the
                                                    waves now   p a r t   the waves now

BLUE
      are on and the   G—
      BLUE
           same but *came on the scene*
BLUE
      —uests on the program this week are two examples of true community spirit, unselfishness, and drive—let *e* let me unutroduce let me Jak and Jac Skrapp rappo *k* "closed-casket" *"closed caske'"* Jack Scrappo and th' 'ther Jak Skrappo whom many   do   think
      at totally different times   **BL** *l*   different
times   *u*   **UE** different *times*   different
times   but wasn't it the case *in fact*
    *different **times***   that you are the two original founders   *different **times***
        of the Experimental Heemio{o} p{o}ole-trilliac pole, c'est   *different **times***
otherwise known as a rotting heeliog of'f a trilliac'd down Experimental Mathematical quite long *t'phone pole plant* and   *different **times*** latently glazed later on pantographically powered regulation TV set works ***diff* *times***
BOM BOM BOM BOM   previously located in West "Bronze" Loose Toothpull?   ***diff***   ***ff***
f   oh ya yi yu ye, *YIP {ain't that}* isn't that so?
whippet
    *Jack **Scrappo***: Yes as a matter of fact I believe it true that you're talking about me {not "my father" and certainly not this other one here [wink wink nudge nudge (to Jak S.

set off to the side) not this one here you know but me I'm right here. ***Why?***

S. Jay*mie* Grey, *intervieweesta*: ***Why?*** Because the telephone pole manufacturing plant established here led to the expansion of the area in many and myriad ways. That's ***why***.

Jack Scrappo: Okay, but what's that got to do with us {*who*? (US, for God's sake, don't you +can't you |aren't you able to **HOT DUG-IN PRONGS** {see me sitting here being interviewed : *right here and beside you* " my word right here and beside you? My GOD " that's right, my God is right : as always my God tends to be always right } and you too Missus *Bedevilment* as you are yes yes) as you as as as as you really really are, } Mr. *Bedivelment* | Missus *Bedevilment* addition plus subtraction *yoo-hoo*   UCK

S. Jay*mie* Grey, *intervieweestickless*: ...there you go does that **SUPERSHARP HOT DUG-IN PRONGS** answer your question?

Jack Scrappo: Uh. *McGockno's Stunners-Up* not really, I—

S. Jay*mie* Grey, *intervieweestickless*'s *shelfpaper copy-person*: Weren't listening, were you?

*Jack(**K**) Sc(K)rappo"closed-boxket"*: Yes I was I merely—wanted to see if you'd give the same answer twice {you know}!

Jay*mie* Grey, *intervieweestickless*'s *shelfpaper copy-person* S.: *I know you're lying but* here we go there we are = Of course I would. Why would the answer change? Truth is truth.

Jack(K) Sc(K)rap.....osed-boxket": Not always.

Yy*mie* Grey, *intervieweestickless*'s *shelfpaper copy-person* S. Ja'*: No? How do you mean?

Ck(K) (K)rap.....newly released three-volume boxed set : The exact words you use to present a true answer, should not ever be the exact same words in the exact same sequence.

Yy*mie* Grey, *intervieweestickless*'s *shelfpaper copy-person* S. Ja' ***purveyor of reasonably priced white-walled horse bedpans*** : Why?

B _Crap_.....*newly released aaaaaa-volume boxed {* **nit-pik** *}* :ecause a relaxed teller would concentrate on the meat of the meaning of the truth, the tendons and sinews of it, and the words would spill out, bits here and bits there, differently, whereas, a lair would not be relaxed and would be internally guilty and fearful of discovery *h* and thus would have prepared *ol* the lie carefully beforehand right *hol* down to the exact words used exact *hold i* timing and cadence even the exact overall posture to assume *ld it se* in the body to steady the face whose *t see w* lips are lying as in careful now careful now *see what ha* don't get caught don't *hat happens w* get caught in a *hen y* lie no no no don't get caught don't get *when you po* caught in a lie no no *pop the wr* no don't get t*he wrong peop* caught don't get *he wrong people in t* caught in a lie no no *pop the wrong people in the m* no don't get *See what happens when you pop the wrong people in the mix* caught that's w **gush** hy you hold auditions because you hold auditions so you don't pop the wrong people in the mix wrong people mix in the wrong people uh the people in the in the mix =duh...***Y' Know?***

Jak "closed-casket" Skrappo: Yes, I do. And I knew back then, too. Very important to recruit the right people for a project. We learned this by trial and error down the years, and it's good we got most of our beginner's mistakes behind us when we got put on this job to redo the classic T-phone pole plant. *Y' know?*

Jaydee Smilieson: Oh, yeah—and by the way, **gush** on that note—you say you got "put" on this job. Who "put" you on this job?

Jak "closed-casket" Skrappo: It was less the case of *who* "put" us on as to *what* "put" us on—or some such combination.

Jaydee Smilieson: Oh? Can you elaborate?

Jak "closed-casket" Skrappo: Sure. After the phone pole plant got tore down, I wandered around some really, really—not 'shamed to say it—confused and barely wanting to live no more. Like a shadow—of something—and that was the difference—most, you see—say they seem no more than a shadow of themselves— *Let's harvest some of that pronto and get it under a microscope* but that's all wrong, **God-d-d-d**, is that all wrong. You can't be a shadow of yourself. Try to step on your shadow, ever? Ever try and do that? No one can. No one dead nor alive. You can't be the shadow of yourself— "*ohhhh*", some say that and stop thinking and give up. No, no. Got to keep thinking. Hard, but possible and you will come to the conclusion I did wha' wha' I was a shadow of the telephone pole plant! And I was drawn to go out them hills sit down on a gush rock and overlook that field hardly anybody knows is up there {mainly because the air up there's too thin to ever be ever survived} *camera-natural* what's all strewn with poles—yah, telephone poles. All kinds all ratings—the last gasped out yield of the plant a'fore she went down. The **H's;** the big ones; "hundreds" of feet long and yards and yards around—**ohh**, not every **H**; not all—that kind our test bed checker couldn't make crack under anything less than some thousands of pounds—and then— out there too—oh, I took it in out there, I did—there were ou gush r daintiers—our **I's**; smaller, but no way small. Still "hundreds" long, yards around, maybe less of both than the primo **H's,** but still not something you'd want laid across your chest (hee ho!) and just as strong, all our babies were *strong*. Then there's the babies. The 6's 7s 9s and 10s. Little ones, cute l*ee*tle ones eh, think so, **NO!** Y' still'd never want to be in the wrong spot with the back of your head targeted for a number 6 even's hot shot. Do you get the romance of this all. Do you? Do you?

Jaydee Smilieson: The way you tell it, yes, I do.

Jak "closed-casket" Skrappo: The sun setting down the hills beyond that yard up there littered with these forgotten gush things is like—like—I—I will just say that the gone t-phone pole plant was like a burnt down church ripped from me killing my need to worship—*it's God.*

Jaydee Smilieson: God?

Jak "closed-casket" Skrappo: Yep! *GOD!*

Jaydee Smilieson: *Okay. So. Then what?*

Jak "closed-casket" Skrappo: It's hard to describe. And a lot is blocked out. It seemed everything was gone to waste. It was like the end point of everything's to end up seeing it gone to waste, but, to have leapt off in time leapt off at the first moment of that final sinking of each thing, leapt off and snag on ɢᴜsʜ another begun rising, then up, ride, *oh oh*, then, *down* and off-leap again out to another and do it this way *again* and *again* and it seemed like a lot of gas *"burnt down for nothing"*, but, of course. You know? Of course { **then,** quieting staring down eyes set down implying that all these cycles of that just kept on and Ah!

Wonderful! } then this not that yes this being the next, *but so therefore* :‖|‖: in this safe *BackWhang!* quiet resting-ledge of "being interviewed for *some reason*"; being interviewed for some purpose some of the purposes may possibly be , **1.** to be "sized up" by a prospective employer {which in itself says a certain slice of the answers will be dried lies plastered to the side of the logic what says yes this one is the one you want to hire slap slap rub down smooth the truth down you *"What? How 'bout it?"* know what's what's what's blah blah, blah, or, **2.** to give answers to the interviewer who'll after while roll them up in a ball *do this* to roll out and multiply to the "hands" of one through *do that* "n" fans 'r followers of [*do this* no no no NO! That cannot be no no *do that* no No— :‖|‖: you know what I mean, ***Bankie***? so so g so the   so *pay tension pay tension here =* **St. Patrick**; after you got through that phase of your life what led to to finally be here *where we're* ***at now***? *do this* eh eh eh eh?   *wait there seems to be something large hung off my side here*   **EH**

<u>*fat shiny brillo*</u>   *"Papoon Stephenson" says do this* wards for the poor o'er & hence get thee *do that* there P *smoothly step over the rubble please/thank you*

          O   nt   PO nt   *"Papoon Stephenson" says do that*   o Pron   to pronto b' pronto bi", prrrronto (ooo) pronto big pronto dat dashed dug up skilliwillian, Pronto. big bass   do this

Jaydee Smilieson: Well, [*whooooooooop!!*] that was some ole hell of an answer, Jak—so how'd that slide you down t' ending up here—down here? +as we said up *St. Patrick* back some dozens of measurable units without which "precise determination" of great truths is mostly impossib-*le*   what the hell's that big thing there hung down off yer back?

Jak "closed-casket" Skrappo: ɢᴜsʜ Nothing not that that would be something I'd just casually answer out loud to any "complete stranger" anyway and especially in *public* like *this* who the *hell* do you *think* you *are*, **anyway** asking *that* (yah, yah, yah) who the *hell* do you *think* you are any-*anyway* who the *hell* do you ***think*** you *are* asking *that* like *this* [this was not what we agreed to {no no no no (*not at all what we agreed to*)}] *who* the *hell* do you *think* you *are* think you *are* who the hell do you think you *are* anyway asking something like *this* that was **never** agreed to, **huh**? Who the hell **huh huh** who the **hell** who the **hell** who the *hell hell* **hell** anyway,   *anyway,*   anyway, *huhhhhhhhhhhhhhhhhhhhhhhhhhhhhhhhhhhhhhhhhhhhhh?*)[(((*)& *(&*^)] bing bang a-rario **hoopla**!|||| Oh, nothing, nothing *at all* what's the next question *Gin* what's the next I am really really having fun here *Gin* I am really having fun aren't you glad you invited me *Gin* I am glad are you glad too *Gin* I hope upon hope that you are glad, too.

Gin
Gin
Gin
Party!
Wonderful!
Uh = My name is not *Gin*. It's **Jaydee Smilieson.**

Jak "closed-casket" Skrappo: Ooo. Oops! Sorry, sorry. *Is my face red*! That was—eh no no, never mind. So, eh.

Jaydee Smilieson: What?

Jak "closed-casket" Skrappo: What's the next question?

smiles   smiles

smiles

<small>pork</small>

smiles smiles

smiles smiles

smiles

Jak-Jaydee   Jak   "closed-casket"   Skrappo Smilieson: ss we thoug 'aydee 'losed-cask' Smilie' 'e thought th' '**dee 'd-ca' Smi'** 'at we were *fried* you kno' 'e <u>ca</u> **Sm'** you *know*—we got put on a really bad [{bad being it was quite t' '**Sm'** 'uite totally wrong for us e' 's 'or **S'** *for us*}] assignment the first time but don't get us wrong it was not **THE GENERAL** <small>pasta-phreak</small> **MANAGER**'s fault so stop trying to say that.

Jaydee Smilieson: Hold it, hold it; *what*?

Jak "closed-casket" *{J.S.}* **Co-Skrappo:** Stop asserting it was **THE GENERAL MANAGER**'s <small>pasta-phreak</small> fault we ended up blowing 'l ***Serenade and Flowers*** ? most our home {whole} loan {load} on an overall plan and detailed entryway mock-up of a revitalized +I don't recall M. Skrappo we ever said anything at all of **THE GENERAL MANAGER** let alone that anything at all was ever the esteemed <small>heep heep</small> great big **THE G** <small>BackWhang!</small> **ENERAL MANAGER**'s *"fault"*. |casa = house| down town great big grid-locque atlantacontractition (y' know? {Nope, don't know}) <small>the buddha says,</small> *do 'dat* |ac<u>c</u>qua = water| that that ha t't taht-that belief in this is known as ***Hunckugatorianism and is banned: a. Everyplace   b. Noplace   c. Someplace in between   d. Everyplace else*** or ***d. This is a dumb question*** okay? Does <small>we do support no such conclusio</small> that SUIT YOU NOW <small>ns</small>

whomp *we've never supported any such conclusions* who ***okay?*** mp *as a matter of fact* *if ever* so you see we were more than willing *faced with a mandatory* *order fr* **Jaydee Smili** *om* "*w* to put shoulder to wheel *ay up high*" *to support any* to grow back the town to within range of its former glory *such conclusions* who we were put to the task which was wrong for us. Looking back it now seems painfully obvious that the design and construction of a memorial site mp 'ho **eson** m' 'p *we would swiftly m* **Ja** *ove to the disablem* **ydee** *ent of their auth* to a historical tragedy where so many were lost (there were several thousands lost there in one afternoon if we remember right the stat sheet) is very different in all ways from *ority* whomp *yes* ya   **Smilies** h yah "Dig that great big hippo +*those g* **O** *reat big hippos* [these here **n:** t the bringing online a manufacturing concern especially one so gross, large, noisy, labor-intensive and relentlessly dynamic as big hippos = them **ayd** there 'n YAH!] YAH YAH!
=   *   *   *   **Jee** YAH YAH YA **Smi** H] y y y y y y y +
lie crank up the amps boss " ***son***   **:** a modern utility pole manufacturing plant (wh ic h is *a l   l*
       Jaydee Smilieson *plomp!* : Okay. But—_so_?
       Jak "closed-casket" Skrappo: So? ***This*** = the long-gone "Sckrappo Plant" was all that and even *more* like that than any other site to be designed could ever dream to ever possibly ***BE***) but instead we did waste some time, at least, detail designing the entryway portal to the memorial site, and got so far as to present to town officers a working prototype of the initial guest arrival experience, but, it was just th' that = *two thousand minutes, that's thirty three and a third* *hours, that's much more than the number of hours in a single* *day, so so ah ah = = ; ; 0 +yhbe!!!!* tell me so ***HOW THE*** ***HELL CAN THIS WORK*** is the flaw we inadvertently built into it where no where ho-hope in a single day it would prove more disastrous than day one at "Disneyland" so we got ourselves bowed out down and gone from that job {that first aborted placard we think may still be viewed in the wash closet of the floor-swept-out supplies locker way down there someplace way the hell down there} so stop whining this

story that **THE GENERAL-MANAGER** tried to set us up for failure how the hell should I know why in Earth am I that cannot be never ne'er *'cause* **THE GENERAL-MANAGER** never *tries* expected to know that who the hell pinned that damn sign on my back who the hell's the joker here uhhhhhhhhhh **THE GENERAL-MANAGER** simply successfully *does* **THE GENERAL-MANAGER** does not fail who the hell's the joker the joker if the **THE GENERAL-MANAGER** wanted to crush us we'd be way back there crushed when/where the who in the hell's the damned joker "0 +yhbe!!!! tell me so *HOW THE HELL CAN THIS WOR* (pick that up) *K*" consta-stain and death knelliellienne **work** got tossed on us round 'bout this place down here there we'd be in the mud in the mud back there *now* ehhhhhhhhhhhhhhhhhh so don't do it because pinning things on **THE GENERAL-MANAGER** simply put will simpl *Who are you?* y not work, err, there comes not later but *now* not before but *now* a day to use your own two feet stand up on them step forward on them step forward yes yes *now now now* yes yes step forward and stop bl yes yes *now now* aming it all on other e no not o yes yes *now now now* n others no more no not no more stop blaming yes yes *now* all on others no more and *now now now* not no no *now* more "Pennsylv *[BackWhang!]* ania" *now now now.*

Jaydee Smilieson *plomp! plomp!* **:** Wow, that's "<u>fascinating as hell</u>". Then, how'd you get swung over into this factory reestablishment assignment and what were the first challenges to be faced to get it all up'n goan *hot-bangers* as you seem to have been very successful in pretty please tell me pretty please pretty please Hawaiian jingoes' "heva smasha *upp* machine" accomplishing more quickly than could ever be expected + *by who? why, by everyone what the hell do you think what, don't you think? + ?* little round sandwiches   eek so   remember   remember   how   they   (*hold it hold it I am* **Jaydee Smilieson** you're *disrupting my interview*) got theirselves way out there *Gimi* for reasons ||well then,

Jaymie, the best I can say for me and my partner here, is that its like if I drop this here pea‖   having nothing to do with one thinking they had a *battery-powered transistor radio* got strapped dead-eye (*whomp whomp I am* **Jaydee Smilieson** you're *disrupting whomp whomp*) into the wriststrapping o' their trusty ole' ***cestas***   (no matter I don't really got a pea here just humor me out okay *humor me out*)   on ago playing out toward each moment's next for them (*whomp whomp whomp whomp* **Jaydee Smilieson** whomp *whomp whomp whomp*) and making it be yah yah ***making it be*** th' each moment's next for them comes out the same every time   ‖it seems, well, seems like quite a crash of no improrortance at all *but to the pea* you see just *but to the pea*‖ th' same over (*whomp whomp* **Jaee Smieson** whomp *whomp*) same o'er 'ame o'er 'me 'm' playing and playing fuh ass lawnh hiss it Stai's up-surripstiting ***easy*** they kept on irregardless irregardless   [sek-cuse me sec-skuse got to do *Andy's gang* snozzle-snore snot snot snot snozzle-snore snot snot snot snozzle-snore not heard of a snozzle-snore dantch-ya? Heck rolloerre, dat got damn Gott me Hapsburg city big snozzle-snores yas yas yas]   they kep' o' sass' Fly! (*whomp* **Je Smon** whomp) Pop! sass' Back! Catch! sass' Fling! Fly! Pop! sass' Back! sass' Back! sass' Back! sass' Back! sass' 'til 't   [so hard to stay upright but somewise *they'll manage* so let those there *be*]   'tweren't no no no moah' *great, great fun* no no moah' (**Sn**) sizz sizz Isn't this game *ain't this game no way* aren't 'll these *Saint John Bosco* kinds'a stupe gaymes *"great great fun"* nope (**0**) not fun nope not fun   ‖ you know our early-day Jai alai was like that ***just like that*** jus' some li'l snot slopped right down there *what they said **what they said*‖*   no no moah' nope not fun no moah' fun   ‖*what they said **what they said*‖*   b' b' b' b' b' bu' bu' bu' bu' but but   ‖***what they said***‖   but but *but {n others no more}* "*Who are you? **what they said** Who are you? **what they said** Who are you? **what they said what they said what they said what they said was*** = "Who are you?"

Party!
Party!
Party!
Party!
Wonderful!

Big Captain Journey says; Pop Willy! = the health implications of sweating up a daily set or two of Jai alai with friends like we made there, were not apparent until several months later. We began noticing we fell asleep effortlessly each night. And stayed asleep the whole eight or nine hours, the majority of nights. We awakened each morning—and this very literally—as the <u>cock crows</u>—as a farm back or two up in the hills had quite a few roosters. We never knew about the roosters until we woke each day refreshed and brightly aware. I mean—the roosters had been crowing, we are sure, every morning for years, but—we were never before able to hear past all the aches and pains and deep thoughts of regret at facing yet another half-asleep pain-filled day—gifted to us both equally by the near-total tossing and turning all-night insomnia, which we are sure—at least I, speaking for myself—do completely believe—had settled into whatever folds, fissures, or deep hidden areas of our brains which regulate the sleep cycle and hardened there tight as some program burnt into some virtual machine where there never again will be decent sleep for either of us and—how 'bout you take it away from here partner, while I wet my whistle a bit.

Okay.

And so on and on they took their viewers down the dark road they'd rolled down every night until the day of the unwanted TV (TVs sold separately) and its associated mandatory wireless network (the components of which are also sold separately). Woke them into (long story short, as its been presented by this time already, in all of its heavy-duty bored-you-to-tears *ad nauseam* selfhood) so we will not bother you again today with that lore turned inside out from its prior mode-tone of telling which was in and of itself turned inside-out from *its* previously told inside-out mode-tone of telling, until not being the time it is but will sleep by so most-instantly, that there's never nothing ever told "right now" since no tale can be told right atop any now since each now is a knife-edged cut off from the great big of time which lies as a *slab o' beef ribs in a meat case* no no no no visible life (which in and of itself is so much less than a *hundredth*-life or even a *billionth*-life [not to mention which's also a *slab o' beef ribs in a meat case*] you see you must see here you see where I'm holding it here hurry up see 'fore we lose our grip and then oh no uh oh there it goes lost I am afraid, *Gimi*—I am so so afraid you ar *smoothly step over the rubble please/thank you* e set on the edge of hitting me with all that before once again right now *Gimi* so—lets move on shall we? That seems best right here now. See see and even as we wrap this up tight right here and now [gimi] you can see in the transcript how often falsities get told and this in the right-faced normal sane tones of each and every normal conversation (whatever that itself means the probing of which meaning would itself consume several reams of paper and pencil scribbled down scribbled out scribbled out right there *Captain*) so we won't take you there no no no no the world is not no more the way it used to be *no no no!*

    Big Captain Journey: Bright though you be, please tell us the rest (as move on from here now we are losing all the other guests which we need to stay put here until their turns arrive) *HA!* *ho what hot trunks you're in there where on earth you going someplace to be* Oh yah I met them when I finally hit into the first wall n' ceiling plastering job I Caim'n Abel'd to snag down that first edition which back then just sat on Main street like a box, but now we all tend to breathe as it's a shrine now (but you know there's no good reason f' the way it came I had up a great big aluminum ladder all careful and shit to wipe my feet in half-quarter thick toweling 'cause *rats* yo never spot-s'posed to mar brand new varnish in general at all let alone the said varnish's rolled o'er a sports court m'member back sigh/school I got tagged back b' Gym fats sprin'd *o'* an overweight sad-sack childhood dreamer of someday 'rriving hot fame yah hot fame to be down the field that just dazzled the night away on with this kind of ball that kind of puck this kind of racket or even having been such a strong case-hard sports game general superstar whapper [don't matter what game what court what rules indoor/outdoor rough-tumble game being at the focal point of the roaring cheers of their surrounding fan-crowd, but—*E* never made it came to be a seventh rate small scholl hydroplastical pompous assed gym teacher getting wrapped off th' beat-bullying of small students everywhere already humiliated in some most disturbing way being forced to wear daily dumb-poppo'ed outfit of wrong gym shorts wrong gym shoes wrong gym shirts and even now here and sometimes out there forced into the "skins" vs. "shirts" hot-tangle of something requiring near-immediate complete forgetfulness cowed already and small as Tip's shit rolled out red carpet &nearly said white but red sounds so right& don't it yah don't it yah don't it God yes it really, really does—anyouch we were on the way to take letters-up some hot chicken of a ripped plastic basket **God** yes **God God** yes on it's last journey up the river of recyclement howl howl so you 'ee my mission was of maximum 'portance but b' this loser *saw me* as an opportunity to take out the "gas of failure" what being the only gas come able to keep 'is pitiful failed/thwarted at every step by both faith and humanity so they jumped me with a yell of Get your ass off my fresh-finished court yah you yah yah **glasses** hey **glasses** I'm talking to you who are you to mar my finish, **glasses**, who are you to add another coat of scuff-stain to my floor so bad so precious no one can walk here **glasses** who the hell are you' think I would let you get away with marring my finish **glasses** don't dare join the club of those bent on permanently marring my very soul's finish what you ask if he's crazy of course he was crazy calling me out like this hey glasses you ass who the hell are you anyway hey glasses you ass who the hell are you anyway hey glasses hey ass hey hey hey who the hell are you anyway anaynwyawya anyywway ay all got big-twisties so it spiked down the worst of my several hot-buttons but thank God the lord is merciful just moments after I buried it deep that's how bad it was *so so so bad* so—there I was up that 'ick' 'y ladder towel-footed safe o' this fresh-buffed gleam of a hard/thick varnished sports court happily living my life latest now-day plastering just quiet plastering calm yes so calm but butt-end that smash out it all tumbled down in me when those new twos came in that door and replayed their new version of that old story for "*Me*"—I became as they entered   that deepseaing plasterboy which from their point of view'd just appeared o'erhead—and they did part around my four solid ladderlegs (Not one of which they seemed to even notice)— and began to play a fast-moving exciting sport *appearing to involve bouncing a ball off a walled-in space by accelerating it to high speeds with a hand-held wicker cesta*—I simply, since having no master instruction defining how what and/or which way or even what not to do in this class of encountered situation when up high in my ladder, fatly dropping plaster-fragflops down on what should have been nothing but now here'd become a (look/see look/see look look look look see-e-e-e *big baby pangolin*) loud-mothed grossout of some hard thrash of a two-person game crying *Fling! Fly! Flail! Pop! Run, catch! Fling! Fly! Flail! Pop! Run, catch!* but my work simply continued as there it was down there flowing that way and here I am up here flowing this way (Pepto *a a* Bismo Pepto *a a a a a a a a a* BI*SM*O!) *heavy flo's-tation encountered gosh-o-gee please inform headquarters immediately* for a few moky-mokies things came out level until the noise reached the top-scraping point *if you see the Buddha coming stop doing that bad thing they don't like* beginning to form 'bout a mold shaped somewhat like *don't dare join the club of those bent on permanently marring my very soul's finish* where from eh where from eh Mustafa bean-soup'd spattered off somebody's great big platter by now overflowed with *don't dare* Fling! *join the club of those bent on perma* Fly! Flail! *nently marring my very soul's finish don't dare join* Run, catch! Fling! Fly! Flail! *the club of those bent* what they're doing's so wrong *on permanently marring my very soul's finish* started down the ladder *don't dare join the club of those bent* Fling! what they're doing's so wrong Fly! Flail! P*on permanently marring my ver* so very, very wrong Pop! Run, catch! *y soul's finish don't* Fling! Fly! Flail! *club of* catch! Fling! Fly! *bent on* got to stop needs to stop *permanently marring* Pop! Run, so turning my painter's cap backwards I did catch! Fling! *don't dare* here's the floor now go face them *join* Pop face them! Run, catch! Flin face them g! *permanently marrin* face them *g* Fling! Fly! Flail! Pop! Run, catch—once chest-to-chest on them I cried up past my top, Stop! You are marring my floor {*count aloud backwards from 1000 while holding your right foot six inches off the ground*} who the hell do you think you are marring up my floor, **glasses**? Who oh why my floor why my floor why the hell are you marring up my marring up my floor, ***GLASSES?*** stop this behavior <u>*cut off this game **Right Now!***</u>

Oh?

Yes ***right now***!

(0)

WHY?

So I must have been taken aback by this very good question and for the first time I became aware of the power of when confronted with the push of an unreasonably harsh situation of authority just dodge the question fast look for an opening then hit them with a sharp ***WHY?*** which should stop them all by itself if hit through in the clear but if there's noise in the way try something like Hold, wait—one question one question.

Oh? Yah? What's the question, little weakling. What's—

WHY! just like that or possibly **WHY!** cut out/cut in just like that really hard—then get ready to deliver another **w-w-w-w-w-w** if necessary watch their *eyes* the need for another will show in the *eyes* and there they *are* here we *go* **WHY?** hut 'em hard **WHY? WHY? W-w-w-w-w-HY! WHY!** *why* **WHY!** *why why why why* w-w-w-w-w-w-*HY!* **W-w-WHY?** *w-w-W-w-w-w-w-HY?* **WHY! WHY? WHY!** right between the *eyes why why why* **WHY!**

Out of steam then yes t'was so, **SO,** t'haz' cleared away there they were again, ***and***—u'—but—made so small by my barrage as to hardly not even matter.

Y'know?

Sure do.

Pa sure so *rty!*

Pa su' so *rty!*

Pa su' rah-rah *rty!*

Clintatonia Party!

Y' Party!

Y' Party!

Y' Party!

<u>**WONDERFUL!**</u>

So-once that thing got taken care of {it being a ***blip*** no no moa tha' 'mere *blip*} we played on. Yes. On and on so 'he ladder w' 'll ***there*** so what we told me and them also, as—being 'll there's something which common m-memories "<u>tend</u> '*to do*' ***best***"—and so yah yes you too, <u>*Shirleycakes*</u> = *[Buddha]* have and so it came to pass that these begun their dissolving in the wake of a frenzy kept on their dissolving in the wake of a frenzy *through no hands of their own sometimes these things just simply happen* kept on their dissolving the wake a frenzy on their in the of a frenzy *no hands_their own these things simply happen* went on with dissolving the a frenzy their in of a *no hands own these things happen* relentlessly rolled on with dissolving a frenzy in of *no hands these things happen* caught up in the gravity on with a frenzy of *no these things* caught up the gravity with a of *no things* caught up gravity with of *no* caught up with of caught up of caught up caught up caught up *the spouses so smoothly stepped over the rubble and proceeded their advance into Jai alai playing mastery* caught *went on playing* caht *went on* caht *on ct c* the work on the new plant was surging ahead of its timeline. *So,* the leaders that be not to mention the actual physical presence of **THE GENERAL-MANAGER** itself had to admit the workers ought to get five minutes more added on/into off the back side of *aha* concatenated into some kind of WAY stop NITPICKING cause you know its not your IDEA stop nitpicking NIT dive so they all did get that five minutes more added on/into each of their backsides, for a grand total of 10,000 minutes/166.6 hours/6.9 days total added on/into each of their individual backsides, which at the going rate let's say of @ $14.13/hour ends up costing the what have you any town/company not just this town/company $2,354 per day/ $859,231.17 per y'r in which case we're not going to do it but you already told them we would do it *smoothly step over the rubble please/thank you* so what and so what they got to know we all make mistakes *yah* but money's different oh yah why's money *the one called* different 'cause *MahJohnglie-McBlanch* we know, we know, what kind of a names' that *s'* simultaneous to that cannot possibly be your name [ho ha hi hee] along with the newly elected or sort of chosen by lot number or simply impassive about most things management soul-grinding heavy crush of the faceless who know everything's ever happened along with every single thing that's ever going to happen (yikes sounds like you *Rennie*) like like like *hold that horse Mammo* your horses your horses but your horses your horses your horses before we get your horse hold your horses into breaktime *Sweeney's* arrival on your horse hold your horses the lunching-bench stacked down in 'is horse layers right off two-faced 'nd same-sighted *MahJohnglie-McBlanch* there's need to be saids sum of the nimbers Sam Slash-dot willerries (zooooooooom) let's as suggested crack-snap our way to the pop and know a bittle tinie about Faith-in-God Jessie Faith-in-God Jessie swept o-er the scene soe halve's are really quarters backed into a corner and thus back-bristled *up* says here's what's what of the illuministicle up on high way out ther *Go'head* this *Go'head* pressed forth out some size of a dollop of Sweet - Child-at-Play^{tm} ultra-pliable rainbow hued modeling clay (OOPS excuse me, did not see you there, *sorry*) garbage = = = = = = ! Really? *Wow!* God has to roller-coaster this flow through this here pinhole *amazing* so you mean they hand in final plans 'bout what each of our futures hold then has to take to the saddle and ride the damn fast plunge of a buck through future's infinite (maybe not) pinhole even though its a few hundred macromills south of the border in terms of their fit-through to get beholding the Lord's son's passage BUT nd the rules even, after all'd impossibly built too large to fit anyway, make sure the inflowing newly modeled of that clay moment exactly but not too obviously matching the plan of the future handed in up there some place back behind and so all to be said now's may seem haphazard chaotic and incomprehensible to some [heck yah maybe even thus so to *most* (and as some scientific researchers perhaps e'en to *all* in a couple fleeting instants important dignitary is approaching look-alive alert 'larm rang [[[Hans, please take the lead on handling this—got time for that have you? That's great. Okay, if you could get a jump on that buh' putting in a few extra hours past quitting time today, that'd be really, really *great*]]] once every three centuries, maybe less, maybe more)] but's all' being safe-steered by the soft yet firm, very loving hands of *God* the new-minted *Sweeney* [[[we all feel we can rest easy now that Hans' on the job]]] *all praise upper management now all can sleep better* so; after Sweeney and McBlanch took their seats in the bench room with the 1,998 other workers, McBlanch spoke up loud enough to hear over the din.

I didn't think they were still recruiting workers for this job. What brought you to apply? Are there still hiring notices at the library and by the clerk's window in borough hall?

No, ah—I never saw any of that. I didn't apply. I just somehow—ended up here.

McBlanch's head cocked slightly.

What?

I'm just here. I don't know. I am here is the only thing I know for sure.

But what did you do before?

I, *{ruffling through files okay—okay here it is so deliver}* I worked in an office.

Really. I never worked in an office. What'd you do there?

Paperwork. Like that.

Oh. What kind of paperwork?

Nothing special, just—clerical work.

Clerical work? Sounds way too boring to me. I like a job outside. Like this one.

Yeah. I like to spend time outside too.

So what made you get out of the—the clerical business?

Sweeney looked down.

What's the matter? I touch a nerve?

No, but ahh, said Sweeney, stretching an arm—I got out because I hated it.

Why?

Sweeney's face snapped around full-on facing McBlanch.

I guess I didn't like it. I guess I just—

A bright tone sounded in the distance cutting Sweeney off as their break was over.

Oh, hey, hold that thought, pal. Got to back. Eh—and the huge break room sounded with the clatter of what seemed to be 2000 bright blue toolboxes being lifted which as it faded was gradually replaced by the shuffling footsteps of 2000 workers returning to the job. In the glass office perched up top on its ninety meter high solid steel legs the S(k-c)rappos stood looking out on the scene, arms folded, taking a break from jockeying the reams of daily paper reports analyses graphs charts they sent off to **THE GENERAL-MANAGER** back up the main office. Every day, as **THE GENERAL-MANAGER** opened the bundle thinking to themself, Okay, let's see, this has to be the day these contain some bad news. Things have been going too well, new projects like this *never* go that well, *unless*—eyy, let's see—Crap. Yup, too good to be true, again--and **THE GENERAL-MANAGER** picked up the reports, placed them in recycling, and sat down at their desk regarding the now-empty space before the desk where the Sk(c)rappos had stood when summoned that long-ago day to explain how they possibly could be ready to start building the plant a full month before the master plan estimate.

Okay, said **THE GENERAL-MANAGER.** Make me believe you're ready to start.

And—from the very last syllable of that question, they began thinking hard, how to answer that question most concisely, most crisply, so that it would **NOT** become true that once more they'd go nowhere **NOT** become true again that they'd fail like that last one and **NOT** have to be once more assigned to something else, because every else gone is an else gone forever, so, they thought long the longest way out back-pack'd when they'd faced the one last knotty problem to solve that day five or six ago they'd stood cross the plans draped over the drafting-table.

I am worried, Jak. I just don't see we're going to be able to do this.

Why not? said Jack. These plans are damned good. I feel good about them. What are you seeing here that I am not?

This plan assumes a certain number of workers to get this done. Where are they going to come from?

From the ads we put out. And the flyers. That we're doing this's been publicized. Remember, that was the first plan we drew up.

I know. But we only got a couple dozen signed in to start.

Okay. Okay! That's a start. And there'll be more. Come on.

What do you mean, come on? Come on what?

Stop being negative.

But the situation here *is* negative. This town went way downhill when the plant closed and all the rest of it. All the people qualified to work on this are gone. What—do you think everybody worked here before were just sitting around waiting for the place to come back to life? There's nobody fit for these jobs anymore.

Hold it. You said—what's you say—you got two dozen or something—how many'd you say you got signed in so far?

Around twenty.

Okay. That's a start. I think you need to be a bit more patient. When did you put out the call for workers?

A month ago. Maybe a month and a half.

So what's the issue? I don't see that's a long time.

The issue's that the twenty applicants we signed up put in for the job in the first five days that the ads were out there. That was forty, fifty days ago, or something. There's not been a peep since. I been telling you nobody's signing up.

What? You told me—what? You said you signed a bunch up and said there'd be more.

No, no no no. I never said there'd be more. I said I hoped there'd be more.

Okay. Okay. So—why's that a problem?

God, said the other—you don't see a problem nobody's signing up?

Hold it. Simmer down. I'm really confused now. You said you had twenty signed up. But now—nobody's signed up? I don't get it!

Hold it, no, listen—

No no no you hold it and listen! I'm completely confused now. The plan has the work starting this week—*and nobody's signed up?*

I didn't say nobody's signed up. I said—

STOP! I think I can quote you as saying something like, *I been telling you nobody's signing up*—you did say those words did you not?

Yes! But that's not what I meant!

Oh!

Oh? What?

You have trouble saying what you mean? God damn, if you got that trouble maybe I got the <u>*wrong person beside me to get this damned telephone pole plant built*</u>!

Listen, listen, said the other, red-faced and fists forming at their sides—you better stop what you're doing, right now.

Stop what I'm doing? How can I stop what I'm doing? I'm trying to get some status of where the hiring for this project stands ***right now***! Don't you think we **both** need to **clearly know** if this project can start next week? **Clearly know**? and on and on and on loss Charlie's snort +awk! and all the Mucus!+ these made the spitting image of two uncomplete humans struggling *Don't you think* whirling **both** need round to be one again but the and about **clearly** if one another human they want to become's already become itself again faster whirling round about here's Jack "closed-casket" Scrappo 'n Jak Skrappo tussling 'ain this project one another fastest whirling about SO faster fastest SO SO faster than fastest **clearly know** they had reached the point of fighting such that the neither of them nearly mattered no no more so out 'f the 'irl-gig stepped agai' the common within them appeared at these times this one finding their states fully repellent {hey hi ho one more time here's a new *red-letter day*!}—the same Tapper Rose [former hero] which in times of trouble like this tended to tubularly gradually reappear *(hots)* stepped toward the door which no one notice'd been banging stepped off from **tabula**

rasa the whirling high flesh and its not magic it only looks like magic blood pointless surge of a spun up struggle of a red-hot cylinder well if it looks like magic that's good enough for me the Jak and their Jack had once more become {and would remain so indefinitely [how long is indefinitely *{WhoaKnock VonParsnip even cried out;* **hoops***!}*] *who the hell knows that question's not on topic* : hey hey hole down how many you got here how 'bout we buy you out one moment *who decides what's on topic? And who, pray tell, does not?* : I am the ones deciding on these drivers] oh yap y oh yap no I am the one *ME*! oh-nooooooooooooooo, *hots* the door to the outer side opened just as far out there *the in a mere blink off three eyes* sun shone most brightly haloing the very who me? head of the knocker : shut up Tapper Rose first find out who's this knocker : yes you! okay we will find out who's this **gock-knocker** |||you better find out\\\you better find out +++ you better you better you better find out o - - - - -- 000000000000 hello I am 777   8 here we have heard (m e r c e d e s – b e n z) you were down here looking for some *workers* so what kind, I asked, and the sheet "read" construction workers and liquid starts to piston up from down below and starts t' overspread out and down all around the circumference of the rim—as this first one spoke, it pistoned them up faster, and with each word more came out over the top of the hills all around, and the mass of them flowed down into a line leading into the "*telephone pole factory worksite*", and, over the next few days the pounding forward of the sound of work being done pressed relentlessly forward and, the walls began to rise it did not matter why so that wasn't asked for fear of the whole thing stopping down into itself and all having been a dream so we stepped back and turned away and listened to it keep happening until it seemed safe to completely believe it was real and forever so we turned and looked and here it was real and if not :*Don't you Get It?*: totally forever at least probably forever : No. *Sorry.* : enough to get the needed work : Okay then.: done so we didn't : *Get out.* : question and as : Hey Pap!: time went : ***Next Airplane Please***: the need to : but :

be able to answer : open my mouth and : questions lessened : comes out *this shit*: and lessened so we forgot :*please prepare my spaghetti dinner immediately!!* : how it all got started and only lived : *(What?)* : in the : *whether you are traveling for "business" or "pleasure"* : present of what is happening : ||said senior flight attendant *Jan* || : right now, *so*— who knows but there it is : || we thank you for having chosen || :go down touch the walls : || airlines to fulfill your *"travel needs"* || : its reals so why its real do'sn't matter because it is. : || today. || : Doc. So. So so.

So i So iii So So So iiii SSSSOOOO luckily caught a hot cab for the travel and[1] after checking in unpacking their baggage and[2] freshening up noting by watch time the appointment with their new f*OCA*l a*DMINISTRA T*Or at the university office. After grasping a half off their full heads of coffees, they cabbed over, got out, went up, and[3] stepped in.

As seen from above they sat on one side of the f*OCA*l a*DMINISTRA T*Or's deeply brown desktop and the f*OCA*l a*DMINISTR A T*Or (as you may now assume also) sat on the other. Speaking to each other somewise animatedly sometimes not simultaneous to passing paperwork to-from each other and writing on tablet typing on pads all the while every few seconds/minutes (no hours no no since the meeting lasted nearly closely as possible to the agreed-upon fifteen minutes) and UP there out the walls circling the space schooled three colleagues of the f*OCA*l a*DMINIS-RA T*Or each dying to go in and grill them about the newly arrived researcher} and : the co*m*versation seemed to go on for a fairly long time and then, *hop friendly* the polesitter rose, pulled up their case and (we must presume e' though the proof's just circumstantial) that this highest Mathematics laboratory in the highest level university in the world had successfully absorbed some sort of "greenhorn" {*but a "greenhorn" answering to no one and nobody*} to do research *plunk* of some rarified style *plunk pl-nk plunk* and they left out the same way they came in in-out-in-out in *'lunk pl-nk l-n pl-nk plun' {doff that beanie cap Booster it is not* *appropriate for this category of equation}* and once they vacuumed out to the low pressure of the yard and stepped out past it no doubt to some bus stop or even the train station but no nah eh yeah the must have do that lodgings if no on-campus but immediately adjacent [nope that's Poole's big suitcase not mine can't help you pal so so *sorry sorry sorry {ahhhhhhhhhhhhh hhhhh hhhhhhhhhh}*] the three colleagues of the focal administrator which had been circling the scene smoothly entered taking up perches across the desk from te f*OCA*l a*D-M-I-{ᴅᴍɪ}NISTRAT*Or {3}. boop

It is true they're from that place?

Did they say what it's like there?

I hardly even believed there was such a place and here I am now going to work with someone from that place.

My parents told me not to ever talk about that place because it'd hear me and come at night get in me start me up and drive me away so my parents were careful they always kept me locked up they never left me idling outside any stores they'd just *uh huh* be a second I' going to get a couple bags of chips do you want anything dear any nothing or thing or at all transylvania

My parents were kind of like that too *why're they all like that?*

They thought they were protecting us, y'know, raising us right you know.

Raising us right by *lying?* That's not right at all, it is very very *wrong.*

The '*OCA*' '*DMINISTRAT*O' lowered the tone of the room, saying seriously, Did you guys know that over seventy percent of the telephone poles on the planet come from that place?

No!

No.

Really?

Yes, really.

glandular   glandular   glandular

        gland

—'s going to work with the astronomical team.

S' really?

Yes, really! But, hold it. *astronomical team why the astronomical team* You know that's a real bad habit you got there *{oooo}* that's a verbal tic you got eh eh or something *say say* you need to cut that out it is just *so so* grating!

Tic? *What* tic.

"Really!" "Really!" Oh, *really,* you don't say oh—yes, really—is that true *is it really*? You got to stop that.

I—uh.

There you were going to say it again. Weren't you?

Ah—I—no I wasn't. I was not.

Oh no. Really? You were *not*? Were you not—*really*?

I—the others lightly tittered diluting the response from the "accused", to—

Nothing.

So = the f**O**c**A**l a**DMIN**ɪs**TRAT**Or said, Okay, get out of here. I got to make a call, okay? You have made me late for something again.

The accused smiled tightly and turned and then—

NO! Don't you dare. Not even as a joke. Get all your asses out my office. Now!

After they'd left and closed the door, the f**OC**—' '---**INISTRAT**Or stared at the blank some minutes, then picked up the phone, dialed, waited a moment, and spoke.

Hey there—yah, me. They just checked in. I sent them up your way. Yah. So be ready. No, no. I don't think so. But you'll have more time to know and decide. Sound good? Yes, I will. Everybody's dying to know. *astronomical team why the astronomical team* Yes, yes. It seems wrong, you know, but—hey, time will tell—hey's that your door knocking? Oh, yes. It will. Tell me how it goes. We're all dying, you know, eh— okay bye so long in the day on   *astronomical team why the astronomical team*   the   d a y   the Sweeney did manage by the   *astronomical team why the astronomical team*   d   a   y   knocking knocking knooo o   *astronomical team why the astronomical team* oo ooooo   oo oo

OO *astronomical team why the astronomical team* O OOOOOOkkkkkkkkkkking to, working together with MahJohnglie-*McBlanch* strike no less than three fifty hard hammerblows on this/that component from off the conveyor belt from up down below {*fifty* being too neat and too clean, we know, yes we know, but; say what—*fifty-one* or *forty-nine* are no more likely to be the number of/when random numbers are getting picked out "*a' hat*" these are just sounds these are not the numbers the numbers are the numbers and not what the numbers are called don't you *get* it why don't you *get* it} 's 'ot to say 'e did'nt strike too close to {*mostly*}this/that fingertip, joint, or connecting spans 'n between let alone never {which would be lying we hate liars we hat aht ahhta t ah ah LIARS *see* how the liars strive to confound us just the mere mention of the name "liars" bu', b-b-b-b, do not fear young one we are here too young ones and all you remember {listen hard this is mandatory} just as numbers are not the numbers the liar {liars} is {are} not the liar {liars} see how clear all becomes up here in this place of the suprerrerly rary-fied air that we breath in air out air feel it flowing up flowing down that's air but remember just as number {numbers} is {are} not the real-world number {numbers} and liars {liar} are {is} not the real-world liars {liar} then air is not the air I is not me nor are you you either {tan tootin (Vic Tanny)} bloom hold it hold it hold it holde; why you claim air is unlike all others *Gimi* why you make air so special is air somehow somewhat kin to God *Gimi* is air somewhat that way but no why you make me child why you make me blaspheme like this **Gimi** trying to slide me down hell be ye Gimi that way ye be ye that way ye *be*? Gimi Gimi please *Sweeney eh Swee'* don't let that be *you okay there Sweeney* Gimi Gimi please don't *what's the mattah' there Sweeney* let that be Gimi Gimi please don't let that be you slam your thumb {thumbs} one time too many Sweeney you slam your thumbs {thumb} *one time too many*? *astronomical team why the astronomical team,* **Gimi**?

    OY!

Big Buckin' Broncos, Batman!

Nah I don't think so eh ah—but—wow how much higher are the walls now? They seem higher and looking down seems longer ah Francis eh Servon what you doin' 'p there on them girders up there wow what are you doing {seen "within" Sweeney where the h *(CUT)* }

Sweeney followed MahJohnglie down the planks to ground level merging them with what seemed a very disorganized great big crowd of on-site workers *{reeking}* pressing forward toward the gate being staffed by a large chested gate-guard whose main feature was an outsized rattling keychain swung loosely off their hip-belt which as every twelfth worker pushed by the hip of the worker jangling the chain made a very very irritatingly persistent sound *why the astronomical team, Gimi?* which as the proceeded why that hell can't they step the hell back what the hell that gateguard getting a thrill off each slid-by tight pass move the damned chain I do not want to have to rub past them like that why the hell you stand right there Gimi why you want me push past so annoyingly Gimi step back please step back step shut up you're overtired too much laughing leads to crying *bu' why the astronomical team, Gimi?* just look at you you are living *proof* {gimi?} gimi living-Proof living *p r o o f* —hold it there pal—eh, pal.

Sweeney turned.

Me?

Yah you where you going? The bunkhouse's up that hill that way there.

Bunkhouse? Oh, no— *but please please why the "<u>astronomical team?</u>"*

Oh yes. Go up that hill over there with the others. Please don't make me mad.

Don't make me mad.

Don't make me mad.

Don't make me mad.

Please please. Don't make me I do not like being mad.

Sorry, no, no. I'm not with those others. I live out that way. Thanks anyway.

Start walk' buh' NO hold it, no. Up to the bunkhouse please. With the others up to the bunkhouse {oh my God what no no that one (just look at them look up and down over them that kind never knows what's going on keep walking they will turn around)}Keep walking, just keep walking (hear them Hey Pal, *hold it*) they will stop turn around and go the other way (Hey pal here stop right there Hold It stop Hey pal) no keep on walking they will tire, stop, turn, and walk away so keep hey pal on turn away damn you no no hey hey **PAL** hey there *PAL* they will and they must hey pal stop turn walk away and ook *what*?   **WHAT!**

Hand on shoulder who's hands touching shoulder no no no musn't be touched who the hell is this—Sweeney turned, saw the guard (said call me guard over pocket it says **GUARD** see there see me I am the **GUARD** and you must stop down tracks in your of cold, dead.)

Who the hell are you, said Sweeney—who the hell are you? Touch me again and you will be sorry. I am going home so turn around and get off me, okay?

No. You have to go to the bunkhouse. All the workers stay there. So go on over here to—

Hold it, *hold it*! My house is (pointing down the road away) *that way*.

No. The bunkhouse. I'll need to call law enforcement if you won't sleep in the bunkhouse.

What? Why the H' *okay yah but we have no idea who these 2000 workers somebody shipped in came from who they are or why they got sent here so* 'ell does everybody got to stay at—this "bunkhouse"? *put up a quickie pre-fab bunkhouse sort of thing up there we don't want* Listen, it doesn't matter why the rules are the rules the big shots make the rules around here *not me these people snooping around town* not me *until we know who they are and why they came here okay yes boss good go make it happen and fast they're up* not me *there already I don't want them* I'm sorry pal, but I'm simply not going to *down in town to get* do that *out of there* okay? *and get that done* so get the hell back off my face, get out of my way, and shut up 'cause I'm *going {as this debate grew more and more heated three police officers in heavy gear with massive guns strapped all over came slowly up, observing}* home!

No. You can't. Come on. To the bunkhouse. Stop making trouble. Come on!

Reaching for, no, don't reach for, no, Get off of me, damn you—don't dare touch me, I AM GOING! Now *{the three police officers slowly sidled closer, ears cocked, hands and faces ready}* then right then *which was to the players on the field their really right now* Sweeney saw a gap between the leftmost *{police officer}* and the rattly-keyed gatekeeper **SO**, took a chance a big chance *to run* through this suddenly pending scrimmage, only to be *no no no* what's this (?) GRIPPED by the arm, what why-y-y-y *why* when, no no no, I need to get home, *no you don't what's your problem hey* I want to get home, I won't go in some *bunkhouse,* and the officer held Sweeney sort of soft but tight enough to say one more step and its *"face down in the dirt time"* and, thee **topt itp** the Gatekeeper stood by the officers saying, so, what's you problem anyway, I mean look back up there all the other 1,999 workers are quietly obeying the rules as all should but you who the hell, who the hell do you think you are, anyway !(?)! *So?*

I'm—I'm—no, never mind who I am! I have the right to go home after work wherever I say and can prove my home to be! So shut up, and step back!

The officer's grip incrementally tightened but, there was slack still so time to give in was off some moments anyway, as the gatekeeper said, No, no. I have been ordered that *every {can you spell every? Sure e-v-e-r-y every. Good. Now—do you know what every means? Sure. The entire group of something like every single lump of coal in that bin you know that you knew **mew mew mew** said Midnight the cat from the four a.m. coalbin **mew mew mew mew mew}*** every last worker on this site is to be lodged at the bunkhouse erected on the hill to the side. That's the law. You understand the term *law,* young rooster? You understand the word l-l-l-l-aw!, Meester cock-a-doodle-doo? Huck Finn in a coalbin at midnight's *"the clue"* so can the next contestant guess, **SPIN THE WHEEL** hosanna!

There's no such law. Who'd make such a bad law?

Top-mayor made the law. Top-mayor is saving this town—

w   top   m
Swee   mayor Swee   Sween
weene   S-Y   SweetopmayorNey ---

That is *wrong*, this is <u>*crazy*</u>. You are a <u>***liar***</u>!

Really? *Why?*

'cause I'm the Top-mayor. That's why and v-v-v- but expecting to immediately feel anyand all disrespect to shatter and fall down away in the grass, no, So what? What's that make you? God or something - that—so why what's *this?*
sweep it away louder

Listen, you idiot—I'm about to blow my top! Are you deaf, or just stupid—I am Top-mayor! And I made no such law!

The grin and—on the officers also why—why is this funny, why's funny, one, the faces of this idiot, and their officers?

Of course you didn't. The Top-mayor did. So, enough now. Up there to the bunkhouse—

JESUS! and the savior obliged by loosing the hand of the officer so the rest being I AM TOP-MAYOR, *YOU ASS!*

Okay. Okay. Got it off your chest now, *Sweeney?*

Sweeney? Oh, no no *that's just*—listen. I'm not Sweeney. I'm Top-mayor. Okay?

My God, you are sick. You just said you're not Sweeney, because you're really Sweeney, and you don't care what laws Top-mayor's made, because you are Sweeney, and know better than Top-mayor, *no.* You're just an idiot—and ain't it funny that out of 2,000 workers suddenly showed up from God knows where taking over the jobs of people who we know who they are—the first random'd-downne one we end up dealing with is *nutty*. **Nuts**! You don't know who you are, eh, I'm Sweeney, no I'm not Sweeney—I'm Top-mayor, hold it, no, and round and wound 'round o'er under their entire selves rapt in time, sped pulling all's puzzling, dark, troubling, and wrong, tight 'round Sweeney's tight to begin with Top-mayorized overfull head, and so; come on with us "*pardner*" have we got a place for you! Come on and come on you will love it it's way better than that bunkhouse they be hootin' and o' hollering up 'til dawn 'n that crazy bunkhouse plus its *no no no come on do not resist **Gimi*** its ready to collapse anyway being built-soe poorly to 'egin with ***Gimi** might as well loosen up stop fighting us you'll need your energy where you're going Sweeney No I am not Sweeney yes you are no you're not I am too what you were not now you are my oh my are you confused no (it can't be us {yes it must be you [**GOD** why does it really have to be anyone at **ALL** stop yelling crazy] no I won't} well yes you better) What d'ya say hold it* **HOLD IT** what did the chief just tell you on the phone?

Chief said bring this idiot down to the office.

Which office?

Top-mayor's office.

No, *no*! I am Top-mayor! Jesus, *I*!

Shut up! Yah, Top-mayor wants to see this looper.

Hey, why?

No no no, no! I am Top-mayor!

Shut up, Sweeney. We know your name. Please shut it off, you're boring us.

Yah. Boring us.

But I am no no no no Party!

But but but Party!

But but Party!

Party! hands over fists big fat Party!

OOF!   *toooooooooooooooooooome*

Wonderful! **SO** *this*
is the place where we'll go now to the **next one** no not hold
it not hold who are you to say what, No no no both of you,
both neither nor one's or the other's can, but, Halt no right
there Shhhhh's, we are taller than any o' the eithers of you
two three or four hold it no shut up five of 'em six or more
send in more very large/loud dogs just like that one these
ones and O *ah really*? Why not these ones here **too
hestaskakula major** no no no those ones *also NO* wrongo
God's said right quite clearly, the sign's **hestaskakula minor
too   hestaskakula major**   no no no those ones *also NO*
wrongo God's said right quite clearly, the sign's
hestaskakula minor no **hestaskakula major** why not **major
+ minor** as some combreratioon of the **to(wo?)o** no no no no
NO it is one or its nothing **Pop** no no no no it is one only or
nothing at all **Pop** it is one or its nothing **Pop** Jak/Jack
Sc(k)rappo boshed killies it is one only or nothing for
breakfast, dear holy Father is that its nothing **Pop** no no
wrong, Holy Father that's why you're the Holy Father, isn't
Pop it is one or its got to tell us the right from the wrongs in
all of its recktafusion—that's granted, but, one or its nothing
Pop no no Magnificent be the **Gloriack't** of it, and no no it
is one only or nothing at all **Pop** it is one or its Equally
magnificent be the **Gloriock't** of it is one only or nothing at
fling **Pop** it is fly flick flack its nothing **Pop** swing squeak
no, shuffle, slack, no swing swang swung, **Brillo**, "Isn't this
game" great great isn't it really "great, great fun" great fun
great fun innnnnnnnnnhale, gasp exhaaaaaaaaaaaaaaaaaaaale,
Isn't this game great, great fun?"

"Yes it's fun."

The spouses came around after another last thrill of a
Jai alai game, on this day being [*at least yesterday*] the very
next day of carefree, undistracted all-out Jai alai playing—at
which they were getting so better over what they thought was
so   much   better   just   yesterday,   which   seemed   to
exponentially grow in size from moment to moment so

noticeable like as though one could stare at a clock long and hard enough to see that no, the minute hand does not proceed smoothly along the marking off of the minutes of time, but, proceeds in jerks fits starts and jerk led to a muse down thee hole where its asked now and then, do all minute hands proceed in this manner *s se see how awful it is to find possible that which was never so before efore fore ore ee e* or or-r o-r or, its this a behavior unique to this make and model of clock, and then, if *s se see how awful it is to find possible that which was never so before efore fore ore ee* this is a behavior unique to this make and model of clock, is the phrase "unique to this make and model", even though for this particular physical clock, that phrase will of course always apply, at least for as long as this particular physical clock remains in working order and is running, but what about the entire set of physical clocks of this particular make and model; or some subset of the entire set; can we have one of the following statements be absolutely immutably true;   1, all clocks of this make and model run the exact same way, or; 2, one and only one clock of this make and model's minute hands moves jerkily and not smoothly, or; 3. multiple members of this make and model run jerkily, and the rest run smoothly, or; 4. an undefined number of clocks of this make and model run one way (smoothly), then another number runs another way (jerkily) and, it may even be possible for there to be more than just two ways for the minute hands of the clocks of this particular make and model to move, up to and including a number equal to the number of clocks of this make and model actually manufactured, *currently* being the operative word here, since one or more of the total number of clocks of this make and model ever manufactured may no longer exist, having been destroyed, thrown out, lost, or whatever, the test being are these clocks still in serviceable existence and being actively used, or **not**? And so, then, we may surmise that *no no no, enough Montressor, we give up, we give, we are sorry, we are soooooooo sorry we ever found possible that which was never so before efore fore ore ee e*

(0)
__Party!__[1]
__Party!__[2]
Party![3]
Party![4]
{spit}

..   ..

...   .

...   .

    S' tha' spouses been = *__bean bean bean__* so after looking up from their watchface (1) and down from the far off wallclock (2) once more both realized but differently that it was time to hit the locker room, get a shower, and head for home. The taller spouse idly slipped off their cesta and leaned slightly to the shorter, saying, Look here. This is getting worn out. See—see there?

    The shorter touched their fingers to dark wear spots on the device.

    Oh, yes. Let's see—does mine—oh, yes. Look here. Mine too. Not quite as bad as yours, but—bad enough.

    We ought to get new ones. I'm starting to feel mine getting a little too loose at the wrist, and—actually, you know—I think I've been holding back my swing a bit because of it—like, that it might come loose in the middle of a game, and—that would be embarrassing. You know?

    Ah, actually, no. I don't know. It might be disturbing in some way, but—hardly embarrassing. Why do you say that?

    I suppose I'm quite conscious of how I appear when I play.

    Okay. But—are you more conscious of how you appear while playing the game than when going about the rest of your day?

    Above at the edge of a high skylight, damp began seeping in from the light rain that'd been falling all day, outside.   *slashroteria*

I, uh—well. I don't know, actually. That's a good question.

They looked across at the vertical stone wall at the end of the court from which hundreds of Jai alai balls had rebounded in the course of hundreds of hot fast 'alai games.

Forsooth the hemi

Off the court I suppose I am conscious of how I appear, I suppose, but not—not all the time, like I am during a game.

Droplets began to form from the leak at the edge of the skylight far above—but none were yet heavy enough to pull loose and fall.

It ought to be the other way around, you know, said the other—for example; I am conscious of my appearance {ahem} off the court only. Never while playing a game.

Really?

Yes, really.

The *drops* at the edge of the skylight continued to multiply and grow. Outside, the rain was beginning to let up—but very slowly.

Okay, well then, said the shorter, standing up and picking up the ball—let's get out of here. Almost time for dinner.

I know what is is, said the other. I know the difference.

Difference? Difference of—what?

What we were talking about. That I feel self-conscious when I play Jai alai, but not at other times throughout the day.

Okay. Tell me the difference. And then come on, we got to go. I'm <u>hungry</u>. Aren't you <u>hungry</u>?

The *drops* at the edge of the skylight continued to multiply and grow. Three or four of the dozens hung there had nearly grown heavy enough to fall.

Oh sure, I'm hungry too, but, just wait—the difference is that when playing Jai alai I am trying to achieve some sort of—of *victory* that will impress others. Jai alai has a win and a lose. Other things do not. There you go—well, okay.

Having said this, they rose and moved to join the other toward the locker room but the other appeared to have abruptly taken an interest in the topic.

No, wait. Everything in life has a win and a lose. Not just Jai alai.

Okay yah, we could debate that, but, even if that's so—but Jai alai is very different.

Different how?

It's a game.

The *first drops* began to quiver as ceiling drops tend to do just before they fall.

Please don't bore me. We covered that already. Everything in life's a game.

Okay, okay. I didn't want to—but let's go ahead and debate that.

Okay. Shoot.

Using the toilet. Is that a game?

What? No. Of course not.

But you just said everything's a game—*did you not?*

Uh. Yes I did. *But I didn't mean things like that.*

Here they go there they come it starts slow but then it
drip

You said <u>everything</u>. Is using the toilet not included in <u>everything</u>?

Of course it is but it's not a drip game—listen—I was only trying to—

Only drip trying to only trying to only trying to **blah blah blah!** Only trying to **what?**

To make a point, that's what. Okay, enough. Come on. Let's go drip drip get some dinner.

You're really good at that, aren't you?

Good? Good at *what?*

At slipping out from under having to deal with things you don't want to face.

Like *what?*   Drip

Think about it. I don't need to tell you. Go get your dinner. That's *so much more important than anything I might have to say.* Go. Now.

... no—they stood faced off considering each other— which way will what's about to fly fly need to step aside get out of the way we think that we do yah think that we why ...

Okay. I'm *leaving.* If you want to come along, <u>*then come*</u>.

With that, the shorter gripped up the ball, turned, and went toward the locker room. As they receded, the taller gazed, drip watching them receding, growing smaller and smaller, as they walked away. Is that true, are they really getting smaller? No, of course not, that's just something called per drip spective at work. They flowed off with the time gone all the way drip nearly to nothing, but no non it's not really they're nothing's just perceived to be so, as drip the mountain wi drip ll f drip it between two raised spread finge drip rtips *if both things fall exactly the right way from each other* huge bridges being crossed are far smaller than your steering wheel *if both things are momentarily in the exact spatial opposition to each other* the Rockies are one inch viewed from thirty thousand feet *just in that same way the same way as those twos* and so forth and *so on* but that's not important—what's important's what's this flowed on over *from behind no*—don't *turn around* it's the roar of the crowd but don't turn around *it's to do with the Jai alai* just sta drip nd up and feel it the roaring *the Jai alai how Jai alai* the pressure the life of it and the roar of it and the high *of the jai alai and the Jai* and the high and the highest of it, so go. O th' *Jai lai no no,* walk away " " off the *Jai alai,* and *lose;* One more down *{no can't lose}* t (.) he droplets fall go who knows one more (0) down *{no no way no must not lose}* much faster now one drip one more down how *{there's a reason* (00000) *for all this a}* fall though the rain's receding (000000000) the drops begin to fall many more *{reason where'd they go{* (0000000000) } *God must* **catch** *them}* fall grown heavy enough to fall so **catch** *them* {'d

(00000000) e'} *must* **catch** *them must, hey! Hey* fall droplets fall who knows **GO it is not too late** s {'d (000000) e'} 'h ore more fall though the rain's receded the drops continue **down please don't make it too late** s {'d s' (0000) 'n e'} 'h to fall drip drop drip drop spatter one more spatter spatter drip drip drip drop one drip drop drip drop spatter spatter drip drip drip drop spatter drip drop   drip   drop spatter   spatter drip drip drip   s {'d s' (000) 'n e'} 'h

                                              drop   spatter

tool late   not too late

     is it too late   no its never *lie* or **truth**   'ngs
{'d s' (0) 'n e'} 'h
            le or *trth*
        th'ngs {'d s' 'n e'} 'h n'w
   l or *th*   *o rt*   *r rr*   ..   ..
.. ...

     ii e   th'ngs dis' [l '' d] 'n
e''h n'w
     Party![5]
     Party![6]
Hey!   'd th'ngs diss'l '' d in e''h n'w m''   Wait up!
I—

Turn 'round, hand up, 'nd say it, th', Don't say it! Don't say. I know what you'll say, so don't say it! *Okay?*

O …   uh a Okay. *Okay*—but, eh, ah—how 'bout that other place for dinner tonight, *eh?*

Yah. Yo. That other place, but showers first.

Oh. Y' Showers first. Of course.   O'd
th'ngs disssolved in each n'w m''l

Go fast though.

                             Go fast
       of course   *of*   *c our*   O'd
th'ngs **disssolved in each** n'w m''l   *se*
     go go go go
O p kupt'd 0 o . oooooooooooooooooooooooooooooooooooooooo w a d
     Yes
old things dissolved in each new meal
old things dissolve in each new meal

old   things   dissolved   with   {in}   ....
each new meal

   ... sizzle le sizzle le working twenty four seven three hundred sixty five {***Good day, senor?***} Nice hat! Nice hat!

  knots